EXPOSURE
— TO —
TRUTH

By Joe McCoubrey

Dedication & Thanks

Where would I be – in fact where would any writer be – without the support of family and friends. I couldn't find the patience or the drive to keep going without the wholehearted encouragement and belief that I get from the women who matter most in my life. And so this one, as with all the others before it, is for Teresa, Brenda, Lynda and Lisa. One big motivation for me is the hope that one day my grandsons Alfie, Rory and Ellis will get to read this and, hopefully, be as proud of this old man as I am of them.

I have my own personal family reading club, which includes my brother Johnny, sister Geraldine, uncles Norman Ennis and Jimmy Millar, aunt Amy Watters, niece Sharon Bolton, cousins Cath Millward and Anne Strain, and God-daughter Norma Ennis. They are a critical bunch, and I can only hope this latest offering passes their muster.

I also want to thank the people whose names have been used with such cavalier abandon. Needless to say, they are neither as good, nor as bad, as I've painted them!

My editing team are the go-to guys for wake-up calls when bad habits or poor research creep into my work. Without the blandishments of Brad Fleming, Mick Keane and Martin Graham this manuscript would not be as polished as it should be. Thank-you for your patience and for the little bits that make me better.

About the Author

Joe McCoubrey is a former journalist who reported first-hand the height of the Northern Ireland "Troubles" throughout the 1970's and 1980's, firstly as a local newspaper editor, and then as a partner in an agency supplying copy to national newspapers and broadcasters. He switched careers to help start a Local Enterprise Agency, providing advice and support to budding entrepreneurs in his native town, and became its full-time CEO. He retired to concentrate on his long-time ambition to be a full-time writer. His previous novels have all been published to critical acclaim.

He lives in Downpatrick, County Down, and is proud of its historic connections to Saint Patrick, Ireland's Patron Saint.

You can visit Joe at: www.joemccoubrey.com

EXPOSURE TO TRUTH

Copyright © Joe McCoubrey 2017
ISBN: 978-0-9954687-4-0

A CIP catalogue for this book is available from the British Library.

Also by Joe McCoubrey:

No Margin for Error

Spent Force

Absence of Rules

Absence of Mercy

Someone Has To Pay

Death by Licence.

EXPOSURE TO TRUTH

Mike Devon is back in his most challenging assignment ever. What starts as an investigation into terrorism in France takes on a sinister new twist when the real enemies are discovered closer to home – within the very Government Devon has sworn to serve. But what links can be found between a British Home Secretary, an American Senator and two of the world's richest men? When all else fails, follow the money. And the bodies!

When a former MI6 agent is brutally murdered after uncovering a trail of lies and deceit that threaten to expose some powerful and ruthless men, his widow and son are caught in the crosshairs. Mike Devon and his team are all that stand between the family and a small army of dedicated mercenaries intent on wiping out the last remaining links to the truth. Devon needs to find and expose these shadowy enemies. There's just one problem - he doesn't know where to start looking. And the clock is ticking.

ENDORSEMENT FOR PREVIOUS WORK
"Sometimes a book comes along that you instantly know......damn, I am now going to have to read this all over again for the sheer joy of the narrative. It means that I will have to swear off other books for a time as very few can provide the utter joy and delight of Joe McCoubrey's superb novel."

KEN BRUEN, the international bestselling author of the Jack Taylor Irish crime series.

Chapter 1

THERE WERE LOTS of things Matthew Hayden could have done in the last few minutes of his time on earth.

He could have phoned his estranged wife and told her he'd finally come to his senses. What would it have taken to let her know she was right about the selfish way he had turned his back on thirty years of marriage to pursue an obsession?

He could have contacted his son, now in his final year at college, and asked for forgiveness for all the missed birthdays, the no-shows to watch him play football, or the fact that he was always too busy to help with getting him through his exams, or his driving test, or the hundred and one things that a young adolescent male could do better with a father around for support.

But Matthew Hayden was not thinking about any of these things.

Typically, if he *had* known he was out of time, his first thought would have been to open his mailbox, attach the file he'd just completed, and send it to a whole bunch of people who would learn a lot about what he'd uncovered over the past few months.

An ex-MI6 operative, he'd been unfairly hounded out of the service over his refusal to drop an investigation that rankled a lot of people at the very heart of the UK's political and security establishments. Something was amiss, and Hayden had been determined to get to the bottom of it. He had made it a crusade; one that had lost him not only his job but also his family and his friends.

Now, it was about to cost him his life.

The file he had just closed was a two-hundred-page Word document hidden in the sprawling sub-directories of his Hewlett Packer laptop and was filled with random names, places and dates. It was a mishmash of copy-and-paste extracts from websites, online newspaper articles, and research notes typed in a confusing smorgasbord of one-line sentences, text-box inserts to highlight key questions, and rows upon rows of SmartArt arrows and other shapes pointing the way along the convoluted path his mind had taken in pursuit of answers.

Most important of all, it was full of secret file excerpts culled from the servers of his former employers, as well as snippets of bank statements, property dealings, and business insider-trading transactions that were supposedly hidden from public purview.

But Hayden knew his way around such things. After all, it had been his job as a security information analyst to find a path through even the most sophisticated firewalls, file encryptions, and password protections. He was good at it, maybe too good. His nose for sniffing out incongruous snippets from the mountains of data that passed across his desk was what had led him to the top of his profession – and had ultimately brought his world crashing down around him.

Instead of slinking away under the weight of the lies, deceit and threats that would have made a lesser mortal swallow the barrel of his service-issue Walther PPK, Hayden had been fired with a determination to fight back the only way he knew how. He moved north, away from London, to take up residence in his parents' deserted moorlands cottage. No-one knew about the place, not even his wife. He would be safe here. All he needed was the right kind of computer and server hardware, a range of software packages that he had copied and amassed during his spymaster years, and high-speed broadband connectivity - a situation he remedied by piggy-backing, undetected, on the vast resources of a multi-national financial institution based ten miles away in Leeds.

He'd covered his tracks well, both physically and electronically. He was supremely confident that no-one would discover what he'd been up to until he was ready to reveal all. Now, it was time. Some of his last keystrokes spelled out the names of two people he had finally unearthed. He had the evidence of their treachery, and was convinced he could bring about their destruction.

The results of the painstaking work would restore his lost reputation. It would allow him to return to the life he'd once enjoyed. It would reconnect him to family and friends. Most important of all, it would exact revenge on those who had so callously tossed him on the scrapheap. He relished the prospect of the come-uppance that awaited them.

The thought of what lay ahead brought a rare smile to Hayden's heavily-lined face. Too many sleepless nights, and too many love affairs with bottles of Scotch had aged him twenty years beyond the fifty-five he had reached to date. He could now put all that behind him. Where would he start? There was really only one place. There was only one man he trusted above all others. It was the final name he had entered in the file.

Mike Devon.

He leaned back in his seat and stared through the window at the rolling fields of the Yorkshire countryside. It was a sunny afternoon with just a slight breeze to stir the trees and make the long, wispy grass dance in the haze as far as his eyes could see. His hideaway cottage was about as remote as it could be. Not a neighbour to worry about for more than two miles, and no traffic sounds to break his concentration.

For a moment he thought he saw a curious pinpoint flash on a distant hilltop. It was followed by what seemed to be the muted pop of a champagne cork. His brain didn't register the small hole that appeared in the glass just in front of him, nor could he understand the heat spike that ripped through the centre of his head. He just sat there staring at the green-shaded landscape, his body held in place by some odd counterbalancing force of nature. A small rivulet of blood trickled down from the centre of his forehead, found a course between his eyebrows, and ran unchecked over the bridge of his nose.

His body suddenly bent at the waist, and his head crashed heavily onto the laptop's keyboard, sending bits of broken plastic scattering across the old oak desk that had once belonged to his grandfather.

The assassin didn't wait for the corpse to topple forward. At barely three hundred yards, the kill shot was almost an insult to his prowess. He didn't need confirmation that the 5.56mm NATO-issued, copper-jacketed bullet had found its target. From that range he quite simply couldn't miss.

He unscrewed the Leupold FX-II scope from his Remington 700 rifle and quickly began storing the component parts into a small brown case, which fitted neatly into the seat storage compartment of his fuel-injected Honda Fireblade motorcycle. He pulled a red and black striped helmet over his head, snapping the mirrored, anti-glare visor into place. Then he straddled the powerful machine and glided gently down the laneway towards the little cottage.

He removed a large package from one of the bike's twin panniers and stepped through the unlocked cottage door. As expected, he found his victim slumped over a computer workstation, and noted with satisfaction that the through-and-through round had left only a small hole as it exited the brain cavity, its force eventually spent against the concrete wall opposite the window.

His assignment hadn't called for a messy killing. He could have used a dum-dum, or some such variant, designed to expand on impact, but he liked things clean. If he'd wanted messy, he would have crept into the building and run a blade across the target's throat. Or he could have pumped a half-dozen 9mm rounds into the man's face, and watched as fright and shock locked the features into a grotesque mask of death.

No, he didn't get many opportunities to practice his preferred sniper's art. Okay, it would have been better from a more challenging vantage point about a thousand or so yards away, but the undulating terrain hadn't provided that option. It was a case of taking what you get.

The gunman lifted the broken laptop, ignored the pools of blood, and closed the lid. He stuffed it into a plastic bag, which he'd pulled from a pocket in his leather jacket, before setting it to one side. Next, he opened his package and removed eight small bricks of C4 explosives, a roll of det cord, and a small triggering device.

Twenty minutes later he crested a hill, unhooked the bike's parking stand, and looked down at the picture-postcard building. He took the triggering device from his pocket, and depressed a red switch. The explosions came at half-second intervals, culminating in a fireball eruption caused by the C4 block he'd wedged against a large gas tank positioned in a small compound beside the rear door.

The little cottage disintegrated into millions of pieces, the largest no bigger than an average suitcase.

The motorcyclist watched for a few seconds before patting the pannier containing Matthew Hayden's laptop secrets. A sharp twist on the throttle handle brought a gratifying roar from the 16-valve, liquid-cooled engine, the front wheel rising against the sudden torque and the rear wheel burning rubber as it fought for traction on the compacted ground.

He couldn't wait to get back to the bright lights of London. He had money to burn and places to go. He would enjoy a break until the next big pay day.

Chapter 2

THE WOMAN'S REACTION was a natural one. She let out a gasp, sank to her knees, and stared uncomprehendingly at the mess that was once her neatly-arranged living room. It took Sonia Hayden several seconds to realise she was the victim of a burglary, one carried out with some kind of animal ferocity, and with scant regard for her precious few possessions.

The place was thrashed beyond recognition. What had she done to deserve this? Sonia heaved and started crying, at first in low sobs, but her desolation gradually developed into a full-blown wail, the pitiful sound echoing off the walls of the small first-floor apartment in Camden.

It was late afternoon and she knew none of her neighbours would yet be around to help. They were all workers, mostly on eight-to-six shifts in various offices and shops dotted around the tight-knit London neighbourhood where she'd taken up residence two years previously. She'd found a job stacking shelves in a local supermarket, but was now the branch manager, a role that had helped her through the worst days of despair, especially after learning that her husband had forsaken all their friends and dropped out of sight.

What hurt most was the fact that she'd been unable to shake him out of his depression, or to convince him they should start a new life together, away from the gossips and the reminders of what they once had. He'd begun a downward spiral that she couldn't rein in, though up until the moment she'd received official notification that he'd transferred his service pension payments to her, she still believed they had a future together.

A sound from the rear of the apartment brought her back to the present. She looked up as a tall, menacing figure walked out of her bedroom and pointed a gun directly at her head. She had enough presence of mind to realise this was no ordinary burglar, certainly not in the way he smiled from behind thick-rimmed glasses and called out her name in that rounded-vowel way of the university-educated, silver-spooned set from Oxford or Cambridge.

"Ah, Mrs Hayden, so good of you to drop in early. I was not expecting this little get-together for at least another half-hour. Did we knock off early from that little job of yours? I must say it is rather obliging of you to save me the trouble of waiting around."

Sonia Hayden processed the information as quickly as she could. This man knew her. He knew about her work and her normal quitting time. He had ransacked her house and was preparing to wait for her, but for what purpose? If only she hadn't stopped early because of a migraine. Maybe if she'd worked overtime, she could have avoided this. No, the bastard would have probably stayed around.

But why?

The thought when it struck her was like a hammer blow to the stomach. *My God, this is about Matthew! They're looking for him.*

The realisation of what could be happening, galvanised her into action. She rocked back on her heels and tumbled through the front door, which was still open from her earlier shocked entrance. She rolled twice on the communal concrete walkway, jumped to her feet, and took off at a sprint towards the nearest stairwell. She had no more than a twenty-yard head start on her assailant, and could already hear his feet pounding on the hallway behind her.

She tried to take the stairs two at a time, but tripped on the fourth step, grazing her knee and banging her head against a wooden balustrade. She had two choices. Stay on the ground to await a certain death, or get the hell up and keep going. She was already running for the push-bar security door by the time the man appeared ten feet above, his gun hand sweeping back and forward as he steadied his aim.

The sound of the 9mm round was like a thunderclap in the confined space. The bullet smashed into the doorframe just as Sonia stumbled out into the open air, narrowly missing a young mother pushing a pram along the busy pavement beside the apartment block.

Sonia stared frantically around the sea of faces, hoping to spot the familiar yellow fluorescent jacket of a Metropolitan Police officer. There were always foot patrols in the area. Typically, there were none this evening.

She spotted a red single-decker bus pulling away from a stop thirty yards away and sprinted after it, her legs powered by a mixture of terror and adrenaline. She reached out to grab the safety bar at the rear of the bus. Her hand locked around the steel pole, which almost pulled her shoulder from the socket, but she clung on and was catapulted onto the pedestrian platform.

She gulped in air, steadied herself and risked a glance backwards. Her pursuer was sprinting down the middle of the road, closing the distance rapidly, his gun still clearly visible in a meaty right fist. Then the bus moved into the centre lane and accelerated away.

Sonia watched the man slowing and stopping. She had escaped, but for how long? She staggered forward into the passenger compartment, flopped onto the nearest seat, and buried her head into her hands. This time there were no tears. She was too angry for that. *What have you done, Matthew? What have you got us into?*

Christopher Hayden crammed his study books into a battered backpack and rushed headlong down the stairs. Five years at the London School of Economics, and never once early for the endless lectures, or group meetings, or the one-to-ones with Mr Albright, the tutor who had brought him to within a whisker of achieving his MSc in the Management of Information Systems and Digital Innovation. Just one more paper. One more hurdle to overcome before finally standing on his own two feet.

It was typical mid-July weather in the capital. The sun beat down relentlessly on the exposed streets, spreading a hazy shimmer that distorted the shapes of people as they scurried about, seeking the refuge of any shadowed areas. What a day to spend indoors trying to grapple with the capabilities for technology-enabled innovation in business and government!

It was his dad who'd fired Christopher's imagination about the power of computer software systems. Ever since he could remember, he always seemed to be perched on a seat watching his father hammering on a keyboard and bringing to life all manner of images on a screen in the study of their former Georgian home, once a haven of happiness and contentment.

"Information technology is the future," his dad had told him repeatedly. "The man who can control a keyboard can control the world. If you have the know-how, you can reach into the deepest, darkest recesses and find ways to make things better. You can bend people to your will, force big companies to act responsibly towards the environment, make governments sit up and take notice, help alleviate poverty and suffering, hold people to account for their actions, and generally be a force for good in a world where evil lurks around every corner."

The memory made Christopher sniffle back a tear. His dad was his idol. What had happened to him wasn't fair. He was an honourable man who didn't deserve the things he had had to deal with. Christopher knew he was innocent, and one day he hoped to find a way to prove it.

Outside the digs he shared with four friends, Christopher began weaving his way through the throng of pedestrians, desperately hoping the 9.40am bus was still parked at the little perspex shelter. Suddenly, he was confronted by two men who blocked his path with outstretched arms.

"Whoa there, Mr Hayden. What's the big rush?"

The men were dressed in matching black suits, white shirts and red ties. The one who'd spoken was holding up an identification wallet, although he snatched it away before Christopher could read the inscription. It was obvious, however, they were some kind of police or security service personnel, judging by the confident, nonchalant way they stood rigid in front of him. Sizing people up was another thing he'd learned from his dad.

"I don't have time," Christopher blurted, and tried to force his way past the immovable obstacles.

"This will only take a moment. We need to ask you some questions about your father."

And there it was. Déjà vu all over again. "Look, I've been through this a hundred times with you people. I don't know where my dad is, I haven't been in contact with him for over a year, and I'm late for an important exam."

The second man spoke this time. "You're at LSE, aren't you? What say we give you a lift and ask our questions on the way? You'll be there in plenty of time."

Christopher glanced ahead and saw his bus pull away from the kerbside zone. "Okay, but can we make it quick, please?"

One of the men swivelled and raised an arm. A black Transit van pulled up to the pavement, and Christopher was bundled towards a side-panel sliding door. As he was about to step into the darkened interior, one of the men pushed him roughly in the back, sending him sprawling against the opposite panel.

"Hey, what the fuck's going on?"

The men closed the door behind them.

Thirty minutes later, Christopher lay battered and bruised on the concrete floor of a deserted warehouse. They'd worked him over pretty good, taking turns with their fists or boots to deliver a succession of blows every time he refused to answer their questions, or told them something they didn't want to hear.

"This is your last chance. How does your father contact you? Where do you meet with him? What has he told you about his activities? Who's he working with?"

Christopher's jaw ached; he was certain it was broken. One eye was closed over and his lips were badly swollen, making it almost impossible for him to speak coherently. Despite his injuries he maintained a stoic defiance. "I can't help you. My father left us a long time ago and we haven't heard from him since. Let me go, please. I won't tell anyone about this."

He watched as the men rummaged through his backpack, tossing books and lecture notes on the ground, before removing his iPad and checking the on-screen apps. They talked non-stop as they scrolled through the menus, before one of them closed the lid and carried the small nine-inch tablet across to the van.

"We're done here," he shouted back to his colleague. "Take care of our little friend."

The second man withdrew a long-bladed knife from a leg sheath and walked forward. Christopher tried to squirm away, but he felt his hair being pulled roughly and he was brought to his feet to stare into a pair of callous eyes.

He registered a blur of movement in the man's arm. He felt the sensation of the knife penetrating his chest.

And then he felt nothing.

Chapter 3

IT WAS THE KIND of set-up Mike Devon enjoyed. A backstreet casino full of thugs, wallowing in champagne and girls, protected only by a solitary bouncer standing guard under a dimly-lit rear entrance porch.

Okay, they probably had all manner of weaponry at their disposal, and weren't all that over-reliant on the single man-mountain to keep away uninvited guests, but it was the way they liked to do things. This was their manor, and you played by their rules. Besides, who would be stupid enough to take on the power of the self-styled *Tunisian Templars*?

Devon smiled at the pretentious choice of name. They were a mixed bag of immigrant layabouts who'd wormed their way into the country to set up a crusade against the forces of law and order. They chiselled and chivvied a position of prominence for themselves in just about every money-making racket going, from drugs to prostitution, from gambling to extortion, and from armed robberies to gangland murders.

Various branches of the Metropolitan Police had had their arms full and their hands tied trying to investigate this merry band for a number of years. But where money is no object, and you can afford to hire the best of the best of the British legal establishment, the end result was usually one quashed case after another. These guys were the kingpins of loopholes and technicalities.

But this type always made at least one mistake.

Theirs was giving Mike Devon's organisation a reason for taking a closer look at their little cesspool. A former operative of Britain's Secret Intelligence Service, better known as MI6, Devon now headed up an elite anti-terrorist group answerable only to the British Prime Minister. He worked regularly with a similar group set up in America under the

Office of the President. Both groups had a certain carte blanche when it came to dealing with the enemies of democracy.

Cloaked behind a bonafide company, known as *LonWash Securities*, the organisation's base was at Charterhouse Street, slap bang in the middle of north London's Smithfield district. Its reach, however, was a global one, with operations mounted anywhere and against anyone considered to be a threat to the UK's national security.

What had made the *Tunisian Templars* a possible threat to national security was the uncovering of a link to a horror attack in Nice, where more than eighty people were mown down by a lorry driven by Tunisian national, Mohamed Lahouaiej-Bouhlel. In the aftermath of the tragedy, Europe's top counter-terror organisations began compiling lists of all relatives and known associates of the perpetrator. Originally from the town of Msaken in north Tunisia, Lahouaiej-Bouhlel had taken up residence in Nice, but had maintained close ties with his homeland. A search of his computer records threw up some interesting names, among them two men who were members of the *Tunisian Templars*.

The *LonWash* tech team, led by Tim Halloran, began a painstaking search for any trails leading from London to Nice. Thanks to their abilities to circumvent secure bank databases, several large money transfers were discovered and traced to a bogus account, which was tied to Lahouaiej-Bouhlel's French address.

The two names which linked back to London were Mehdi Naybet and Marouen Badri, the latter recognised as the leader of the *Tunisian Templars*.

Having established a connection – albeit a tenuous one – between London and Nice, it was time for Devon to act. He was not trying to build an evidence-based case. It was not what he was about, never mind the fact that time was of the essence. Who knew when these people, including their cohorts in place anywhere across Europe, would next strike?

Devon's agents mounted a two-day surveillance on the Templars' base in Southwark, one of five boroughs which make up the London Docklands area. By day, the premises operated as a cocktail bar situated behind a ground-floor frontage of opaque glass and neon signage. By night, the action switched to the first floor, apparently accessible only from a nondescript rear entrance, where gang members and their friends met regularly for extra-curricular activities.

Devon broke cover from the shadows of the alley and strode purposefully towards the door where the sentry turned quickly at the sound of footsteps. The closer he got, the bigger the man appeared to become.

"Ere, where do you fink you're going?" Not Tunisian then; definitely some hired-in muscle from the East End."

Devon smiled. "I'm going inside and I'd be obliged if you'd open the door for me."

The mountain tilted back his head and roared with laughter. It was a stupid mistake, one he had no time to regret. Devon straight-fingered a jab into the folds of flesh below the giant's chin. At best, it temporarily cut the flow of air into the man's lungs; at worst, it smashed his larynx. Judging by a strange gurgling sound and the way the bouncer's eyes bulged in their sockets, it was the latter.

Devon swivelled on his feet and smashed a forearm into the side of the man's head. The mountain swayed several times before he pitched forward, hitting his head on the concrete apron that surrounded the door. Devon knelt to feel for a pulse. There wasn't one. He searched his victim's pockets for a set of keys, and was midway through testing them in the lock when he heard footsteps.

He didn't turn round. His team had joined him from the shadows.

First up was Alan Doyle, his second-in-command. A big, brash, ex-military veteran, here was a close friend of more than twenty years, dating back to a shared assignment which had cost Doyle his right arm in an IRA shoot-out. He now wore a prosthetic limb, a cumbersome extension most people would have found awkward and limiting. In Doyle's case, he boasted it was his best part, and had actually helped to improve his shooting skills.

Next to Doyle was a red-haired packet of trouble in the shape of Chelsea Horgan, a former CIA black-ops specialist, whose hand-to-hand combat skills were matched only by her deadly precision with any manner of long-range armaments. She had merged seamlessly into the *LonWash* fold, and was rarely to be seen away from Doyle. The two had become an item, and planned to marry just as soon as they could find the time.

The last member of the squad was Alfie Cheadle, a fresh-faced recruit who had been plucked from the ranks of the Special Air Service, arguably foremost among the world's elite special forces units. At just twenty-four, Cheadle had crammed in more action assignments than most soldiers twice his age, earning him the respect of his peers for the cool, calculating demeanour he demonstrated, even in the most intense life or death situations.

The group took up kneeling positions beside Devon. They each carried suppressed Glock 19s and shoulder-mounted MP5 submachine pistols, and wore combat utility belts crammed with spare magazines, C4 explosive units, fragmentation grenades, and several knives. At face value, it was probably way too much overkill, but it was a *LonWash* motto always to be prepared.

The final pieces of gear were black balaclavas, which each team member pulled over the head, adjusting the eye and mouth slots into their proper positions. Whatever way tonight's action went, Devon knew there would be survivors, potential witnesses who could confirm the assault was not the work of a rival gang – a scenario he'd already put in place for the inevitable follow-up police investigation.

Devon found a key that fitted the single mortice lock, and stood aside to usher his team into the building. Instead of putting a man on post outside the door, the proper security arrangement for this gang would have been to stand a sentry on the inside, usually with a CCTV monitor covering the alley. But when you operated under the illusion of infallibility, why take unnecessary precautions?

They were about to find out why.

A single bulb provided sparse illumination of the stairwell. Devon counted twenty risers, each covered by a threadbare carpet, heavily stained in a way that suggested the cleaning lady never made it to this part of the building.

The team was all mic'd up, with small earpieces and voice-activated throat plates. From here in, they would stick with their comms and various hand signals. Doyle pushed his way to the front, taking the first two steps in a giant leap. He was followed quickly by Horgan, leaving Devon and Cheadle to bring up the rear.

A small landing at the top of the stairs led to a single corridor running east to the centre of the building. The sound of voices and laughter could be heard coming from a number of closed rooms, a sure sign, despite the lateness of the hour, that the party mood was still in full swing.

The corridor ended against a set of double doors, half panelled in wood and half in red-stained glass. The four *LonWash* agents bunched against the door and peered through the coloured screens into a large bar-type lounge, kitted out in seated-cubicle areas, and with enough chandelier lighting to power up a night-time soccer match.

Doyle tested the door and began a silent countdown using three fingers. By prior agreement, Cheadle remained in the hallway to provide cover in the event that gunmen started pouring out of the side rooms. He knelt on the ground, placed the MP5 at his feet, and held the Glock in a two-fisted sweep across the corridor.

Doyle, Horgan and Devon stepped into the lounge, their presence so far unnoticed by the partying throng of about thirty people, most of them women in various stages of undress. One man looked over the top of a cubicle, then another, then pretty soon all eyes were turned towards the intruders.

There's always that curious moment of inertia caused by people trying to process what's happening. A hush descended on the room and no-one moved for almost ten seconds, until a long-haired youth buried his right hand into his jacket and started to withdraw a short-barrelled weapon. Before he was able to pull it clear, a small round hole appeared in the centre of his forehead, sending his body crashing backwards in a death spasm.

Devon took a pace forward. "Nobody else needs to die here tonight. We've come for Mehdi Naybet and Marouen Badri. Point them out and walk away."

Several women started screaming, others crouched below tables. The remaining eight men exchanged glances, trying to read each other's thoughts, and hoping someone else would take the initiative. In the end it might as well have been choreographed. Three men made a grab for holstered weapons. The three died on the spot.

The remainder raised their arms in the air, shocked by the fluidity and lethality of the hooded assailants. One of the group found the courage to speak. "No more shooting, please. The men you want are not here. They are out of the country on business."

Devon signalled the men to step away from the cubicles and line up in front of the bar counter where he kept them covered while Doyle and Horgan patted down the group, relieving them of an array of weapons.

The sound of an unsuppressed MP5 tore through the saloon. Cheadle had obviously encountered some other resistance from the side rooms. Devon and Doyle took off at a sprint, reaching the swing doors in time to see a man tumble out into the corridor, his chest a mess of blood and gristle. Two more bodies were also spread across the hallway.

Devon stepped through the door. "What've we got, Alfie?"

"There are at least another two men in the room at the farthest end of the corridor. Can't tell if everyone has been cleared from the first two rooms."

This was not a situation Devon wanted to drag out. He cleared his throat and shouted a warning. "Listen up. We have grenades and will use them unless you step outside with your hands in the air. The men we want are not here, but we *will* kill all of you unless you do what you're told. You've got five seconds to decide."

He had reached three in his countdown when the door

opened and two men stepped out, their hands laced against the back of their heads. Another man inched out from the nearest room.

"Is there anyone else?" Devon barked.

"No, no. Just the women."

The captives were herded into the main lounge. Devon knew the situation was a bust as far as Naybet and Badri were concerned. The man who'd told him the duo were out of the country had been too scared to lie, besides which none of the remaining men looked remotely like the grainy photos his team were able to procure before this evening's action. He needed to close things down as quickly as possible.

"We're leaving now," he yelled at the cowered group of men and women. "Our gang is taking over this part of town and we want all of you out of here within twenty-four hours. The next time we come back we will not leave any survivors. We will take two of you as hostage to make sure you do what you're told."

Forty minutes later, the full *LonWash* team was back in Charterhouse Street. Two men selected for interrogation were safely tucked up in the building's basement cells. Devon was angry at missing his prime targets, but they might get enough from their prisoners to develop a new lead on the whereabouts of Naybet and Badri.

He knew that under the distinctly persuasive questioning of Doyle and Horgan, the two Tunisians would be only too anxious to spill their guts.

Chapter 4

THE PAST TWELVE hours were a nightmare for Sonia Hayden. The bus conductor had dealt with hysterical passengers before, but a quick glance at the cuts and bruises on her legs convinced him that her story of being chased by a gunman was probably not as whimsical as it first appeared. He'd heard a lot of excuses for people not having the fare, but this one had a definite ring of authenticity about it.

The bus pulled over at the first sight of a policeman, and Sonia was transferred to the custody of a young constable who ordered up a squad car that whisked her to the local station on the edge of Camden. After an hour of questions, Sonia finally snapped.

"Look, this was no random burglary. My husband used to work for MI6 and I've no doubt the assault on me this morning was somehow related to what he'd been doing. I need you people to stop messing around as if this is some kind of everyday occurrence. I demand to speak to someone in the security services, and if you don't make that happen in the next ten minutes I'll contact my MP and let him know why this country's in the fucking mess that it is. Is it any wonder we're under attack when our policemen can't take their heads out of their asses long enough to see what's really going on?"

She knew it wasn't fair. In their shoes she would probably have done the same thing, but she needed to get out from under a petty investigation and find out what the hell was going on. Her outburst did the trick.

An hour later she found herself on the fourth floor of the New Scotland Yard complex at Broadway. The man sitting opposite her, Commander John Hall, head of the SO19 anti-terrorism group, was definitely taking her seriously. He, of course, had the benefit of reading a large security-sourced file before he started the interview. He had also time to study a report of an explosion that took place the previous day.

"I'm sorry to have to tell you, Mrs Hayden, that we believe your husband may have perished in a blast at a cottage outside Leeds yesterday......."

"Oh my God, this can't be happening.," Sonia screamed. "What was Matthew doing in Leeds? Are you sure about this?" It was the kind of news she'd been dreading for months. She'd steeled herself for the moment, but now that it was happening she felt the weight of the world collapsing in on her. Normally a strong-willed woman, she found herself in a situation that was way beyond anything she could have envisaged.

"I'm truly sorry, Mrs Hayden, but there seems little doubt. We traced the ownership of the premises to your husband's deceased parents, although the title deeds were transferred some time ago to an alias we now believe your husband was living under for several years. Because of the extensive nature of the explosion, it will be quite a job to make a positive identification of the body that was found at the scene, but you must prepare yourself for the worst."

"What kind of an explosion was it?"

Commander Hall cleared his throat, clearly reluctant to go into detail. "At first it appeared to have been a gas-leak, but investigators found traces of a military-grade explosive, which was why my office was contacted immediately. It's very early to be speculating, though of course it does throw a different light on what happened to you. There could be a connection, but until we know more I don't want to get ahead of ourselves."

Sonia wiped away tears and sat upright. "Let's not dance around the subject, Commander. I'm sure that file in front of you has all the sordid details about Matthew's dismissal from MI6. I'm not going to bore you with protestations about his innocence, suffice to say that he came up against powerful enemies, any one of whom could have been intent on silencing him forever. That's where you need to start looking."

"What I can't understand, Mrs Hayden, is that you say you've had no contact with your husband for almost two years, yet somehow you've become embroiled in whatever he was working on. You must know something about what he was doing, or who he was dealing with. Perhaps, he wasn't as innocent as you believe. Maybe, just maybe, he got mixed up with the wrong people, which was what got him fired in the first place."

It was a line the policeman had to take, if only to gauge the reaction of the spirited woman facing him across the large walnut desk that separated them. He was trained to look for any telltale signs of subterfuge, any of a hundred-and-one facial or body language give-aways that told him he was being lied to. What he got was not something he was not prepared for.

The chair opposite him suddenly went bouncing across the room, as Sonia Hayden rose and back-kicked it with all the power she could muster. Before he could react, she flung herself across the desk, her hands stretched out searching for a chokehold above his starched collar. She had turned into a wild animal, clawing and screaming, and crying, her eyes blazing with a scary mix of hatred and anger.

"You bastard! You're just like the rest of them. My Matthew devoted his life to helping people, only to be shafted by those he trusted the most. How dare you sit there in judgement of a fine man, a man you know nothing about. How dare you soil his memory with your sordid accusations."

Hall fought her off, grabbing her wrists and pulling her across the desk to envelop her in a bear-hug. He waited until the fight went out of her, before gently lowering her onto his chair, where she hunched over and tried to get her emotions in check. She was a pitiable sight.

"Mrs Hayden, I truly don't believe your husband was a bad man. I'm sorry I had to say the things I did, but I promise you we'll get to the bottom of this. Our forensics people are still working at your apartment, so we can't let you go home yet. We'll put you up overnight at a nearby hotel, under armed police protection, and arrange for fresh clothes to be brought to you. Now, is there anyone we can contact? What about your son?"

"No, no, leave Christopher out of this. He has exams to finish tomorrow. I'll contact him afterwards."

It was a long night for Sonia. Despite taking two sleeping pills provided by a police doctor, she tossed and turned on the strange hotel bed, trying to chase away the hundreds of memories of Matthew that flooded her brain. There was never a moment during the long estrangement when she hadn't believed they would get back together again. It was difficult now to come to terms with the reality that she would never see him again.

Shortly after 10.00am, she rose, showered and changed into clothes that had been brought from her home by a woman police constable. She made a cup of tea from the hotel's courtesy breakfast trolley, and settled into a small armchair to await an escort back to New Scotland Yard.

There was a loud rap on the room door, followed by a familiar voice. "Mrs Hayden, it's Commander Hall. Can we talk, please?"

Her mind didn't register the oddity of a senior policeman doing chauffeur duties. She crossed the room, opened the door, and attempted a smiled greeting that seemed to be lost on the solemn-looking visitor, whose appearance out of uniform surprised her.

"Don't worry, Commander, I won't bite. I apologise for my outburst last night...... what's wrong, you look as if you've seen a ghost?"

Hall closed the door and gently ushered Sonia towards the armchair. "I'm afraid I've some more bad news for you. It's your son Christopher. He was found earlier this morning in an abandoned warehouse...."

"Oh, dear God, no. Is he... is he dead?"

Hall shook his head. "No, but he's in a bad way. Someone beat him and left him for dead. Luckily, an old caretaker found him in time. He was stabbed and lost a lot of blood, but the hospital has managed to stabilise him. I've just come from there, and the prognosis is good."

The resolve she'd built up over the past two hours began to disintegrate. A carefully-crafted determination - forged during a sleepless night - to look the world in the eye and fight for the restoration of her husband's reputation, seemed suddenly to be meaningless. In its place was a cold dread, a stark realisation that her world had imploded, and there wasn't a damn thing she could do about it. Her son needed her attention. Nothing else mattered.

"This can't be happening," Sonia whispered faintly. "I need to go to my baby."

"Of course," Hall responded. "I'll take you there myself."

At that precise moment in another hotel, in another part of the city, a white-haired man stood in front of a full-length mirror, congratulating himself on the choice of a dark-blue Lora Piana cashmere suit. He had six of the designer outfits to pick from, even though this was meant to be little more than a short stopover prior to business meetings in Paris and Germany. Perhaps he would get to wear them all at least once before returning to his home in Austria.

This was a man who embraced the trappings of wealth. He loved making money, almost as much as he enjoyed spending it. Despite his reputation for chucking it around, his personal balance sheet showed it always came in a great deal faster than it went out. At forty years of age, his wiry six-foot frame had an athletic bearing, accentuated by the sepia tones of his Mediterranean heritage. The premature hair discolouration, caused by a genetic melanin deficiency, was not something that bothered him, particularly since one of his many "pretty woman" companions had likened him to Richard Gere, but with more panache and gravitas.

She'd got a little extra in her pay packet for that particularly piece of connivance.

He smiled at the mirror and turned towards a large writing bureau, where one of three mobile phones pinged a Beethoven ringtone. There was no caller ID. He didn't need one.

He lifted the phone to his ear. "Is it done?"

"We had only one small hiccup. The father and son have been eliminated, but the wife managed to escape. I have men out scouring the city. It's only a matter of time before we find her."

The air in the hotel room suddenly turned ice cold. "This is intolerable. I don't pay you people for excuses. How hard could it have been to take care of one insignificant family? I'm leaving for Paris this afternoon, and this thing had better be wrapped up before then."

"I can assure you it will be done."

"It had better be. Now, did you manage to get hold of his computer?"

"Yes, yes, we have everything, including the son's iPad and notebooks. I am arranging to deliver these to your technical department for analysis. They will learn all there is to know within a matter of hours."

The man brushed a small white hair from the lapel of his jacket, and watched it float to the carpet. Perhaps he needed to pay a visit to his favourite barber before his first meeting of the morning.

"Are you still there, Boss."

"Of course I'm still here, you idiot. You let me worry about computers while you concentrate on finishing what you started. Find that woman, and kill her."

Chapter 5

THE HALF-FULL bottle of Laphroaig Islay single-malt whisky was passed around the table, its contents quickly disappearing into an assortment of glasses and mugs. It was an after-action tradition at *LonWash* to toast a successful mission, even though this one felt to Devon like an abject failure.

He was, however, buoyed by Doyle's customary infectious optimism. "We'll run Naybet and Badri to ground soon enough. We've smashed their operation, and there's nowhere for them to go. The tech team are checking all airports and ferry terminals in case they're stupid enough to try for an easy getaway, so all in all, I'd call that a good night's work."

Devon tilted back his glass and lowered three fingers worth of the Scotch nectar. "I'm beginning to feel better already. When're you going to take a run at our friends down in the basement?"

Doyle grinned. "No hurry. Let them sweat a bit. By the time I finish breakfast, they'll be glad to get everything off their chests."

"Okay," Devon replied, "let's aim for a noon update with the people at GIGN." He was referring to the *Groupe d'Intervention de la Gendarmerie Nationale* the leading arm of France's national security services. Despite the current uncertain climate about a possible reduction in inter-state co-operation in the aftermath of Brexit - the name given to Britain's much-heralded exit from the European Union - Devon's team enjoyed a close relationship with the vaunted French agency, thanks mainly to its former commander, Claude Bartran.

Hardly a day passed without Devon remembering the diminutive Frenchman, once regarded as Europe's top terrorist hunter. It was Bartran who'd taken a bullet meant for Devon during an operation against a sadistic assassin in the aftermath of previous attacks in Paris. The entire *LonWash* team had attended the state funeral, during which Devon had pledged his full, ongoing support to GIGN. It was a promise he intended to keep.

The door to the operations room was thrown open as Tim Halloran made one of his usual out-of-breath entrances. He was head of the *LonWash* geek-squad, a less than flattering in-house soubriquet for a collection of some of the country's top computer geniuses. In a previous life, Halloran had been a leading cyber security expert with GCHQ, the Government Communications Headquarters based at Cheltenham, northwest of London. He'd spent his time there engaged in rewriting existing data capture techniques and devising new SIGINT software that had become the benchmark for signals intelligence-gathering throughout Europe. It was those accomplishments that had brought him to the attention of *LonWash*.

Devon had a soft spot for the computer genius. On more than one occasion, he'd let it be known that without Halloran's input, the agency would be just another cog in the machinery of anti-terror warfare. It was the tech boys who elevated *LonWash* to a level that put them ahead of the competition, and not just because they refused to be hamstrung by oversight or playing by the rules. They knew where to look in the kind of cyber-space places others could only dream about.

Devon raised an eyebrow. "What's up, Tim?"

"Sorry for the interruption, Mike, but I've just come across something that could be interesting."

"I'm all ears."

"Do you remember an ex-MI6 agent by the name of Matthew Hayden?"

Devon had been expecting an update on the current operation, and frowned at the diversion into a new subject. "Can't say I do. Has this anything to do with the Tunisian gang?"

"No," responded. "Hayden was one of the guys I wanted to

bring on board a few years ago, but he was rather set in his ways at MI6 and turned down the approach. I had a lot of dealings with him when I was at GCHQ at a time when we were forced to share data with the other security agencies. He was the best computer man I'd ever come across, and he would have made a great addition to our team. You must remember me mentioning him?"

"Yes, I vaguely recall you going on about him, but what's this got to do with anything?"

Halloran drew up a seat. "I've just found out he was murdered yesterday. Apparently his house was wired with explosives. By all accounts there's not much left of him."

Devon could see the news had affected his tech chief. "Wait a minute, wasn't Hayden caught up in a scandal some time back? There was talk that he'd gone off the edge, that he'd been sloppy in his work, and that lives were put at risk."

"Bollocks!" Halloran slammed his fist on the table. The room went silent. "The man I knew wouldn't have allowed his standards to dip. He was too much of a perfectionist and a patriot to let a diminution in personal performance get in the way of the job. He was stitched up for something that he'd come across, maybe something that others didn't want to come to light."

In all the years he'd known him, Devon had never seen Halloran so worked up. He tried to tread carefully. "Look, Tim, there was probably another explanation for what happened him at MI6, but I don't see how we should be getting involved."

Halloran jumped from his seat, his face a mask of crimson. "Jeez, Mike, an ex-MI6 agent gets blown up in England, and that's not something we should be concerned about? What if he had stumbled across some terrorist plot, or was silenced because he knew too much about...about.... something.... anything. I only know that this stinks to high heaven."

"Okay, Tim, you win. What do you know about Hayden since he left the service?"

Halloran slumped reluctantly back into his chair. "That's the problem. He'd dropped out of sight for the past two years.

Nobody knew where he was, or what he was up to. It was as if he'd vanished from the face of the earth."

"The way I see it," Devon said as gently as he could, "this is a matter for MI6. He was one of theirs, so let them do the digging."

"What if I told you that shortly after Hayden was blown to bits, someone tried to kill his wife, and that his son was later found half-dead from a knife attack?"

Doyle decided to intervene. "I'd say that adds a whole new dimension to things. It's one thing to assassinate an agent, quite another to go after his family. There might be a lot more to this than we first thought."

"I agree," Devon responded, "but first we need to let things take their course with MI6. I'll put in a call to the section chief Peter Ramsden and see what they're doing about it. We'll keep an eye on it, but in the meantime we stick to our own current operation."

Halloran looking pleadingly across the table. "Fair enough, Mike, but would you mind if I do a bit of ferreting around? I won't tread on anyone's toes. They won't even know I'm looking."

"Yes," Devon chuckled, "you do have a way of doing things unseen. Feel free to do what you do, but I must insist there's no let-up in the search for Naybet and Badri. That's the number one priority."

The man was looking into a mirror again. This time it was a small hand-held rectangle that was being swayed around the sides by the head stylist at the exclusive Knightsbridge salon. "Excellent work, Carlos, I'll call with you again in another few weeks."

He pressed two fifty-pound notes into the hairdresser's palm and walked towards the entrance. His mood was brightening in line with the noonday sun, his thoughts already turning to lunch at the Dorchester. All things considered, this was a good day.

It was about to take a decidedly downwards turn.

A mobile vibrated in his jacket pocket. He fished it out, hit the answer button, and stepped out onto the brightly-lit pavement. "This had better be good news."

There was a pause before a gruff voice responded. "Sorry, Boss, the news is not good. We still haven't found the woman, and we've just heard that the son survived the attack. He's been rushed to hospital. I don't know how this could have happened."

The man looked around for a quiet spot away from the crowded footpath. He spotted a small goods service alley and moved quickly into the opening. "I'll tell you how it happened," he exploded. "It happened because you hired imbeciles instead of trained professionals. When I pay for a job, I expect it to be done, and when it isn't done right I clean up house and start over again. Do I make myself clear?"

"Yes, yes, Boss. We've found out which hospital the boy was taken to. I'm sending half the team there now; the others will continue to look for the woman."

The man kicked out in frustration against the alley wall. "For fuck's sake, use your brains, idiot. Has it not occurred to you that the mother will know by now of her son's plight, and that the first thing she will want to do is to visit him? You can stop your search, and send the full team to the hospital."

"I hadn't thought about that. What do you want us to do, bearing in mind there'll probably be a police presence? Shall we wait until we can isolate the woman and boy?"

"No, moron, you don't wait for anything. You get to that hospital, you find them and you kill them. If anyone tries to get in your way, you kill them too!"

Chapter 6

THE LARGE CAR park at the front of the hospital building was full, as it usually was just before the start of the afternoon visitors' stampede. The head of the six-man assault team had planned it that way; the more people milling about, the greater the confusion and the better their chances of slipping away.

They didn't need space for their minibus. They simply pulled up to the main entrance door, leaving the uniformed driver to await their return. To all intents and purposes, they were an official police contingent, able to park wherever they wanted and go anywhere they pleased.

Unlike the driver, the six men who marched across the hospital lobby were dressed in matching black suits, their leather soles clacking noisily off the tiled flooring. The receptionist watched them approach, already bracing herself for yet another query or demand about one of her patients. She recognised the type.

"Yes, officers, what can I do for you?"

If the leader was flummoxed by her assumption they were a police unit, he didn't show it. On the contrary, it suited him that she'd jumped to a wrong conclusion.

"We are here to take over security for Mr Hayden."

The receptionist raised her eyebrows. "That's strange. There's already a full police team here."

"Yes," the man responded. "We're here to relieve them. We're what you might call specialist officers. Could you direct us to where we should go?"

She shrugged and consulted a clipboard. "That would be room 321 on the third floor. The lift's over there in the corner."

The man followed the direction of her arm, thanked her, and took off through a small crowd gathered around a coffee machine. His team fell into step.

There was a bank of four lifts, each with its door shut, and about a dozen people staring blankly at the small red arrows, willing one of them to turn green. The group forced its way in front of one of the steel doors, ignoring the irate glances. By coincidence, it was the first door to ping open.

One of the men held out a hand to deter anyone from stepping into the carriage. They needed privacy on the short ride to the third floor. As soon as the door closed, the men removed 9mm Glock pistols from shoulder holsters, and watched the silent hand-signals of their leader.

The lift opened directly across from a nurses' station on a brightly-lit corridor. The men peeled out in two groups, one turning left, the other to the right. As expected, they immediately saw two armed policemen, stationed at either end of the corridor, with another standing sentry outside a single-room ward, the number 321 jutting out on a small arm above the door.

The cop at the door was the first to die. He was positioned midway between the lift and his colleague at the top end of the corridor. The group's leader drilled a hole in the centre of the man's forehead as he turned to look at the approaching figures, his brain barely able to register the threat before it was shut down.

Two of the intruders raced past the fallen figure and unleashed a merciless barrage at his colleague, barely thirty yards away. He was caught in the act of trying to unsling his Heckler and Koch MP5 when the bullets tore into his protective vest and sent him jerking against the nearest wall. The Kevlar jacket might have saved his life had it not been for three stray bullets that impacted six inches higher than intended, entering his throat and cutting off any chance of survival.

At the opposite end of the corridor, the remaining policeman faced a similar onslaught, this time from three pistols on full auto. Blood patches appeared on his arms, legs and head as he was pitched backwards against a window, the toughened glass giving way under his weight and the impact of several rounds. The body crashed through the opening and fell three floors onto a concrete walkway.

Screams rose from the open office where nurses and doctors scrambled for safety. Two visitors, who had been standing on the corridor side of the station, buried their heads in their hands and crouched in terror against the flimsy wood counter.

The group leader ignored the pandemonium and waited for his men to join him outside room 321. All six ejected their magazines, rammed in fresh ones, and operated the slide mechanisms on their weapons. After a silent count of three, the leader kicked open the door to the ward and rushed in.

Six Glocks swept the area in search of targets. They found none. A freshly-made bed stood forlornly in the centre of the room, flanked by empty visitor chairs, while a curtain flapped gently in a breeze caused by an open window. The door to an en-suite bathroom hung open, revealing an empty space, save for a shower convenience-seat and two steel bins, marked by typical hospital-disposal warning stickers.

Two floors directly above Room 321, Commander Hall heard the faint sounds of gunfire. He knew exactly what was going down, although the shock of an attack took several seconds to sink in. He'd never really believed an attempt would be made on Christopher Hayden's life, insisting on a last-minute relocation of the patient only as part of standard operating procedures for witness protection.

The young man was still in a coma, oblivious to what was happening, but his mother jumped from the seat at his bedside. "My God, is someone shooting inside the hospital? Has it anything to do with Christopher or me?"

He gestured to the woman to sit down. "Keep calm, Mrs Hayden, they can't reach us here." Despite his reassurance, he walked across the room and swivelled the door's locking mechanism, his hand already reaching inside his coat for his mobile phone. He needed back-up, and he needed it now.

SO19 operations centre, please state your credentials.

It was a direct-line number known only by senior Met Police officers.

This is Hall, 1414 Charlie Hotel, priority one alert. Full tactical team required ASAP at Rosemund Hospital. Officers down, I repeat, officers down. Extreme caution, tangos still at this location.

There was nothing to do, but wait. And pray.

Hall pulled a Glock 22 from his waistband. He had a full fifteen-round magazine, with an extra round already chambered. He didn't carry spare mags; never had the need to do. In fact, he couldn't remember the last time he'd fired his weapon in the line of duty. He hoped to God, his training and monthly firing-range sessions would help get him to auto-pilot mode when push came to shove.

He had a defenceless woman and a young boy to protect. Whoever came through that door would find a man not prepared to sell his life cheaply.

The leader ordered his men to start kicking in every door along the hospital corridor. The bitch and the brat had to be somewhere!

He raced into the nursing-station annex and grabbed a young woman by the hair, pushing the barrel of his pistol roughly against her temple.

"Where did they move the occupant of Room 321 to?"

The woman's voice was cracked with fear. "I don't know, I just...just came on duty at lunchtime...I don't know."

The man clubbed her with the pistol putt, threw her unconscious body to the ground, and sought out his next victim. A white-coated intern stepped forward, his stethoscope dangling across the front of his chest. "There's no need for more violence. The patient was moved to an ICU ward on the fifth floor. That's all we know."

The man snarled. "What number, what ward. Hurry up!"

The intern's confidence started to drain. "There are two main intensive-care wards and other private rooms on that floor. I really couldn't say exactly where they took him."

"Well, fuck you," the leader snarled. Then he fired point blank into the young medic's chest.

The gunman let out a sharp whistle, motioning his team to join him. "We're heading to the fifth floor. Use the stairs at either end and approach in teams of three. We're running out of time, so let's do this quick and dirty."

Commander Hall heard the noise of banging doors and knew the assailants had reached his floor level, even before the first screams of terrified staff and visitors penetrated the walls. He tried to get Sonia to lock herself in the bathroom, but she refused to leave her son's side, her body standing rigid at the foot of the bed, as if to stop any bullets reaching Christopher.

The sounds outside were coming from both directions. This was a well-orchestrated attack, closing on his position from both flanks. Hall knelt and aimed his Glock at the closed door, just as gunfire erupted in the corridor outside.

It wasn't like the erratic firing he'd heard from the lower floor. This was sustained bursts, with barely a let up in the shooting frenzy. Suddenly, it stopped, and he could hear footsteps thumping heavily on the tiled flooring. A shadow fell across the slit at the bottom of the door.

Hall moved his finger from the guard into the trigger ring. The door rattled. He started applying the final piece of pressure that would send an initial three-round burst towards the target.

A voice interrupted his concentration. "Commander Hall, this is SO19. Are you alright?"

"Identify! Hall yelled.

"This is 3885 Delta Tango."

Hall fell back on his haunches, relieved by the verification of the unit's call-sign sequence. He rocked forward, stood up and unlocked the door. Two men in full SWAT gear nodded, their heads almost covered by visored combat helmets, and their hands full with MP5's.

One of the men threw back his visor. "Looks like we got here just in time. Four tangos have been neutralised, but two got away. Team Bravo is in pursuit. We've secured the hospital, awaiting back-up teams less than two minutes away."

"Great work, Sergeant," Hall replied, noticing the man's stripes. "Casualties on our side?"

"First reports say three officers and one civilian found dead on the third floor."

Hall shook his head, bewildered by the speed of events. How had this got out of hand so fast? What the hell were the Haydens mixed up in?

Chapter 7

IF THERE WAS ONE thing drill instructors taught their men above all others, it was the old maxim of *get your sleep in when you can*. Too many operatives had allowed fatigue to cloud their judgements, or slow their reactions, simply because of failure or stubbornness to grab a piece of shuteye during missions. There were those who allowed adrenaline, or fear, or tension to get in the way. No matter how hard they tried, they couldn't switch off. The trick was to train the body to accept subconscious demands to power down. Only the elite managed to achieve it.

Devon had never found it difficult. He could go from an all-action state of alert to total serenity within a matter of minutes. While others struggled to get their emotions under control, Devon would be sound asleep wherever he could find a space for his six-foot frame. Usually it was on damp ground, or wedged into the corner of a derelict building, or – has had happened on more than one occasion – on a precarious observation platform in the crook of a tree.

This time he was in the comfort of his own king-size bed. He'd left the *LonWash* offices just before 6am and here he was, eight hours later, still buried below one of his wife Emma's many floral-patterned duvets. He would probably have stayed there for another few hours were it not for the sudden pressure he felt on his chest.

"Daddy, daddy, wake up!"

Six-year-old Michael was doing his best to use his father as a trampoline. Devon came alert instantly, grabbed his son in a playful bear hug, and rolled across the bed in a mock wrestling match, which Michael always seemed to win.

"When you two are quite finished, there's a dinner waiting to be served."

Devon looked up to find Emma standing at the foot of the

bed, feigning indignation. "Hi, Em, what time is it?"

She lifted a discarded pillow and flung it playfully at his head. "I'd say it was time a certain someone had a shave and a shower and presented himself in full dress in the dining room. You've got twenty minutes to shape up."

With that, she sashayed from the room. Devon watched her go and marvelled at her stamina. She was a corporate lawyer who specialised in international mergers and acquisitions for some of the biggest multi-nationals on the planet. She worked mainly from home, and somehow juggled her heavy business schedule with being a full-time mum. She was also Devon's biggest supporter when it came to his job, even though it had twice put the family in the direct line of fire. Instead of diminishing her resolve, the incidents had hardened her belief that her husband needed to continue what he was doing. For his part, he never kept anything from her. He'd learned long ago to accept that she coped best with knowing where he was, and what he was doing, rather than having to deal with wondering and speculating every time there was a news-flash about some incident or other across the world.

The couple had a full-time nanny to look after Michael and to help with general chores. Apart from delegating the nanny to school-runs, Emma was a hands-on mother who spent as much time as possible with her son, and usually ended up doing most of the housework herself.

The Devons could afford the luxury of home-help, thanks to a generous inheritance from Mike's parents, not to mention the lucrative fees earned by Emma's legal work. In many ways, they could retire to a less hectic lifestyle, but the thought of not being involved, not making a difference, didn't sit well with either of them.

Devon reported to the dining room on schedule. Dressed in blue jeans, a T-shirt, and his trademark combat boots, he settled into a chair, tousled Michael's hair, and savoured the plate of heaped food. Nobody made a traditional fry-up quite like Emma, though he'd had to teach her some of the quirks of the *Ulster Fry* he'd enjoyed during a stint in Northern Ireland at the height of the so-called Troubles. It was all there. Fried potato bread, soda farls, beans, bacon, sausages, black pudding, and three eggs, sunnyside up.

Midway through what could only be described as a food-scoffing session, Devon glanced up at the muted television screen mounted on the kitchen wall. There seemed always to be breaking news banners every time you tuned into one of the twenty-four-hour news channels. According to the familiar red bar across the bottom of the screen, this one was about at least four deaths in a shoot-out at a London hospital.

Emma followed his gaze. "Wondered how long it would take for you to notice that. The news broke about two hours ago. They're speculating it could be one of those terrorist attacks linked to ISIS. Apparently a young doctor was amongst those killed."

Devon bolted from his seat and grabbed the remote-control handset. He listened intently for several minutes before muting the sound and seizing his mobile phone. "Can't be terrorists. We'd have been notified before now."

He waited impatiently for the dial tones to stop their infuriating sounds. Finally, a voice cut through. "Hi Mike, guess you're ringing about the hospital incident?"

There were times when Devon could throttle Doyle for his laid-back approach. This was one of them. "Cut the Sherlock crap. What's going on? Why wasn't I contacted"

Doyle ignored the anger. He was used to it as being just part of Devon's way to get attention. "Cool the jets, oh great one," he intoned playfully. "There was nothing to disturb you about. This terrorist angle is a load of baloney, although we do need to take a closer look at what went down."

"Okay, give me what you've got."

Devon listened without interruption while Doyle succinctly laid out the details. It was a typical no-frills summary, with no personal commentary or hypothesis, just the salient facts.

"So, you're saying someone tried to get at a Met Police witness?"

"That's about the height of it, Mike, but here's the rub. This was no ordinary witness. This was the wife and son of Matthew Hayden."

The news hit Devon with the force of a runaway train. "Jeez, what's going on? Maybe Tim was right about us needing to stick our noses into this. I'll be back at the office within the hour. First, I have a long overdue phone call to make."

The man with the silver hair and the Lora Piana suit wasn't prepared to sit about waiting for a phone call. He'd heard all he needed to hear from the television stations. Four gunmen were dead, so was a medic, but no mention of the woman or her son. The mercenary and his team had failed again!

It was time for a different approach.

He was back in his hotel room, his flight to Paris already cancelled, and his mind racing through the options for cleaning up this mess. There was only one man he could really trust. He thought about the quirky individual, about his fanaticism for racing motorbikes, and about his one hundred per cent success rate for getting the job done. He reached for one of the encrypted mobiles and hit a speed-dial sequence, satisfied the loner would jump at the chance for his biggest-ever payday.

The conversation was short and sweet. The independent contractor gratefully accepted the assignment. The reward was not the size of the bounty, but the scale of the risk involved. That's what turned the crank of his thirst for danger. He was addicted to the challenge.

"Just one question. They're bound to relocate the targets. How will I find them?"

The silver-haired man smiled. "Leave that to me. Just make sure you're ready when I give the word."

Peter Ramsden, head of MI6, Britain's Secret Intelligence Service, took Devon's call at his Vauxhall Cross office overlooking the Thames. He was one of the few mainstream security agency personnel to be privy to the sanctioned clandestine operations of *LonWash Securities*, and had benefitted personally from their input into countless operations.

"Mike, to what do I owe the pleasure?"

There was no need for preambles between the two men. "Tell me what you know about Matthew Hayden, and about what's got everyone in such a twist lately."

There was a long pause before Ramsden spoke. "Look, Mike, this isn't something you should be involved in. Without sounding too harsh, I'd be grateful if you'd keep your oar out of these particular waters."

"That ain't going to happen, Peter. Some of my people have a history with Hayden, and we intend to get to the bottom of this. Whatever he was tied up with could have serious ramifications for national security, and that's not something I'm prepared to take a back seat on and, frankly, neither will the Old Man."

The Old Man in this case was General Sir John Sandford, the founder and majority shareholder of *LonWash*, and now the Prime Minister's senior security advisor. One of the most influential figures in Whitehall, Sir John directed virtually all anti-terrorism policies, and had a big say in who was hired and fired at the top of each agency.

"Mike, there's no need for a full-scale intrusion here. The matter's being dealt with by the SO19 Commander, John Hall, who's taken a personal interest in the case, and will make sure Hayden's wife and son are protected. Let's leave it to him to do what has to be done."

Devon knew Hall from several meetings he'd attended of the COBRA committee, the Government's think-tank on anti-terrorism policies. Hall was a good man, the kind you'd want in your corner when things got hairy. He was an up-from-the-ranks policeman who commanded the respect of his men. But was he really the right man to be pitched into this situation?

"This is hardly an SO19 matter, Peter. We both know this could lead into areas that require a different approach...."

"For fuck's sake. Mike, what part of staying out of this don't you get?"

Devon could feel the heat rising. It was time to stop pussyfooting around. "Here's the part that gets me, Peter. We have an ex-MI6 operative blown up at his home in the middle of nowhere, followed by separate attempts to murder his wife and son. If that's not enough, we then have a military-style follow-up assault on a London hospital in broad deadlight, with no care for how many bodies are piled up, and you think we should take a back seat?"

Ramsden responded in a more conciliatory tone. "I'm just saying, let the Met deal with it for now. We'll monitor things at this end, to make sure all the bases are covered."

Devon was not ready to back down. "Take a step back, Peter. You were there in MI6 when Hayden was drummed out of the service. What went on then? How come an apparently top-notch intelligence gatherer suddenly found himself in hot water?"

Another long pause. "That's classified, Mike. I'm not going to speculate or rake through old coals."

Devon had to rein in his mounting frustration. "Classified, my ass. We both know that if I make one phone call, the Old Man will see to it that things get unclassified in a hurry. What is it you're not telling me?"

"Okay, here's the best I know. I was a deputy chief at the time. There were rumblings that Hayden had gone off the reservation, that he'd started some kind of a personal crusade against our political masters. He was caught digging into the personal bank records of more than a dozen politicians, and had even ordered illegal wire-taps on some of the country's most senior Government ministers. When he was confronted about it, he spouted all sorts of conspiracy theories, but refused to offer any tangible evidence against any one individual. It appeared as if he was throwing a very wide net in the hope of finding something untoward. The chief at the time tried to give him a way out, but he insisted on being allowed to continue his work. In the end he left us with no wriggle room. He had to go."

"That all seems plausible," Devon responded, "but if these were just wild speculations about conspiracies, what got

Hayden killed and his family almost wiped off the map? What the hell was he claiming he'd found? There has to be more to this."

"All I know is that he believed there were some high-level conspiracies involving pay-offs to people to look the other way. He didn't know if these were run-of-the-mill bribes involving business transactions, or if they represented an undermining of national security. As I say, he'd become almost delusional about everything."

Devon knew Ramsden was doing his best to fill in the blanks, but it was a giant jigsaw with far too many missing pieces. "There's one way to get to the bottom of this," he told the MI6 chief. "Take a look back at the electronic trail of data that Hayden was working on. Who knows what a fresh pair of eyes could do with seeing the kind of things he was gathering intel about?"

This time the pause stretched into a highly uncomfortable silence.

"Are you still there, Peter? Did you hear what I said?"

"Yes, Mike, I heard. The problem is that when I took a look earlier today, the file on Hayden has gone missing from our records vault, and all trace of his work has been wiped from the agency servers."

Chapter 8

JUST WHEN HE thought his day couldn't get any worse, Commander John Hall found himself sitting uncomfortably in the centre of a large office, listening to a tirade that had already gone on for the best part of fifteen minutes. More than a tirade, it was a full-scale dressing down, complete with several thinly-veiled threats about his job being on the line. Hall had no doubt that the man delivering the rant was on the look-out for a scapegoat.

"So, let's summarise what London has had to put up with during your watch over the past few days." The Home Secretary, swiped a hand across a small mound of files on his desk, sending sheets of paper billowing downwards onto the opulent, blue-patterned carpet. It was a typical show of anger and aggression from a man who was all smiles and affability when things were rosy, but who was clearly out of his depth when the going got tough.

Unfortunately, as the most senior Cabinet figure next only to the Prime Minister, the Home Secretary's shortcomings were not up for discussion. Being in charge of the Home Office, he was responsible for the country's internal affairs, a remit that covered all policing and matters of national security. He was, effectively, Hall's boss, and seemed to enjoy letting him know about it.

"As I was saying, there is the little matter of a shoot-out in a back-street casino where six Tunisian men were killed, apparently in some kind of gangland reprisal, though of course the press is having a field day looking for terrorist links. As if that wasn't bad enough, we allowed a hospital, of all places, to be the scene of a gun battle, which claimed the life of a young junior doctor. Once again, the press is looking for terrorist links while you sit there spouting about a witness protection operation, one that - to put it mildly – was both ill-conceived and poorly managed. Is there anywhere within that summary that makes you believe I shouldn't fire you on the spot!"

Hall was used to this kind of political hyperbole. When shit hit the fan, politicians were quick to find a patsy to blame. Someone had to take the fall, provided it wasn't the duly-elected representative who was always keen to be front and centre of the good news stories, but grabbed the first backseat he could find when the heat was turned up. Hall knew he had to tread carefully.

"The casino attack seems to have been nothing more than a turf war. There was no recent intelligence to suggest a build-up of tensions between rival gangs, though of course it takes little to spark a confrontation. We're still investigating, but all the signs are that it was unrelated to any terrorist threat."

"And you'd stake your job on that?"

"No, I wouldn't!" Hall responded emphatically. "I'm not about to be backed into a corner so early into an investigation. We both know there can be surprises when you shake a tree hard enough, so let's wait and see what drops out before we rush to full judgement. Believe me, every possible angle will be covered."

The Home Secretary shifted direction immediately. "And what about the hospital?"

"I admit the hospital episode could have been handled differently. On the face of it, this appeared to require nothing more than simple precautionary protective measures on our part. There was no way to foresee that a group of armed men would show up to finish the earlier attempts that were made on the lives of a mother and son, whose only importance seems to be their connection to a former MI6 agent."

"And yet they did, Commander, and the lives of hospital staff and the general public were put at extreme risk. Hardly the Met's finest hour?"

"May I remind you, sir, that three of our officers died protecting this family, and that if it hadn't been for the follow-up actions of our other teams, many more people might have perished." It was the first time Hall had lost his cool since the interview started.

"Yes, yes, of course. The bravery and sacrifice of these men must not be forgotten." The politician was quickly covering his bases. "I will see to it that the public is made aware of the heroic way in which they performed their duties. You have to realise, however, that my disquiet is not about the gallant conduct of your men, but the manner in which they were put in harm's way in the first place. Arrangements should have been made to care for the young man away from such a vulnerable area. There are umpteen private clinics that would have afforded you better control of security, not to mention greatly reducing the exposure of the general public."

Hall had to concede the point. However, things had happened so fast after the Hayden boy was found near to death that he hadn't had time to put together a more detailed operation. Even now, with the benefit of hindsight, he was not so sure he could – or would – have done anything differently. One thing nagged at him. How had the gunmen discovered the boy's whereabouts so quickly?

The Home Secretary was still talking. "I'm also struggling to understand why the head of the capital's anti-terrorism unit was personally babysitting this family. Don't you have better things to do with your time? Is there a personal interest here that I should know about? Are you otherwise involved with this woman?"

Hall couldn't contain his anger. "That's bloody nonsense! I never met Sonia Hayden until two days ago when she presented herself at The Yard because of an attempt on her life. This followed the news of her husband's murder, something which, by the way, now merits a full-blown security investigation. We put her up in a local hotel under police protection, and the following morning I was informed about the assault on her son. I personally escorted Mrs Hayden to the hospital because it had become clear that someone, or some organisation, was trying to obliterate all trace of this family. There has to be a very big motive behind these attacks, and the obvious starting point is Matthew Hayden's previous job."

"I'm well aware of Hayden's background," the Home Secretary said. "Arrangements have already been made to transfer investigative responsibility to MI6, so you are hereby ordered to stand down. The Hayden family will be moved from the hospital to a new location, under new protection measures, which doesn't include SO19. Now, Commander, you have a lot of other things on your plate. I suggest to get to them and forget about the Haydens."

The Audi A8L 3-litre TDi roared to a stop between two ten-foot pillars, the driver drumming his fingers impatiently on the steering wheel as he waited for the remote-control command to kick in. Finally, the electronic gates swivelled inwards and activated a necklace of lights that illuminated the long driveway to the imposing three-storey house in the centre of the compound.

Manicured lawns and professionally-sculpted flower beds fell away on both sides of the tarmacked road. The car's headlights caught the shimmer of water at the bottom of a fountain enclosure, which was surrounded by a cluster of topiary trees, one in the shape of a full-size elephant. Motion-sensor CCTV cameras swivelled from a half-dozen locations to zero in on the vehicle as it drew to a stop beside the front door of the house.

Dave Millward climbed out and stomped angrily up the steps. Normally, he would pause and look lovingly around his creation, conjuring up ways to add to the features or enhance the design of his life's work. Tonight, however, he had more pressing matters to attend to.

Millward had somehow managed to escape from the hospital firefight with his long-time friend, Mark Jennings. The pair had made their way across town, swopping taxis at regular intervals, before walking the last mile to a rented garage where he'd stored the Audi. He'd dropped Jennings off at a London address and was halfway to his Surrey estate when he'd received the call from the Paymaster.

It was a conversation that had not gone well.

So, the fucker thinks he can dump me?

Millward made his way into a large drawing room, poured a glass of brandy, and flopped into an armchair. He lived alone, always had done. He was a career soldier, first as a special forces operative with tours of Iraq, Afghanistan, Brunei and Africa, followed by a post-service stint as a mercenary in more hotspots than he could remember. Along the journey, he found a more lucrative sideline as a fixer, a somewhat genteel description for a profession that became little more than a paid assassin.

His combat skills were never in doubt. An expert in short- and long-range weapons, he was also a top-notch hand-to-hand fighter, who specialised in an eclectic mix of martial arts. Above all, Millward was noted for his attention to detail in mission-planning, a gift that had earned him widespread admiration among the men with whom he served. He had taken those strengths into civilian life, and quickly established a profitable agency, known only to those who lived within the darkside. It was here he was contacted by the Paymaster, the only pseudonym he was permitted to use.

It mattered little to Millward that the voice on the other end of the phone appeared to belong to a callous, pompous individual. He paid well, and the work kept rolling in, along with extravagant payments that had swelled Millward's bank accounts in a dozen countries.

Because of that, he'd suffered the Paymaster's often gruff tones and downright nastiness. Lately, however, the demands had become almost hysterical, the deadlines tighter, and the risks increased to an unacceptable level. The attack on the hospital was the last straw. It needed more planning; an extra twenty-four hours would have made the difference between success and failure. He'd allowed himself to be bullied into a doomed venture, one that had cost the lives of four friends, men who'd worked with him for many years.

And what was his reward? Chewed out by a jumped-up little fucker who'd ranted about no longer having any confidence in his work. Dumped on the scrapheap without payment for services already rendered. Cast aside with no compensation for the families of the men who'd died.

That's what he thinks!

Dave Millward had an ace up his sleeve. Despite the Paymaster's insistence on anonymity, Millward had tracked him down a year ago, thanks to an old Army communications buddy who'd inserted a nifty piece of GPS back-tracing software into the burner phone that had arrived mysteriously one day via courier post. It was meant to be the only safe form of communication between the two men. In fact, it proved to be the Paymaster's one big mistake.

Millward hit paydirt with one of the calls. The GPS tracker showed it coming from a London hotel, less than fifteen minutes away from his then location, perusing top-of-the-range motors in a London saleroom. He'd grabbed a taxi, hightailed to the location and settled into the foyer, drinking coffee and watching everyone who came and went.

He remembered being alerted by a voice at the concierge desk. It was one he'd recognised almost immediately. He'd turned to watch a white-haired man being given theatre tickets, handing over a large wad of cash, and disappearing out into the street without so much as a glance in Millward's direction.

In less than an hour he'd learned all he needed to know about the Paymaster. The information was filed away for a rainy day.

He was now ready to pounce. He threw back the last of his brandy, and slipped into a familiar planning mode. He'd get what was due to him. He'd make the bastard squirm while he completed online transfers of funds, making sure that what ended up in his accounts would allow him to spend more time in his beloved garden. After that the Paymaster would cease to exist.

And then, Millward decided, he would finish the job on the Haydens. It was a matter of professional pride.

Chapter 9

THE BRIEFING ROOM at LonWash Securities was frequently the scene of frenetic activity. Too many bodies, not enough space, and a volume of chatter capable of drowning out the noise of a good-size industrial grinding machine. When the room was full, as it was today, there was usually some crisis or other to deal with, or some deadline to meet.

Things were slightly different this time.

There was no immediate mission panic, no clock or calendar to keep an eye on, no apparent reason why everyone should be in a flap. And yet, the air was charged with electricity.

Devon had called together the agency's full frontline team. Doyle, Horgan, Cheadle and two other operatives, Terry Hunt and Jim Cross, were bunched together at the coffee counter. Tim Halloran and his three most senior technicians were already seated along one side of the conference table, each staring at a tablet computer, making sure they were keeping up to speed with whatever data was flowing into the mainstream servers down the corridor.

At the head of the table sat a solitary figure, patiently waiting for things to come to order. This was Sir Clive Oliver, renowned among London's financial sectors as the successful chairman of *Paxoil*, a business he'd developed from modest roots to become one of the world's leading oil companies. What most people didn't know was that these days Sir Clive headed a second, secret operation, one that took him into the murky waters of financial terrorism, a threat identified as being the new kid on the block where national security was concerned.

Sir Clive had helped *LonWash* isolate and bring down a Russian billionaire who had come close to collapsing the UK economy through a series of Stock Market manipulations. The near-miss had prompted the PM and General Sandford to persuade Sir Clive to establish a covert watchdog team whose sole purpose was to scour financial markets for any unusual activities. Although all major Stock Exchanges have their own oversight and investigative arms, they are limited in what they can achieve, often facing complex financial rules, which either slow down investigations or result in little more than slap-on-the-wrist outcomes. The tie-up between *LonWash* and Sir Clive's clandestine operation meant that more immediate – and direct – actions could be sanctioned.

Six monitoring and surveillance officers worked for Sir Clive in an office at Gracechurch Street, close to the curiously-named Threadneedle Street, home to the Bank of England since the early part of the eighteenth century. The team worked shifts, ensuring there was always at least two operatives on duty on a 24/7 basis.

At the age of seventy-five, Sir Clive still cut an imposing figure, with a thick growth of mousey-brown hair and the clean complexion of a man in his forties. He always wore three-piece pinstripe suits, tailored to the precise contours of his six-foot frame, and sported a matching tie and breastpocket handkerchief in the colours of his former Royal Fusiliers regiment. He'd never lost the shoulders-back-chest-out posture of his military days, and spoke in a rich baritone voice that tended to get attention.

Devon drew up a seat beside Sir Clive and signalled the team to take their places. He waited for the scraping of seats to subside before starting the briefing. "We have two topics on the agenda – a follow-up operation against the Tunisians, and what to do about the attacks on the Hayden family. Let's see how we divide our resources."

He pushed a button on a laptop, and the head-and-shoulder photos of two men appeared on the wall-mounted screen behind him. "Meet Mehdi Naybet and Marouen Badri, two gentlemen we unfortunately missed during our little casino soiree. We know they are linked in some way to what happened in Nice, so our priority is to find them. According to their confederates, who are enjoying our hospitality in the basement cells, the pair had already left for some sort of business trip, either in America or Germany, depending on which one of our guests is to be believed. Unfortunately, what we learned from their interrogations, is that they really don't know much, so we have to follow both leads. We also have to assume the missing men may not even have left the country."

"How do we go about finding them?" Cheadle asked.

"That's probably down to us," Halloran interjected. "We'll scour all flights out of the country over the past week, using facial recognition searches against airline passport databases. We'll do the same at ferry crossings and the Channel Tunnel, although these are less likely to throw up any hits because security procedures are not up to the standard of airports. Also, we'll scan mobile networks to see if we can trace any activity on the phone numbers elicited from our prisoners. If they have modern GPS sets, we might get a location. We'll check names against passenger lists, though experience tells us they'll be travelling under aliases, and we've already begun scouring for any credit or debit card transactions linked to their personal accounts or those of the casino."

"Just what I'd expect, Tim," Devon told him. "It's important we run these bastards to ground, but I want you to keep yourself and half the team in reserve for the next part of our meeting."

"Where do I come in?"

"I'm glad you asked, Sir Clive," Devon beamed. "Basically, I want you to bleed the *Tunisian Templars* dry. Clean out their bank accounts, and find me a list of all transactions, particularly money transfers involving sums that you consider to be outside the normal business of a casino. Get us a list of recipients of their largesse, and see if there's a pattern of activity between them. I want names, addresses and where-they-shit-last details of anyone who pops up on your radar."

"Is that all?" Sir Clive responded without the slightest trace of sarcasm.

"No, it's not. I'm giving you a layman's shopping list, but

your people will no doubt think of things I know little about. Feel free to be expansive. These people are part of a terrorist-funding network, and the more we learn about them, the better chance we'll have of stopping them."

Sir Clive smiled. "You know, for a layman, you've covered most of the angles. However, I'm sure we can come up with a few frills such as their online purchasing histories, where they like to eat out, and where they buy their clothes. Unfortunately - although we can take a wild guess - we can't advise you on their toilet habits!"

That brought a round of laughter from the group. Devon rose and accompanied Sir Clive to the door.

"I take it," the septuagenarian said, "you want all this by yesterday."

The photos on the wall screen had changed by the time Devon retook his seat. They were replaced by a single picture of a smiling man, chomping on a cigar and holding a glass towards the camera.

"This," said Alan Doyle, who had moved to the top table, "is Matthew Hayden, clearly in happier times before he was shoved out of the MI6 door, and subsequently blown to pieces for reasons as yet unknown."

Doyle continued to give an outline of Hayden's career and finished with a summary of the events of the past few days. He nodded at Devon for a recap on his conversation with MI6 chief Peter Ramsden.

"It seems to me," Devon concluded, "that something's rotten over at Vauxhall Cross. How can a senior intelligence agency lose a significant personnel file, while allowing its servers to be sanitised of all references to Matthew Hayden's work? Coincidences belong in the land of the fairies, not in the real world of espionage."

"How much do you think Ramsden knows?" Doyle queried.

"Peter's a good guy. I think he's embarrassed by what's happened, and is trying to put a brave face on it. If I was to guess, he's getting pressure from above, meaning any follow-up investigation by MI6 will be perfunctory at best. We can't expect much help there."

Doyle raised his eyebrows. "We don't need their help! Let them play silly buggers if they want to, while we do their job for them. There's bound to be a way around deleted hidden servers and deleted files. Isn't that right, Tim?"

Halloran shifted uncomfortably. "In most cases that would be true, but there are some bright boys over at MI6, and if they wanted to permanently get rid of data they'd know all the tricks in the book. Naturally, I'll take a sneak look, but I wouldn't hold out much hope of unscrambling things. What we need is access to Hayden's personal computer."

"Not going to happen," Devon sighed. "Whatever he had in that cottage of his was turned into little more than dust. There must be other ways of finding a trail?"

"Ordinarily," Halloran replied, "I'd guess a man like Hayden would back up his work to remote servers, or supporting hardware storage drives, or even simple data pens. He could've hidden these anywhere, including safety deposit boxes, or railway station lockers, or at other sites such as....."

"Such as his wife's new home, or his son's student digs?" Devon finished the thought for him."

"Yeah," Doyle agreed, maybe that's why they were targeted?"

Halloran waved down the enthusiasm. "It would make things neat and tidy if we found something at those locations, but surely the assailants would have stumbled across them already? My guess is that the odds are slim to nothing, which means we'll have to do it the hard way. We'll trace everything and anything connected to Hayden over the past few years. Maybe if we turn over enough stones, something'll fall out."

Devon leaned back in his seat. He'd made a decision. "Tim, use all the resources and manpower you need. Let the other team work on the Tunisian investigation, but concentrate everything you've got on finding what there is to know about Matthew Hayden's life since he left MI6. There are no budget limits on this."

He got up and turned to look at the screen-projected photo on the wall. "I'm becoming more and more convinced this man was shafted, and it's our job to find out why. I just wish we could talk to his wife and son, sooner rather than later."

"Not gonna be easy," Doyle told him. "They're under SO19 protection, and we all know how territorial those bozos can be."

A new voice boomed across the room. "So, when did *LonWash* start caring about territories?"

All eyes turned to the door.

Chapter 10

FEW PEOPLE could command an audience the way General Sir John Sandford did. One look at the broad-shouldered, six-foot-six bear of a man, was enough to grab anyone's attention, but there was more to it than that. Much more. The shock of white hair, the penetrating stare, and a John Wayne-like swagger marked him clearly as an authority figure, a man to be either obeyed or stepped around at great haste. There was no room for grey areas. He had that kind of effect.

And yet, the old warhorse was renowned for his bonhomie and innate good nature. In a long and distinguished military career, which had taken him to some of the world's worst hellholes, he had never lost his humanity, nor allowed his troops to be placed needlessly in harm's way. If a fight could be avoided, Sir John did his utmost to make it so.

When all else failed, however, and action was needed, a small door opened to reveal the General's flipside. He became a merciless, implacable foe, particularly where the defence of innocents was concerned. The rules of engagement and any false sense of fair play went out the window. He hit his enemies hard, and he kept on hitting them, until he won the day.

He'd seen too much evil to trade niceties with men lacking conscience or honour. The new breed of radicals and extremist warriors concerned him most of all. It was why, after his military days had come to end, he'd started his own corporate enterprise. *LonWash Securities* came into being ostensibly to handle a number of private government contracts in places like Iraq and Afghanistan. The cover allowed Whitehall to channel funds into the agency, though no one ever checked what was actually delivered for the large sums involved.

The General had persuaded successive Prime Ministers

that more direct action was needed against the nation's enemies. This had to be done away from political oversight, and the constraints faced by established agencies like MI6, MI5 and various other anti-terrorist groups in the UK. Financial support was also provided by Washington, where a similar organisation worked closely with its British counterpart in rooting out world terrorism threats. The London-Washington tie-up had been quickly truncated to *LonWash*.

Sandford established a base in a five-storey building on Charterhouse Street, not far from the Victoria Embankment, and with easy access to all major city routes. It had a large underground car-parking area where the agency stored and operated a fleet of specially-converted vehicles, including highly sophisticated, armour-plated surveillance cars and vans. Beneath the car park was another level for the building's maintenance machinery, with large rooms for generators, electrical switchboxes, and a water filtration plant. One room on this level had been converted into a fully-soundproofed firing range; another was used for four, single-room, holding cells.

Sir John was convinced his greatest success was landing Mike Devon as his senior operative. He'd chosen Devon after watching him successfully complete an infiltration mission against the IRA in Northern Ireland, and later made him a substantial shareholder and the agency's new boss. By that time, Sir John had recovered from an assassination attempt funded by a Russian oligarch whose plans to wreak havoc on the London Stock Exchange had been left in ruins through the intervention of *LonWash*.

General Sandford "moved upstairs" to become Britain's most senior security strategist, though he still retained direct links with his beloved agency.

It was why he'd gatecrashed Devon's latest briefing.

"I haven't left the building for more than the proverbial five minutes, and I'm hearing defeatist talk," Sandford boomed, before flashing a smile at Alan Doyle and squeezing into a gap at the top of the table.

Devon inched across and warmly shook his mentor's hand. "Glad to have you on board, sir. I'm hoping you're here to help us with the little jurisdictional problem that Alan was referring to?"

"It *is* rather coincidental that I walked in at that precise moment, but I do have some updated info for you. It seems that our esteemed Home Secretary has pulled the rug out from under SO19, and wants the problems with the Haydens moved out of London. It doesn't do to have gunmen running amok on our streets, so he wants the targets spirited away to avoid a repetition of the scenes at Rosemund Hospital."

Devon was stunned by the news. "These people need proper protection, not swept under the carpet. Who's going to be looking after their welfare, not to mention trying to find the real truth behind what's been happening to them?"

"I would have thought that was obvious, dear boy!"

"You've lost me, General."

"Let's just say that calls were made, and influence was brought to bear on the right people. The upshot is that two hours from now, Sonia and Christopher Hayden will be transferred to the protective custody of *LonWash*."

Doyle slapped a palm on the table. "Well done, sir. Maybe now we can start to get to the bottom of this."

Devon nodded in agreement. "That's the best possible solution. We have a safe house outside London, and enough muscle to keep the Haydens under wraps. I worry though that sinister forces will be working against us, and not all of them will be on the wrong side of the fence."

"Tell me what you know to date," Sandford stated.

It was not often one got the chance to pick one of the country's best strategic brains, so Devon launched into a full report, including the proposed actions outlined earlier in the briefing. As he spoke, he could visualise cogs whirring inside Sir John's head.

"That's about it," Devon finished, glancing expectantly at his boss.

"It seems to me," the General said, "you're covering all the squares on this particularly nasty-looking chessboard. I don't like this mysterious loss of data from within MI6. It smacks of collusion, no matter how honest and misguided it may have been, and it does raise some questions that make me think we should tread very carefully indeed. I know Tim and his tech team can surf the ether world without leaving traces, but this time we must be doubly sure."

"I will be, sir," Halloran responded.

"I know you will, Tim. I bring it up because to all intents and purposes our only remit here is the protection of the Hayden family. Nobody must know we're doing anything else until we're good and ready to confront those with their hands in the cookie jar. I don't know how high we'll need to reach, but don't be afraid to follow this wherever it leads. If someone's trying to cover his tracks, I want him found. Remember our old intel adage, and start looking in the least likely places. Rats tend to scurry to the farthest, darkest corners."

"Consider it done," Devon said with more confidence than he felt. "Now, what about the details of the handover?"

"The SO19 Commander, John Hall, will personally escort the Haydens to this office. The boy is sufficiently recovered to make the trip, although he *is* still confined to bed and will need ongoing medical attention. Our own surgeon will examine the patient here before transfer to the safe house and I've arranged for some security-vetted nurses to remain with your team until this thing is over."

"You seem to have covered everything, General."

"Just one more thing, Mike. The SO19 man, Hall, wants to be kept in the loop. I'd say you can trust him implicitly, but it's your call."

Devon needed only a second to process the request. "I've met Hall and I liked what I saw. We'll do what we can, but we'll have to tread carefully. The fewer people who know where we're at, and what we're doing, the better for everyone."

The ringtone told the white-haired man all he needed to know. It was not one that was used on a regular basis. Unlike his other mobiles, this unit was rarely active, reserved only for those occasions when direct contact was unavoidable.

He hit the answer button and waited. The caller was a careful individual. A sequence of odd electrical shrieks and pinging sounds signified the use of encryption to block any trace of the origin of the call, or what was being said. A third-party listener would hear meaningless electronic babble. Clear dialogue was available only to the intended recipient.

"You have something for me?" white hair stated blandly.

"The targets are being transferred from hospital this evening to the offices of a private security firm located in Charterhouse Street. They are due to arrive precisely at midnight. This situation has become much too messy. Can we be assured it will be sorted out this time?"

White hair didn't like having to deal with the surly behaviour of others. He was not used to being told what to do. He was the one who gave orders, and handed out the dressing-downs to others. He had no masters, except.... except for this man and his cronies. He was forced to bite hard on his lower lip. "Yes, I agree this has not been handled with our usual aplomb. Your information will ensure the job will be finished by a new, more reliable contractor."

"See to it that it is."

The phone went dead.

It took several seconds for white hair to compose himself and reach for another mobile.

Chapter 11

An ambulance and an unmarked police car drove down the basement ramp midway along Charterhouse Street. Devon and four of his team stood guard either side of the entrance, and followed the vehicles to a cleared area beside the building's only service lift. The gates leading to the street were quickly shut, although no attempt was made to increase the dim lighting of the spacious interior.

Three floors above the ramped entrance, Chelsea Horgan made one last sweep of the empty buildings opposite the *LonWash* offices. She was staring through a night-vision-enhanced Schmidt and Bender telescopic sight attached to a bolt-action L115 sniper rifle, traversing it slowly across the darkened windows along the length of the street.

She had been in position for more than fifteen minutes, part of an orchestrated operation to ensure a smooth transfer of the Hayden family into the care of *LonWash*.

Devon was taking no chances.

As expected, so late in the evening in a non-residential area, there was no movement in any of the surrounding office buildings. Horgan deftly dismantled her gear in the blacked-out office, and stored the suitcase in a locker bolted to an inner wall. She eased into the main corridor, walked to a flight of stairs, and ascended to the agency's newly-converted staff accommodation floor.

She was just in time to watch Devon emerge from the service lift ahead of a posse of people surrounding a fully-equipped hospital bed. She could make out the shape of a young man, apparently unconscious, and hooked up to an intravenous drip and a number of portable gadgets that trailed behind on a double-shelved, aluminium trolley. Walking beside Devon, Doyle, Cheadle, Hunt and Cross was a man she didn't recognise, and a red-eyed woman she guessed was Sonia Hayden. A doctor and nurse completed the sizeable entourage.

The bed was wheeled into a large, air-conditioned room that had been prepared in advance. It was tastefully decorated in pastel colours, and contained a single bed, several armchairs, a writing bureau, and a dressing table, a thoughtful last-minute accessory insisted on by Horgan. An en-suite bathroom completed the self-contained arrangements for mother and son.

The room was fitted with bullet-proof windows, though they were somewhat superfluous. Shutters were fastened and curtains closed as an additional belt-and braces security measure. Even the best sniper in the world can't hit what he can't see.

Christopher Hayden's bed was wheeled against one wall. The nurses busied themselves with plugging the equipment into mains sockets, and settling the patient's pillows and bedclothes. The doctor nodded at Devon and his team to leave the room to allow him to carry out a complete examination.

Out in the corridor, Devon introduced Commander Hall to his team. After a round of nods and perfunctory handshakes, Hall looked uneasily at Devon. "I have to say, Mike, that this has all been done with indecent haste. I don't for a moment doubt the capabilities of your team, but it beats me why the Home Office was so fired up about farming out this family, especially when the boy is still in the vital early stages of recovery. Given what's already happened, there are a lot of risks involved, and my men are not happy at being stood down."

Devon had received a full medical briefing before the transfer. Christopher Hayden was one lucky young man. The stabbing had missed his vital organs and - because he'd been discovered within ten minutes of the assault - doctors had managed to induce a coma to mitigate the effects of body-shock. A blood transfusion had regenerated his circulation and he'd been fed a concoction of antibiotics and steroids. As soon as he emerged from the coma, he was subjected to a barrage of sensory tests, all of which he'd passed with flying colours.

Shortly before transfer he was given a dose of mild sedatives to help make the journey comfortable, although it was agreed in advance that he be kept at the *LonWash* offices before being taken on the longer journey to the safe house, approximately a hundred miles outside London. It was likely he would remain at Charterhouse Street for at least thirty-six hours.

"I'd feel no differently in your shoes," Devon told Hall, "but the reality is that we both have to get on with things as they are. Sonia and Christopher will be safe in our hands, probably much safer than in any of the public facilities you would be forced to use. Much as you may not like it, we are a better bet at this moment than SO19, no offence intended."

Hall's nostrils flared. "No offence, my ass! It's easy for you to take the high ground, but you're not the one being shafted here. I've lost men on this assignment, and it sticks in the craw that I'm being told to walk away without being given the chance to lead a follow-up investigation into why my officers were killed. You should know better than anyone how hard it is to take that kind of thing lying down."

Devon felt for the man. No team leader worth his salt could sit on the sidelines in the aftermath of an action in which he'd lost men. All the old clichés jumped into his mind.

Leave no stone unturned.

Kick down every door.

Move heaven and earth.

They all applied. The bottom line was that he could simply never walk away. And, he knew with certainty, the same stubbornness and determination to put matters right applied equally to Hall. Despite whatever orders had been handed down, the reality was that Hall would keep appearing at the fringes of whatever events were likely to occur in the coming days and weeks. This pent-up policeman would need careful management.

"I'll keep you posted every day," Devon promised, "but I must insist you and your men stay at arm's length."

"Tell me at least where you're taking them. I want to be able to visit them."

"Are you mad?" Devon exploded. "How do you think the hospital location became compromised? Someone, somewhere within SO19, or your affiliates, blew the whistle. That's not going to happen while they're with us. This is now a strictly need-to-know operation and .... you don't need me to finish, do you?"

Devon was determined to lay down a marker. He had no intention of provoking Hall into a war of words, but he needed his message to get through, no matter about private feelings and sensitivities. This was not a subject to be danced around.

To his surprise, Hall didn't bite back. Instead, his tone was one of resignation. "Don't you think I don't know something rotten went on behind the scenes? I can vouch for my men, but how can I be sure of others who were tied into our operation? I'll keep out of your hair for the sake of Sonia and Christopher, but I'll get to the bottom of this, I promise."

"The investigations into the attacks on the Haydens have nothing to do with us," Devon lied. "Our only job here is to protect the people who've been put under our wing. That's all we'll be concentrating on. I guess you'll do what you think you have to, but that's not my concern."

"I'm grateful for your frankness," Hall said. "I'm not walking away from this, but I respect your position. Will you at least honour your promise to contact me on a daily basis?"

Devon grasped Hall in a firm handshake. "You have my word."

The Honda Fireblade rested on its parking stand in shadows at the southernmost entrance to Charterhouse Street. The rider's red and black striped helmet was still fastened around his head as he stood observing the arrival of the ambulance. No detail was missed, particularly the confident bearing of the men who stood guard at the entrance and ushered the convoy into the basement with all the hallmarks of professionals.

A slight movement at a third-floor window also caught his attention. There was just enough moonlight cutting through the gloom to enable him to make out the silhouette of a crouching figure, and the outline of a long-barrelled gun as it was pulled away from the window. Now that *was* impressive!

This was no two-bit private security firm. This was the real deal. He'd expected a show of muscle-bound second-raters, more concerned with a sense of their own importance, a trait usually underlined by idiotic posturing, holding their hands to earpieces, or wearing sunglasses even in the dead of night! He'd come across too many Johnny-come-lately movie followers not to notice the difference between those who thought they knew how to do the job, and those who simply got on with it.

The team guarding the basement entrance at Charterhouse Street belonged clearly to the latter.

There was an economy of movement and an understated way they went about things that showed they knew what they were doing. Ex-military? Certainly. Honed into a cohesive unit? Without doubt. Strategists and forward planners? The evidence, as demonstrated by the upper-floor sniper cover, was plain to see.

Suddenly the biker's assignment took on a whole new dimension. This would not be as easy as he'd anticipated. This would require his full skillset.

He almost rubbed his hands in glee at the challenge that lay ahead.

Chapter 12

HOME SECRETARY Charles Manning sat behind an enormous Regency walnut desk and stared at the study's hand-carved double doors, willing them to remain shut. This was not an evening for entertaining guests, much less the two men who were about to barge in for what they euphemistically called one of their *little chats*.

Apart from a housemaid and three officers of the RaSP Command, the Royalty and Special Protection squad attached to the Metropolitan Police, Manning was alone in the country manor that had been his ancestral home for eight generations. He was the last in a distinguished lineage stretching back to the days of heroes such as Horatio Nelson and the Duke of Wellington, and statesmen like Gladstone and Disraeli, men who had forged Britain's rich history, usually with a Manning standing alongside them, if the fanciful ramblings of the latest holder of the name was to be believed.

Charles Manning was neither a hero nor a statesman. He was a dreamer. His university days had been noteworthy only for their mediocrity; his rise to power made possible by wealth and the cronyism that was rampant among the aristocratic elite. There had never been the possibility of an heir, not least because he preferred the company of rent boys and high-class male prostitutes - all of whom were well paid to overlook his physical shortcomings - but there was also the little matter of Manning's innate abhorrence to sharing anything with anybody. He was self-deluded, bordering on ego-mania, a man who considered others as little more than pawns in whatever grand scheme happened to be his flavour of the day.

He was a bully - of the highly dangerous and most unpredictable kind. He thought little of destroying lives and careers, usually on a whim, and often because it was easier to get rid of a problem than deal with it. And it usually worked for him. Right up until the time he crossed paths with the two gentlemen who were at the moment passing through the manor's front-gate security checkpoint.

It had seemed to be a perfect confederacy, the convergence of three people who could scratch each other's back to the mutual benefit of their respective bank balances. Manning had needed the money, large sums of it, to fund his lavish lifestyle and cover the mounting costs of a high-maintenance property that should have been disposed of years ago. But stupid pride and a sense of infallibility had set him on a different course.

Billionaire industrialists George Roper and Giles Grimand had offered to help. All they'd wanted in return was having a man on the inside, someone who could open a few political doors, and maybe steer policies in a direction that best suited their interests. The right nudge here or there could, they told him, lead to lucrative opportunities for those who knew what to do with them. And Roper and Grimand had proved more than capable in that regard over the ten years of their *little arrangement.*

The referendum which had led to Britain's exit from the European Union was a case in point. The industrialists had known there was a potential fortune to be made from *Brexit,* provided they built up a fund of foreign currencies to take advantage of a plummet in sterling values in the event of an EU withdrawal. To help their cause they'd surreptitiously ploughed a few million into the anti-Europe campaign, and forced Manning to convince a number of high-profile politicians to throw their hats into the ring in favour of an independent Britain.

Their efforts had garnered a few extra billion for bank deposits across the world.

Unfortunately for Manning, not all his dealings with the duo had been quite so entrepreneurial. He'd learned to his cost that their schemes, for the most part, were of a far more sinister nature, often involving death and destruction, and almost always requiring a treasonable act on his part. He was in too deep to be able to extricate himself from their clutches, a reality that had led to many, self-pitying, tear-filled episodes in the solitude of this mausoleum he called home.

Roper led the way through the double doors and marched to a seated area surrounding a sturdy coffee table, covered with a solid-silver tea service set and trays of sandwiches. Grimand flopped into an armchair and waited for his partner to begin proceedings. No smiles or pleasantries were exchanged between the three men.

"Get out from behind that ridiculous oversized desk and join us," Roper barked at Manning. He waited for his host to shuffle across the carpet and take a seat before resuming what appeared to be a well-rehearsed speech. "I don't much care for having to travel here to remind you of your commitments, and to warn you that unless this little matter is quickly resolved we will have to rethink our continued relationship. Now, tell me you have some good news."

Manning ignored the obvious threat. He'd prepared his own speech, in much the same way he tackled sensitive matters of state at Cabinet meetings. He'd lived by the old adage of getting your retaliation in before the other guy, even if this particular confrontation was way outside his comfort zone. "You can drop the holier-than-thou act, George. We both know what's happened here, and why we find ourselves in a mess. At your insistence, I've been dealing with a third-party contractor – a man of your choosing, no less – and if there's any blame to be spread around, it's most certainly not at my doorstep."

The two visitors exchanged raised-eyebrow glances. Roper leant forward, his scowl replaced by a thin smile. "Nice to see you've finally grown a pair, Charles, but don't underestimate the seriousness of the situation, or your part in it. The fact remains that it was down to you to get rid of our little problem, and yet here we are no closer to a resolution. What we need to hear from you is that you are on top of things, and that we can be assured this matter will be put to rest, so to speak."

Manning was determined to remain bullish. "Must I remind you that had it not been for my timely intervention the discoveries made by the MI6 man, Hayden, might already be a matter of public record. Because of my contacts, I was able to nip things in the bud and ensure his secrets were buried after I arranged for him to be put out to grass."

Grimand, who until that point had remained stoically silent, slammed his palm onto the coffee table, and fixed Manning with a withering stare. "You fucking imbecile! That was the start of our worries. Instead of putting him out to grass, you should have buried him. The situation didn't call for the man to be sacked, it required a more permanent solution, one that would not have given him the opportunity to keep digging. It was precisely because he was allowed to go free that we ran the risk of always having to look over our shoulders."

"I know, I know," Manning said apologetically. "In the circumstances, I believed enough attention had been drawn to Hayden without making things worse by adding his death to the rumours that were flying around. It was better to watch him drop off the grid, cut off from his former colleagues and friends."

"All very plausible and extremely stupid," Grimand said. "There was never a chance a man like Hayden would simply disappear and forget his life's work. He was clever enough to sever all ties and run to a bolthole where he assumed we could never find him. We would have most certainly lost his trail if he'd stayed away from computers and stopped data-mining in places he shouldn't have. But that's where he made his mistake. We'd taken precautions with new gateways and firewalls, although our tech people admit it was only by chance that they came across his electronic snooping. Thankfully, we were able to back-trace Hayden's whereabouts from what little information was salvaged from his incessant trespassing."

Manning's face brightened. "Yes, yes, and need I remind you that I took care of the problem as soon as the location was passed to me."

Roper rose and towered over the Home Secretary. "Aren't you forgetting that the wife and son are still alive? Who knows what he told them, or what arrangements he made to provide them with access to a safety deposit box, or some other hidey-hole, in the event of his death. Until the entire Hayden family is accounted for, we will not be able to rest easy."

Despite a sick feeling in the pit of his stomach, Manning refused to be intimidated. "I was able to discover the new protection arrangements for the family. Our contractor was on site to witness the handover and he is confident a resolution will be found within the next forty-eight hours. It's just a matter of sitting tight until he concludes this unfortunate business."

"We shall see," Roper responded.

The limousine swept through the gates and accelerated away from the manor, the speedometer touching sixty in less than six seconds. The tall hedgerow flashed past the soundproofed rear compartment as Roper filled two crystal glasses with generous measures of malt whisky. He took a long swig before wiping his mouth and turning to his companion. "What did you make of that?"

Grimand settled into the luxurious leather seat, savouring the bite at the back of his throat. "You *know* what I think. The man's a buffoon, a liability. We have to cut our ties."

"Patience, my dear Giles. We need him to clear up this little mess before we do what has to be done. I intend to arrange things so that Manning ends up being the fall guy. My people are currently working on planting disinformation on his computers and deleting all transactions that could possibly lead back to us. His greatest service is yet to come. His death will be a quite illuminating one for the authorities."

"Don't hang around too long, George. Our investors are becoming a bit jittery, maybe even to the point that they will see you and me as expendable. These are not the sort of people to show an understanding nature, despite the many things we've achieved for them. I say we kill Manning now, and take direct control of the operation against the Haydens."

Roper took another swig from his glass. "I agree we need to tread warily. Let's give it another two days. If nothing happens we'll go to plan B and deal with the problems ourselves."

Both men continued the rest of the journey in silence. A gloom descended on the limousine's rear compartment, leaving the pair with conflicting fears and emotions about what might lie ahead.

Chapter 13

IT WAS DIFFICULT to imagine that barely thirty-six hours had elapsed since Christopher Hayden had been left for dead on a deserted factory floor. The young man was sitting upright in bed, wolfing down a hearty breakfast, and jabbering incessantly to Tim Halloran who was demonstrating a number of features on a specially-adopted tablet computer that sat between them.

The 10-inch gadget was loaded with an array of software programmes, none of which could be found on sale to the general public, and all requiring levels of operating knowledge that only the most advanced user possessed. The youngster was in his element, which was why he was bombarding Halloran with a series of questions, and showing impatience to move quicker through the sub-menus.

The *LonWash* tech chief had prepared the tablet as a replacement for the one stolen from Christopher during his ordeal. Halloran guessed correctly that for a student - especially a potential Master of Information Systems and Digital Information – to lose his gateway to the internet, was something akin to the loss of a limb. Where would he be without the ability to devise imaginary solutions to everyday processes, or track down the latest information on algorithmics, or even tackle more mundane matters such as dipping in and out of the world of social media?

There was also a secondary motive behind Halloran's largesse.

He'd spent an hour probing the boy about any contacts he might have had with his father. He needed to know of the existence of any email addresses, cloud storage systems, access to remote servers, or ghost user accounts. He'd convinced Christopher to trust him by revealing that knowledge of his electronic footprints could be turned to his advantage, particularly since whoever had stolen his iPad could access even his most closely-guarded secrets.

Halloran set up a new email address, and showed Christopher how it could "delete and grab" messages flowing into his old accounts without anyone realising the transfer had taken place. Equally, a new cloud system, one that Christopher had never heard of - simply because it was part of Halloran's own sophisticated network - was installed on the tablet to provide guaranteed future security for all transactions. It too had the ability to stealthily retrieve all previous storage files from the student's former system.

The more Halloran showed him, the more animated Christopher became. Theory and hypothesis had morphed into reality, in a way that years of university lecturing could never have achieved. For the first time, he began to truly understand what had driven his father, and why he had become so engrossed in and obsessed by his work.

The search of Christopher's emails and storage files elicited nothing of interest. There were no messages from his father, no hidden files, no clues to what Hayden senior had been working on.

Another door closed on Halloran's meticulous search for the truth.

Across the room, Devon watched the discussion and marvelled at the boy's recovery powers. He was a gangly youth, probably around six feet, with a thin-frame and the beginnings of a designer stubble that showed traces of blonde and ginger to match the mop of unruly hair that tumbled down to his shoulders. There was a gaunt look to his oval face, and high cheekbones that appeared ready at any moment to push through a thin layer of skin. In contrast to the overall look of anaemia, the eyes were aflame with vitality, providing a glimpse of the pent-up energy that lurked within.

All things considered, Devon decided, there was a resilient and determined streak to be admired in Christopher Hayden. There was little doubt he was looking at a young man who would go places and make his mark, if he were allowed to flourish. Devon intended to see to it that he got the chance.

"What happens now?"

Devon suddenly realised his mind had wandered while Sonia Hayden was speaking. They were sitting in armchairs at the farthest end of the room. "I'm sorry, what do you mean?"

The woman smiled at him. "I think you were a million miles away. I was asking about how long we will have to spend in custody, and when will we be able to get our own lives back. Christopher has to finish his degree and I have to return to work sometime soon."

"I apologise, Mrs Hayden. I *was* preoccupied with other thoughts, but rest assured they were about the wellbeing of you and your son. I can't give you a definitive answer, other than to say this matter will not be resolved anytime soon. Your safety is of paramount importance, which means you will both need to stay with us for quite a while yet."

Her shoulders sagged in resignation. "I was afraid you'd say that. You need to know, Mr Devon, that I'm not a wallflower. I've been through a lot these past few years and the last thing I need is to be mollycoddled. I was proud of my husband and it was difficult to watch what happened to him. He didn't deserve to die, and we didn't deserve to become targets for whatever he was mixed up in. I won't let these people continue to wreck our lives, so you need to be straight with me and tell me what we're facing."

Devon now knew where her son got the fire in his belly from. "Okay, Mrs Hayden, I'll tell you what we know. During his time with MI6 your husband appears to have stumbled across something that was so big that it got him fired. I can only guess that he continued to pursue his investigation and that eventually things came to a head. He needed to be silenced and so too did you and your son."

"But we don't know anything."

Devon placed a reassuring hand on her shoulder. "Yes, but whoever is behind this is taking no chances. They are intent on wiping the slate clean, which means your husband must have uncovered some pretty damaging stuff against some powerful and ruthless people. I can tell you from experience that they won't stop until they get what they want. Until we find out what the hell is going on, there's no chance of you or Christopher ever being safe."

Sonia sat in silence, as if processing the information, before speaking again. "What I don't understand is why MI6 didn't help Matthew in the first place? Why did they fire him and leave him exposed to the mercies of these people? Surely, if everything Matthew did was part of his job, they would have supported him, unless.....unless...."

"No", Devon said emphatically, "I'm convinced Matthew was no traitor. There's no doubt he rubbed people the wrong way, but that shouldn't have been enough to hang him out to dry. I don't know why MI6 cut him adrift, but I can promise you I'll find out."

"Aren't you part of the same organisation?" Sonia asked suspiciously.

"No, we're most certainly not. We *do* work with them on occasion, but we are totally independent. I have to say that until now I've never doubted the professionalism or integrity of the people we've done business with at Vauxhall Cross. They're almost beyond reproach, yet something's badly amiss in their handing of your husband. I won't kid you that it's gonna be easy to peel back the layers, but you have my word it won't be for a lack of effort on my part."

The woman's face brightened. "Somehow I get the feeling you mean what you say. For the past few years I've had to live with not trusting anybody. Until now, I thought we were abandoned and alone, that we would have to live under this cloud for the rest of our lives. You've given me hope, Mr Devon. Thank you for that."

"Let's not be so formal. Please call me Mike."

"Okay, Mike, I'm Sonia. Now, what do you want us to do?"

Devon stood and walked towards the hospital bed. He wanted both Haydens to hear what he had to say. "I'm not going to pretend you have an easy road ahead. Trust me and my team, and do what we say. We will relocate from here at noon tomorrow to a safe house in the countryside. Things will get a bit claustrophic, so prepare a wish-list of everything you both need, including clothes and personal items. It's a big budget, so don't be afraid to ask for anything."

"That's great," Matthew beamed. "Can I get a 4TB Macbook Pro to go along with my new tablet, and maybe a pair of Nike Air Max trainers?"

"Christopher!" his mother scolded.

The white-haired man never saw it coming. One moment he was standing over a packed suitcase, the next he was lying face down on the carpet, a million stars dancing across his blurred vision.

There was a sharp pain on the back of his neck, and he could feel pressure on his lower back. He tried to move, but the pressure increased, keeping his face pinned to the floor, and forcing him to turn his head to one side to clear his airways. There was an intruder in his hotel room!

Through the haze he could hear a voice. "I'm going to let you up now. I have a gun pointed at your head, and I will fire if you don't do exactly as I say. Get up and sit on the bed with your hands clasped behind your head."

He did what he was told. There was too much menace in his visitor's voice to contemplate doing anything else. Gradually, his vision cleared, allowing him to see beyond the long-barrelled weapon to the face of his assailant. It was not a face he recognised. "Who are you? What do you want?"

"I'm offended," Dave Millward responded. "After all the time I've spent in your employment, and you don't know who I am. It pains me to realise I was just a voice on the phone, someone to be used and then discarded despite all the successes we've enjoyed together."

The penny dropped. "Are you Millward?"

"The very same."

"Why are you here? Our business has been concluded."

A scowl swept across the gunman's face. "That's where you're wrong, Mr Valentine. Yes, I know your name, in fact I know all about you, Rudi. Playboy millionaire, fixer of problems, and all-round scumbag. You owe me money, and I'm here to collect."

"This is nonsense! You've been paid well for all your services. It's not my problem that you fucked up on your last assignment, a fiasco which has cost me no end of trouble. I don't see how you think I owe you anything."

Millward pulled back the hammer on his suppressed Glock 22 and watched Valentine squirm. "Here's the way I see it, Rudi. You hired me to do a job and that job is not yet completed. I intend to honour the contract, only this time you will pay in advance, with a little extra thrown in. A number of my men died on this job and I reckon their families are due a bit of compensation. You really don't have a choice."

Valentine's shoulders sagged. "It's not as simple as that. I have people to answer to. They pay the bills, not me, and I doubt they would be sympathetic to your problem. These are serious hard-hitters, not the sort of people you want to offend. I suggest, for your sake, we forget this conversation ever took place."

Millward pressed the tip of the suppressor hard against Valentine's forehead. "Either I get my money, or you get a 9mm bullet playing havoc with the inside of your brain. You have exactly ten seconds to do what I want. Get out your fancy laptop, make an online transfer of funds to the usual place, and maybe you get to live a bit longer."

"Alright, alright, I'll use my own funds. Do you mind if I lower my hands and get my laptop from the top drawer of the desk?"

Millward stepped back and watched the man power up his computer.

"Let's just round things to an even million."

"Are you mad...that's not what we agreed."

"That's the new going rate. Just do it."

A minute later Millward's mobile pinged. He glanced at the screen to read a message from an off-shore bank confirming the transfer had been completed. He waited another thirty seconds, knowing that pre-set arrangements within the account would send the new funds to several other accounts in different counties. A second pinged message informed him the transfers had been made.

He sat on the edge of the bed, keeping his gun trained on Valentine. "Now, tell me everything you know about the current whereabouts of the Haydens. Who is the new contractor, what arrangements have been made, and how do I recognise him? I want chapter and verse."

Chapter 14

THE SQUAD ROOM adjacent to Commander John Hall's office was unusually busy. The SO19 big hitters were all there, split into teams of four, huddled around workstations and wipeboards, in a scene typical of the fervour afforded to a Code One terrorist alert.

Except on this occasion they were not dealing with an imminent threat. Their thoughts were focussed on exacting payback for the colleagues who had died at the Rosemund Hospital.

Hall had been warned off any follow-up investigations. Well, fuck MI6, and everyone else for that matter. These were SO19 losses. And nobody was going to tell John Hall to look the other way.

The men and women bumping into each other in a frenzy of activity felt the same way. They'd lost close friends. And they too wanted answers.

The wipeboards were peppered with photos of the gunmen who'd carried out the attack. Some were prints pulled from the hospital's only CCTV camera in the foyer; others were head shots snapped at the city morgue. As yet, no matches from the Met's extensive database had been found.

Hall had been particularly intrigued by the foyer video of the gang's team leader. It was obvious the man knew the location of the camera. Throughout the short two-minute playback, he'd kept his face averted, or moved his arm strategically to block the possibility of a direct line of sight. His men had not been so circumspect, a mistake Hall hoped could be turned to his advantage.

His teams were concentrating their efforts on the faces that could be seen. The leader and one other man had escaped, leaving three bodies – and lots of raw DNA material – now lying on mortuary slabs. It was only a matter of time before positive IDs were completed.

Hall and his people were using every means at their disposal. The first facial-recognition-software trawl of the general database might have drawn a blank, but the searchers had moved on to other databases, in particular those held by the Ministry of Defence. He was betting the farm that at least one, if not all, of the perpetrators had worn a uniform in a previous life. The way they'd moved, and the ease with which they had used their weapons was not something you learned at a Sunday School picnic.

Just one confirmed identification would have a domino effect. Hall had learned a long time ago that no man was an island. There were always family members, friends, enemies, known associates, frequent haunts, habits, and a hundred-and-one other connections that make up an individual's profile. It was a matter of pulling on the first thread and watching even the most carefully-constructed persona beginning to unravel.

Hall knew that within a few hours he'd find his starting point. It would take him inexorably, one step at a time, to where he wanted to go.

Straight to the door of the murderous leader of the pack.

Three miles across the city another office was also in a state of high alert. Devon was presiding over three separate briefings, each sparked by updated intel within the space of five minutes, and all demanding immediate action.

A lengthy email from Sir Clive Oliver was the easiest starting point. It was set out in a no-nonsense, bullet-point format that summarised research, outcomes and recommendations. It was probably how the financier tackled his usual mergers-and-acquisitions proposals, but it fit equally well with the style required for this purpose.

Devon fast-tracked through the salient points. Sir Clive's team had used bank accounts and credit-card transactions to track Tunisian fugitives Mehdi Naybet and Marouen Badri on a flight from Heathrow to Logan International in Boston.

From there, they'd hired a car at the Hertz desk, and later checked in at the Envoy Hotel, booking two separate suites under fictional names. Within twenty-four hours they'd checked out, moving across the city to the Courtyard Hotel in Copley Square, this time using new aliases. As of twelve hours ago, they were still there, though the report included a proviso that they could have "done a bunk" and gone anywhere.

Two recommendations were appended by Sir Clive. He believed it was time to cut the pair's access to funds. A few simple keystrokes would, he said, close all bank and card accounts, leaving the men high and dry, and vulnerable to erratic behaviour. The wily old financier considered, however, that it might be best to move *LonWash* assets into the area prior to pushing the button. In that way, the chances of locating the pair – in the event they were no longer at their secondary hotel – would increase substantially.

"Desperate men usually resort to desperate measures, which are bound to attract attention," Sir Clive concluded.

His second recommendation was equally practical. Assets on the ground could commandeer Hertz GPS tracking records for the hire car and follow the fugitives wherever they went.

The email ended with the letters *QED*.

Devon smiled at the Latin flourish. *Quod Erat Demonstrandum* – "that which was to be demonstrated." In other words, he'd been asked to do a job, and here it was completed, like some mathematical formula. The old boy had class.

"I can't fault anything in Sir Clive's summary," Devon told the assembled gathering. "We'll get our Washington cousins to hotfoot it to Boston, but I want at least one of our own team there as soon as possible." He became aware of Doyle fidgeting in his seat. "Something tells me, Alan, that you have someone in mind."

His number two was caught unawares. "No, well, yes…. we should send Chelsea. She's due a bit of time off to visit her parents in Chicago. Why not kill two birds with the one stone?"

"Excellent idea. We'll discuss the details at the end of the briefing. Now, let's turn to the second matter in front of us. Where are we with unravelling the last few months of Matthew Hayden's life?"

This was Halloran's bailiwick. The team sat back in their seats, waiting for the usual tour-de-force style that hallmarked the tech man's presentations. It quickly became clear, however, that something was amiss. His usual chirpy demeanour was replaced by a hangdog scowl as he talked through a succession of cyber searches that had dead-ended without adding to the scant information already known about their subject. "Finally," he announced without enthusiasm, "we hit on a possible new lead early this morning. We managed to find an integrated internet-systems facility in Leeds which appears to have been hosting the antics of an intruder for more than a year. We're working on the assumption that the intruder was Matthew Hayden."

"Surely that's good news?" Devon asked.

"I'm afraid it's all a bit of stretch at the moment," Halloran told him. "We took a punt on searching high data usage within a twenty-mile radius of Hayden's cottage. This was the best we could come up with. It's a large financial office block with the kind of state-of-the-art communications infrastructure a company such as this would need for world-wide trading. It's the perfect set-up for someone looking for a free ride, while at the same time covering their tracks. We think that's what Hayden did here."

"So, why the glum look? This has got to be some kind of a breakthrough?"

"We're grasping at straws here, Mike. There's no doubt the Leeds company's system was hacked, but even if it was done by Hayden we'll have a devil of a job trying to pick up his trail. He'll have us bouncing around like a ping pong ball at an Olympics final, with no guarantee we'll ever stop it, much less score a point. This could take weeks to unravel."

It was not what Devon wanted to hear, but he did his best to hide his disappointment. "Don't worry about rushing it, Tim. We're in this for the long haul. If you're telling me this is going to be a marathon, then so be it. I'm just glad we have a gold-medal winner leading our team."

Halloran beamed at the compliment, gathered his papers, and walked confidently from the briefing room, followed by two of his white-coated lab technicians.

"Now," Devon announced to the remaining team, "let me run through the arrangements for transferring Sonia and Matthew Hayden to the safe house."

Thirty minutes later the group broke for a much-needed rest.

"If you two think you're going to use this trip to run off and get married on the sly, you've got another think coming. I'm not about to be cheated out of the chance to wear a tux and give a Best Man's speech. Tell me that's not going to happen."

Doyle and Horgan exchanged glances. They were sitting either side of Devon's desk, a red glow working its way slowly up Horgan's freckled face. "Are you saying Alan's coming with me?"

"C'mon Chelsea," Devon teased, "do the maths. What good is this big lug going to do hanging around here while you're four-thousand miles away? And don't think for a moment that he didn't know what he was doing when he proposed you for the mission. He wants to meet the folks and get his feet under the table."

Horgan caught the mood. "He can be devious when he wants to be. I suppose it *is* time Mom and Dad ran the rule over the man who's kept me in London these past few years. Do you think they'll approve?"

"Personally, no. They'll think their daughter could have done a lot better, though he does have a few redeeming characteristics. Guess they'll just have to accept him the way he is."

Doyle squirmed in his seat. "I *am* still here, in case you two haven't noticed. And, by the way, who said anything about you being Best Man?"

"Aha," Devon scoffed, "you do have marriage on your

mind! About time too, but not until after you get back from America. Emma has her heart set on being Matron of Honour, and I for one would not want to disappoint her."

All three fell about laughing. It seemed every time Devon brought up this particular topic, he added more and more detail. They were used to his banter, although they'd often wondered how much he'd guessed. They'd already made their plans, which most definitely included the Devons, but had decided to keep him in the dark until the last possible moment.

"Okay," Devon announced, "now that we've got that settled, we can turn our attention to less important matters. This is an official mission, so you'll take the company jet, and be ready for recall at a moment's notice, in case things get hairy here."

The company jet was a Dassault 2000Ex, housed in a rented hangar at a private airfield near Stansted. Powered by two Pratt and Whitney Canada engines, the jet was capable of 0.8 Mach speed that would shave crucial hours off the time needed to get the team where they wanted to go. It was a registered diplomatic transporter, and came with an Iridium ST3100 Aircell unit, which provided instant access to satellite communications. Two full-time pilots were on standby to man the aircraft at a moment's notice. The jet was the most impressive part of a large *LonWash* fleet, which also included a Bell 407 GXP helicopter, a highly-manoeuvrable six-seater with a top speed in excess of 150 miles per hour.

"Thanks, Mike," Doyle said with feeling. "That'll make things a lot easier. We want to stop off first at Chicago to meet Chelsea's parents, and this will save us all sorts of time and bother."

"No problem. Just get on site at Boston as soon as you can. Find out who Naybet and Badri are meeting, and what they're up to. When you get what you want, take both these jokers alive and find space for them on the Dassault for the return journey. There's a lot more we can do here to persuade them to give up their dirty secrets."

"Consider it done," Doyle and Horgan chirped in unison.

Chapter 15

THE DOORS TO THE underground garage at Charterhouse Street opened at exactly noon. Despite constant maintenance, the metal rollers shrieked across the recessed runners, sending small friction sparks dancing in a light breeze that snuffed them out instantaneously. The grating sound attracted no attention on the deserted service avenue.

As soon as the doors recessed to their full opening span, an armoured Range Rover, with familiar black-tinted windows, roared up the ramp onto the street and turned sharply left in a squeal of rubber. It was quickly followed by an ambulance with roof-mounted flashing lights and an urgent siren wail that bounced off the walls of the buildings, and brought curious faces to the windows of a dozen offices.

The vehicles had gone barely fifty yards before another armoured Range Rover and ambulance appeared from the bowels of the *LonWash* basement, and raced away in the opposite direction. Those who knew what to look for would have understood what had just happened. It was a classic decoy operation.

The man striding a Honda bike at the end of the street knew exactly what was going on.

Knowing was one thing; doing something about it was a different matter. He could follow only one convoy, but which one? Was the first ambulance a decoy, or was it the second? It was a classic case of heads you win, tails you lose. He shrugged his shoulders in resignation and set off in pursuit of the first vehicles, the choice made for him purely on the basis that they had passed closest to his vantage point, and could be tailed easier than having to ride to the opposite end of the street to pick up the pursuit of the second convoy.

Anyhow, he reasoned, if he *was* being led a merry dance,

his employer would find the true destination and let him know in due course. In the meantime, he settled into a steady speed, keeping at least four vehicles between himself and his target.

Dave Millward was also caught out by the decoy convoy. He'd been told of the noon transfer by the white-haired paymaster, Rudi Valentine, who'd also named and described his new contractor, and his love of motorbikes. Millward had known what to look for, and how to plan for all eventualities, including covering both ends of the street, something the lone-wolf Honda man couldn't accomplish.

Shortly after leaving Valentine's hotel, Millward had rounded up the only other survivors from the hospital fiasco, and quickly put together a new team. His closest ally, Mark Jennings, and the minibus driver, Jason McDermott, were joined by five new recruits, ex-mercenaries who normally sat around in pubs and clubs waiting for their next big pay day. Twenty-thousand in cash per man got them off their asses and into action quicker than they could reload a standard magazine-fed pistol.

The group had been split into four pairs, each with their own transport. That gave Millward two cars at either end of Charterhouse Street. Whichever direction this Mickey-Mouse security firm chose for the transfer, Millward had it covered. He just hadn't reckoned on them using both routes in a double-bluff manoeuvre. Maybe they're not so Mickey-Mouse after all?

Millward and Jennings shared a car parked at the right-hand exit, with a second back-up vehicle parked farther up the road to provide a leapfrogging pursuit. It was the same set-up at the opposite end of Charterhouse. All the angles were covered. It was simply a case of sitting back and seeing where they were being taken to.

Alfie Cheadle sat behind the wheel of the first Range Rover

and powered the 3-litre engine up to 80 miles per hour as he swung onto the northbound M11 motorway. Behind him, the ambulance kept pace, refusing to allow any vehicle into the narrow gap between it and its protection detail.

In the blacked-out interior of the ambulance, Terry Hunt scrutinised the traffic through the one-way rear window. Twenty miles into their journey, the only anomaly he'd spotted was a Honda motorbike that had followed them from central London. The convoluted course that had taken them to the motorway from Charterhouse Street meant it was no coincidence the same bike was still with them.

He activated his throat mic. "We have a tail, Alfie. It's a powerful-looking race bike about two hundred yards back. Can't see any evidence of other pursuit vehicles."

"Got that," Cheadle replied abruptly. "We'll be stopping shortly for tea at the service station. We'll find out his intentions soon enough."

To the south and west of Cheadle's position, the second Range Rover had picked up the M25 heading towards the port of Southampton. Driving at a more sedate rate, Chelsea Horgan kept her eyes peeled for the link to the M3, and the directions towards Basingstoke, the largest of a number of towns that dotted the rural Hampshire countryside. Located just over fifty miles from London, it was an ideal environment for a safe house.

Alan Doyle fidgeted in the passenger seat and kept glancing at his watch. "We're going to be cutting this fine."

"Don't be such a worrier," she chided. "Our flight to Chicago isn't due for departure for another three hours, Besides, aren't you forgetting that it's a private jet and will wait for us as long as it needs to. Makes you feel important, doesn't it?"

His craggy features broke into a grin. "I was forgetting that. Maybe I'm just nervous for this transfer to go smoothly. I'll be glad if things go off without a hitch and we get into the air. I hate delays."

"Maybe you're just nervous about meeting Mom and Dad. Relax, they'll love you."

Doyle ignored the comment and pressed his comms unit. "Any movement back there?"

Jim Cross was perched on a bench in the rear compartment of the ambulance. "Can't spot anything, although to tell the truth the traffic is so hellish behind us that I doubt I'd see anything unless it had flashing arrows pointed at it."

"Just because you can't see them, doesn't mean they're not there. Keep your eyes peeled."

The lead Range Rover gave no notice of its intention to swing off the motorway onto the service station slip road. The ambulance driver, who'd been warned in advance about the manoeuvre, slipped behind the Rover, ignoring the horn blasts from drivers already in the turn-off lane.

Behind the convoy, the motorcyclist couldn't react quickly enough to the sudden change of direction. He was forced to rocket past the exit, hoping he could pick up an alternative slip road farther ahead.

Two cars, which had settled into the line of traffic almost a quarter of a mile behind, had no such problems. They eased into the slip road and followed the ambulance convoy as it entered a large car park dotted with articulated lorries facing a row of fast-food buildings. It was a busy stop-off point, judging by the number of vehicles, although there were ample parking spaces in the sprawling thirty-acre site.

The driver of the first car watched the convoy reverse into two side-by-side bays and kill their engines. Nothing happened for two minutes, and then the Range Rover driver climbed out of his vehicle and walked towards a Costa Coffee shop, stopping at regular intervals to scan all areas of the park. The man waited for the driver to disappear into the complex before lifting his mobile phone and pressing the preset number for Millward.

"They've stopped for coffee at a service site on the M11.

Only one man has emerged from the vehicles. Our friend on the motorbike overshot the turn-off, so I guess we'll not see him for a while. This looks like a golden opportunity. What do you want us to do?"

"Sit tight, do nothing!" Millward roared. "Use your brain. If they were the transfer vehicles they wouldn't be stopping for a rest after forty minutes. You've got the decoy! Keep an eye on what happens, but do not blow your cover. If they move again, use only one vehicle; I want the other car to watch out for the motorcyclist and follow where he goes. He's bound to show up again, and it's imperative we trail him back to his lair. I have unfinished business with that bastard."

Millward was delighted by the news. Fate had dumped the main convoy into his lap in a fifty-fifty throw of the dice that had turned up a pair of sixes in his favour. He would let this little pursuit play out for another half-hour or so before deciding what to do. If the opportunity presented itself, he would move in on the ambulance, forcing it off the road with a quick tyre-shredding burst from his MP5. His back-up team could deal with the Range Rover while he finished off the ambulance occupants.

All he needed was a break in the heavy motorway traffic.

Worst-case scenario was tailing the convoy to its final destination. Thank goodness he'd packed the RPG into the car trunk. He'd a feeling it could come in handy.

He slapped Jennings on the knee. "Looks like we got the sixpence in the apple pie. Get ready for some real action within the next thirty minutes."

Five minutes before the end of Millward's notional timeframe, the ambulance signalled a left turn off the motorway onto a ramped roundabout offering a number of exit options.

Millward studied the large signpost. "They could be heading for Basingstoke. This is the opportunity we've been waiting for." He punched his mobile and issued instructions to the second car.

The convoy swung onto the roundabout, a long looping circle that took them past exits for Epsom, Basingstoke and Reading, before reaching the final turn-off.

"They're heading back to London! What the fuck's going on?" Millward yelled.

Chapter 16

THE BELL 407 GXP glided over the rooftops and landed expertly on the helipad atop the *LonWash* building. As soon as the skids kissed the black-and-yellow-patterned grid, the pilot powered down the rotors and hand-signalled to a group of figures standing beside a doorway to the main office complex.

Devon waited two minutes, as instructed, before reaching for the stretcher grips and nodding to Halloran at the other end. They hoisted Christopher Hayden and carried him across to the helicopter. Using seat belts and extra snap-clip bungee straps to fasten the stretcher across one row of rear-cabin seats, they stepped back to allow a nurse, a doctor and Sonia Hayden to climb into the remaining seats.

Devon closed the door and climbed into the cockpit beside the pilot. He donned a spare set of earphones and waved at Halloran as the engines powered up. When the rotors reached full revolutions, the pilot eased the mixing unit lever, which combined the collective and cyclic controls, and brought the chopper into a smooth, vertical take-off. As soon as he reached a desired height above the rooftops, he gently twisted the stick and banked right on a flightpath that took them across London on an easterly bearing.

The city of Cambridge was forty miles and fifteen minutes directly ahead of them. It would, however, take less time to reach their true destination, a large country estate sandwiched between the university city and the town of Bishop's Stortford. It was a property that had come into *LonWash* ownership several years previously, when General Sandford had decided on the need for a remote training base, something along the lines of a scaled-down version of the CIA's Camp Peary facility near Williamsburg, Virginia.

Every three months, at least twenty recruits were put

through their paces at the Bishop's Stortford complex. These were men and women undergoing training for *LonWash* private sector contracts, such as bodyguards, couriers, or riot-control policing. They had access to advanced driving courses, hand-to-hand fighting in a variety of martial arts, and keep-fit regimes that included punishing cross-country hikes, mirroring many of the SAS disciplines on the Brecon Beacons in Wales. The estate was sectioned off into urban street scenes, specialised combat houses, and large platform structures to teach rapid abseiling descents. The main building contained lecture rooms for seminars on a range of subjects as diverse as make-up artistry, document forgery, counter-surveillance techniques, and the use of modern communication gadgetry.

Only ten per cent of trainees would make the grade. The leavers would never know about the other side to the *LonWash* operations. Those who passed the initial intensive programme would advance to weapons and explosives training and CQB, the close quarter battle techniques required by field agents. These were the elite who would find themselves eventually in various corners of the world, undertaking the most dangerous, and lucrative contacts on behalf of their new employers.

Somewhere within these ranks, Devon might find himself a new addition to the anti-terrorism ranks. This intake was usually no more than one person per year.

A section of the estate's signature mansion house had been prepared for the new visitors. The Haydens, the medical staff and a four-man protection unit were allocated en-suite rooms, their own kitchen and dining area, and a large library-come-television lounge. The recruits were told the new arrivals were corporate clients who required 24-hour protection, which would mean extra shifts for everyone on site. A new guardhouse had been erected at the entrance to the estate, perimeter patrols were increased, and additional floodlighting installed at a number of blind spots leading to the house.

The trainees' briefing, prior to the arrival of the

mysterious guests, had hammered home messages about the potential dangers of the assignment, and their need to embrace a golden opportunity for on-the-job training.

Devon's arrangements were about as watertight as he could make them. The use of trainees was little more than window dressing, a show of strength intended to deter anyone mounting a surveillance on the property. His main frontline of defence was a small group of agency A-listers comprising Alfie Cheadle, Terry Hunt, Jim Cross and Dan Gosling, who had been flown in from an assignment in Hungary to bolster the experienced ranks. These four would arrive later in the day and remain at Bishop's Stortford for the duration.

Devon was not foolish enough to believe the training camp was an impenetrable fortress. There was no such thing. The trick was to make sure its existence couldn't be discovered, which was why he'd gone to such elaborate lengths to stage the ambulance convoys. If Charterhouse Street was being watched – and that had to be a very big if – he needed to draw attention away from the helicopter transfer.

Content the ploy had worked to perfection, he glanced out the window as the Bell 407 descended and lined up for a landing directly in front of the mansion house.

He had barely stepped onto the manicured lawn before learning how wrong he'd been.

Dave Millward racked the slide on the MP5 machine pistol and ordered Mark Jennings to close the gap to the speeding ambulance.

All four lanes of the M3 were busy with afternoon traffic. It was the usual mix of articulated lorries, delivery vans, and private cars, leapfrogging each other in an endless blur of motorway madness, fuelled by an urge for constant overtaking, combined with a hopeless craving for a clear road ahead.

Millward's target stuck rigidly to the second lane. Collateral damage was bound to be high. He pictured what would happen after two long bursts of 9mm carnage - one to the front tyres and one through the driver's window. By the time the ambulance slewed across the carriageway, most likely somersaulting into adjacent traffic, he and the occupants of the second pursuit car would be clear of danger and ready to assault the Range Rover.

He spoke urgently into his mobile phone and ordered the second car to close ranks. Both vehicles moved away from the inner carriageway, bullied a path into the third lane, and throttled up to almost 100 miles per hour. The distance to the ambulance closed rapidly.

Millward depressed the window button and rested the MP5 barrel on the doorframe. He calculated no more than fifteen seconds to target.

"Alan, Alan, we've got movement!"

"I see them," Doyle retorted. "Put your foot down."

Horgan stomped the accelerator to the board as Doyle hit the comms button to alert the ambulance driver. "You've got company. For Chrissakes, gave her everything you've got and stay with us."

Through the rearview mirror, Doyle could see the menacing shape of a gun barrel as the first of the two speeding vehicles closed to within mere yards of the rear of the ambulance. He realised in an instance that it could not outrun their attackers. He spoke quickly into the mic again before ordering Horgan to switch lanes. "As soon as you move over, feather the brakes!"

Doyle's plan was to cut off the pursuers in the third lane while the ambulance continued its path on the second lane. He knew Horgan could switch between the brake and accelerator with enough skill to prevent the pancaking of vehicles travelling behind. The idea was all very plausible in theory, but who was to say how other motorists around them would react?

The initial manoeuvre had the desired effect. The driver of the car with the weapon protruding from the window, slowed at the sight of the Range Rover's braking lights. It was a natural reaction. He was sufficiently experienced, however, not to hit the middle pedal too hard, with the result that the cars in his wake mirrored his actions.

The miles-per-hour rate in the third lane dropped by twenty in a matter of seconds. While Horgan dictated the pace, the ambulance raced ahead in the inside lane, leaving her to concentrate on blocking off any attempt by the attackers to give chase. She weaved the big SUV between lanes in an obvious demonstration of her ability to counter whatever their pursuers came up with.

Doyle marvelled at her driving skills. But how long could they hold off determined gunmen? It was time to take the fight to the enemy.

Millward cursed at the turn of events. Just another few yards and he would have had them! The Range Rover's actions had taken him by surprise, and now all he could do was watch the ambulance disappearing into the distance. For a moment he thought about breaking off the engagement.

But it was just for a moment. Millward was not the cut-and-run type.

"Right", he muttered, "let's see how you cope with a flanking movement." He screamed into the phone, ordering his back-up vehicle into the second lane before nudging Jennings to switch to the outer lane. "We'll come at him from both sides. Start shooting as soon as we get close to the fucker."

Jennings expertly nudged across the lanes, gunned the accelerator, and moved swiftly towards the driver's side of the Rover. Millward steadied the MP5, waiting for his chance, and watching as his back-up car gobbled up the ground on the left side of the SUV.

Horgan caught everything in her mirrors. Their only chance of avoiding a catastrophe was to take advantage of the heavy traffic, particularly a white pantechnicon truck hurdling along less than a hundred yards ahead. She glanced in her wing mirrors. The timing had to be right on the money.

She watched as the pursuit vehicles closed in or either side. In another second, the firing would start. That was when she made her move, gunning the engine and moving to within mere yards of the rear of the pantechnicon. At the last possible moment, she swerved to the left, scraped the side of the Range Rover against the large truck, and bounced into the inside lane.

Ignoring the loss of her mirror in the collision, she fought to regain control and hold her speed to match that of the truck roaring uncomfortably close to her side window. She'd shielded them from one of the vehicles, whilst the other could only stay in her slipstream. Job done. Well, almost.

Doyle thumped the dashboard in triumph. "Attagirl! Now let's see if we can't do something about these other jokers."

He lowered the passenger window, hung the top half of his body outside the car, and pointed the Glock 22 directly at the driver's window of the pursuit car. He had no intention of pulling the trigger, not when the risk of causing a pile-up was too great. It was an intimidatory tactic, one that worked a lot quicker than he could possibly have imagined.

The driver took one look at Doyle's smirking face, and started to apply his brakes. As soon as he found an opening, he switched lanes and roared past the truck, leaving the Range Rover sheltered from further danger.

"What about the ambulance?" Horgan yelled urgently.

"Already on it," Doyle responded. He hit his mic button and ordered the ambulance driver to pull over to the hard shoulder. "Open the rear doors, show an empty interior, and hide in the grass embankment. That should tell them they've been chasing a false trail, so I don't expect them to take any further action. Stay put and we'll be with you in a matter of minutes."

Chapter 17

IT WAS NOT THE news Devon had been expecting. He continued listening to Doyle's report as he walked out of earshot from the helicopter passengers, who were making their way through the front door of the mansion. His anger had reached boiling point, so much so that he had to fight an urge to fling the mobile phone across the lawn.

"Are you sure everyone's all right, Alan? How the fuck did this happen? Where did I go wrong?"

"Steady, Mike, don't beat yourself up over this. I admit we didn't see it coming and for a while it was hairy, but we got lucky. They had to be watching the base; it's the only thing that makes any sense. I gotta say, these were real pros, the sort of guys who knew how to stay invisible until the last possible moment. It was as if they'd appeared out of nowhere."

"That's not what bothers me," Devon fumed. "We knew from the hospital attack what we were dealing with. What sticks in the craw is that they were tipped off about Charterhouse Street, and were hanging around outside waiting for us to make a move. How the fuck did we miss that?"

"Yeah, but it's got to a be a narrow field of suspects. You kept things tight at our end, so that leaves only a few possibilities."

Devon's mind was already in overdrive, trawling through the possibilities. The doctor? The nurse? The SO19 Commander? Who had they talked to? None of it made any sense, unless he was prepared to throw out a lifetime's experience of reading and trusting people. No, he was certain it was none of them. But who else could it have been?

"Mike, you still there?"

"Sorry, Alan, I was thinking this through. Jeez, I've just

remembered, we need to contact Alfie's crew. Maybe there were two teams involved. Have you heard anything from them?"

"All taken care of," Doyle reported. "Chelsea got in touch with them the moment we got clear of the motorway. They didn't spot anything untoward, although they're doing a final sweep of the service station area before they head back."

"Where are you now, Alan?"

Doyle explained they'd picked an exit from the M3 at random and were using minor roads to head back to London. They'd abandoned the ambulance in a garage forecourt to reduce the risk of being spotted, and he was confident they'd lost their pursuers.

"Good job. I'll arrange for the ambulance to be picked up tomorrow. In the meantime, get yourself to Stansted. You've a flight to catch. Get Chelsea to contact Alfie again and arrange for them to meet you there. I'll send the chopper to bring them home."

There was an awkward pause before Doyle replied. "Look, Mike, maybe it's not such a good idea that I go to America. Things are getting a bit iffy around here, and you could do with all hands on deck."

"Nonsense! We're well covered. Besides, we can't lose sight of the fact that the Tunisians are still our number one priority."

The platter of crabmeat sandwiches remained untouched on the coffee table in the centre of the private lounge at *The Shannon Club* in the heart of Knightsbridge. Despite the late-summer temperatures being enjoyed in London, a fire crackled in the large hearth, and a red-coated steward was doing his usual rounds of shuttering the ornate windows of the four-storey building. Dusk was settling over the city; it was time to close off the pampered members from the rest of the world.

Only two of the august body of gentlemen were at that moment enjoying the privileges of the lounge, one of six similar facilities within the building to provide privacy when demanded. Large chunky-framed paintings adorned the walls, and a Union Flag stood limply in the brightest corner of the room. Regimental plaques, a variety of sheathed swords, and a glass showcase of guns added clutter to the surroundings, and provided clues to the Club's military origins.

The two men staring at the plate of sandwiches had no associations with the *Shannon's* glorious past. They were of the breed of new members who had bought a place at the table by substituting money and influence for the lack of tradition and heritage. They had little affinity with the club, other than the opportunities it afforded to mix with the right people and to wear the coveted blue-and-gold tie which seemed magically to open doors that would otherwise be shut to them.

George Roper and Giles Grimand knew how to play the game. It had helped get them this far, and would continue to guarantee their success, provided they stuck by the rules. An easy thing for them to tolerate. The riches were too great to do otherwise.

Right now, however, their minds were on more squalid matters.

"We should have heard something by now," Roper moaned. "The transfer took place over eight hours ago. Why hasn't Valentine called with news? Ring him and find out what's happening."

"Dammit, George, I've been trying his number every ten minutes for the past hour." Grimand was becoming tired of his partner's incessant bleating, more so because he himself was now getting anxious about the lack of news. "Obviously, there's been another cock-up and Valentine is refusing to face the music. I must say, the choices of hired help are beginning to look like poor decision-making on our part. We need to wipe the slate clean and start again."

"Yes," Roper agreed, "I had hoped for better things from Valentine. Unfortunately, we can't stay around here, so we'll have to trust him to complete the job. Other business is awaiting us in America, and that means we should leave sometime soon, preferably by the earliest flight in the morning."

Grimand nodded his agreement. "The two gentlemen who will be looking after our interests there, have already set up a base in Boston, but I don't trust them to get things done properly unless we're there to hold their hands."

The manager of the Savoy Hotel stood outside the penthouse suite, his eyes fixed on the *Do Not Disturb* card hanging below the brass doorknob. Ordinarily he wouldn't contemplate checking in on one of his special guests, particularly one who had always insisted on the utmost privacy, even to the extent of foregoing the daily replenishment of towels and bath gels.

However, the fact that this guest hadn't responded to a number of telephone messages, coupled with the non-collection of a valeted suit, meant something was not right. The well-dressed gent simply never missed a day to order fresh attire from his extensive wardrobe.

The manager rapped hard several times on the door before reluctantly swiping his master keycard, and stepping into the room. He was immediately bewildered by an odd smell, a strong, bitter stench that went far beyond the usual mustiness caused by unopened windows. He reached for a pocket handkerchief to protect his nostrils, pausing midway to stare in disbelief at the body slumped awkwardly across the bed.

The large pool of blood and the sightless eyes fixed on the ceiling, told him it was a corpse, even before he took a hesitant step forward to see a neat round hole in the centre of the forehead.

The hotelier's stomach heaved, projecting its contents across the legs of the late Rudi Valentine.

The Honda rolled to a stop beside the boundary wire at the private-jet section of Stansted airfield. The rider had double-backed on a motorway slip road in time to pick up the Range Rover and ambulance heading back to London, and had tailed them on a circuitous route that ended here.

He was on a small service road, which afforded him a panoramic view of the complex whilst keeping him relatively sheltered from traffic using the main entrance roundabout. He quickly opened one of his saddle bags to retrieve the Leupold scope, but even before he unwrapped it from its protective pouch, he saw it would not be needed. By good fortune, the vehicles had stopped outside a hangar, about 120 yards from his position.

He squatted behind the bike, as if checking the chain, his eyes constantly taking in the activity in front of him. Another Range Rover, a clone of the car he pursued, was already parked, a tall man and a slim redhead leaning against the bonnet. Two men alighted from his pursuit SUV, and were joined by the driver of the ambulance as they made their way over to the waiting couple.

The biker dived into his saddle again, this time extracting a strange-looking webbed dish, akin to a folded-down satellite receiver. He flicked a switch to extend the unit into something that looked like an upturned umbrella, and inserted a battery pack with wires attached to a set of earphones. When everything was in place, he toggled the settings and aimed the dish at the group of people.

The 26-inch parabolic microphone he was using had a recommended optimal range of 150 yards, well within the distance needed. He turned down the volume to block out the incessant static, and continued to twist a small knob until faint traces of voices sailed into the earphones. He yanked the volume to its highest setting.

"Leave vehicles here.....pick-up in.....minutes......Stortford and.... Alfie....already offered but the boss....Chelsea and I are......Chicago....."

Suddenly an explosion of sound vibrated in the biker's ear. He pulled off the headset and reached instinctively for his Beretta 92 Compact pistol, his eyes already sweeping in a wide arc for potential threats. It took a few moments for him to register the approach of a helicopter as it swept over the hangar and touched down close to the huddle of people.

He watched as three men walked forward, climbed into the helo, and waved at the couple remaining beside their Range Rover. The biker turned away as the chopper lifted off and flew directly over his position. It was lost to sight within a matter of a few minutes.

He turned his attention back to the airfield as a jet taxied out of the hangar. The man and woman hoisted bags from the rear of their vehicle and made their way towards an airstair, which had folded out from the side of the plane. He made a note of the tail registration number in case Valentine might be able to trace the craft when they next spoke.

He could not yet know there would be no further discussions with his clandestine paymaster.

He was also unaware that he had picked up his own tail from the motorway.

Chapter 18

THERE WAS A LOT for Alfie Cheadle to weigh up before reaching a decision. Terry Hunt, who had first pinged a red-and-black-striped bike on the outward motorway journey, had just spotted an identical machine as the helicopter swooped over the airfield perimeter. Both men agreed it was no coincidence.

Cheadle had two options. He could order the chopper pilot to bank back towards the target in an attempt to follow the cyclist, or even force it to a stop. The big downside was that the area was too built up to be able to achieve either goal.

The second option was more realistic. He could radio Alan Doyle to stall his take-off and give chase to the motorbike in the SUV. The chances were that Doyle could probably run the target to ground, but at what cost to delaying his flight to America? A pursuit of this nature could take hours, and it was no gimme that it would be successful. Was it worth side-tracking a valuable mission on a whim?

In the end he read the situation the way he hoped Devon would. Stick to the plan. Deal with the unknown variables when you've a better chance to control them.

"You did the right thing," Devon told him twenty minutes later when the Bell landed at Bishop's Stortford. "I want Doyle and Horgan in Boston as soon as possible and there was little point in you playing hide-and-seek with a biker who held all the aces, especially in the warren of London streets that he could have reached within a matter of minutes. Whoever it was, we'll get another chance at him."

Devon led the way into the mansion and ushered Cheadle, Hunt and Cross towards a small lounge where Dan Gosling was already stretched out on a fireside armchair. After the group completed their handshakes with the Hungarian field agent, Devon motioned them to sit down. "You four will be the main protectors of the Haydens. This won't be a stroll in the park, especially now we know the gang after them were resourced enough to put pursuit vehicles at either end of the street when we exited earlier. It goes without saying that you'll have to be on your toes twenty-four-seven."

He knew it was a superfluous observation, but it had to be made. Heartened by the nods of agreement, he turned to Cheadle. "Alfie, I'm putting you in charge of the operation here. You might be the youngest team member, but you've earned your stripes in numerous operations which called for a wide range of disciplines. I trust your instincts, especially your feel for threat assessment; something which is going to be tested to the full if we are to keep our guests safe."

"Mike, I don't know what to say. I'll not let you down."

"Course you won't," Devon told him. "Now, here's the way I see it. Use the trainee contingent for the grunt jobs. Keep them busy and keep them visible, but remember they're only rookies. Try not to put them in harm's way because that's where you four come in. You're the first, middle and last lines of defence, so make sure all bases are covered. I'll leave Alfie to work through the details with you."

As Devon rose to leave, Cheadle cleared his throat. "Can I ask what you'll be doing?"

A shadow crossed Devon's face. "I intend to find the source of these leaks. I'll be flitting in and out, but right now I'm heading back to the city for two meetings which probably won't come under the be-nice-to-people bracket."

MI6 chief Peter Ramsden was the first to bear the brunt of Devon's wrath. "C'mon Peter, no more pissing around. Something stinks here at Vauxhall Cross; it was something that got a good man killed, and I'll be damned if I'll let the same thing happen to his wife and son. What is it you're not telling me?"

Ramsden's face reddened to match that of his visitor. "I'm not going to be lectured to in my own office. You might think your cosy little arrangement with General Sandford and the

Prime Minister gives you right to ride roughshod over the rest of us, but I'll be damned if I let anyone speak to me in that tone. Either show some respect or take your tantrums elsewhere."

"Fuck you and your sensibilities, Peter. This is not a matter of ego-tripping by either of us, particularly since the facts point in only one direction. I hardly need remind you that what is supposed to be the most secure server in the country had an employee record wiped clean by someone from within MI6, most likely the same someone who waltzed into your vaults and made off with a bunch of files without, it seems, anyone even knowing the thefts had occurred. You tell me what part of those two events makes you think that MI6 deserves any respect?"

"Yeah, well fuck you too, Mike, and your high and mighty moral ground. We both know things can happen, even in the most unlikely places, but that doesn't give you the right to sling mud over an entire organisation. I'll vouch for my people, just as much as you would do for yours, and I'm not talking blind loyalty here. Okay, someone put his hands in the cookie jar and so help me I'll get to the bottom of it."

Devon kept the steel in his voice. "Okay, let's ratchet things down a notch or two, but only on the understanding that you level with me."

"I thought that's what I *was* doing," Ramsden countered.

"When were the records purged? Was it immediately after Hayden was drummed out, or was it something that happened only lately?"

"As far as we can tell, it took place within days of Hayden leaving the service. There was no reason to check until things started to blow up over the past week."

Devon had his first answer, but he wanted more, much more. "Who would have authorised such a move? You were here at the time, so who are the key suspects?"

"Just so we're clear," Ramsden snorted, "at that time I was one of four deputies, with no dealings in Hayden's department. His chief officer was a woman called Elizabeth Gray, sadly no longer with us. She died in a car accident while holidaying in Spain almost a year later."

"Nothing suspicious about her death?"

"No, it was thoroughly checked, as you might imagine. We *do* take the death of our people rather seriously."

Devon ignored the barb. "What about higher up? Who had overall control?"

"The service chief was Sir Simon Pegg, an old schooler who ran a tight ship and was admired greatly by everyone. I don't see him having anything to do with it."

"Have you asked him?"

"Can't do, I'm afraid. The old boy died recently, and before you ask, it was natural causes, a heart attack brought on by spending far too many years in this nuthouse."

Devon kept up his pursuit. "He could still have ordered the whitewashing of records."

"I would have to say it would have been completely against his character."

"What if he felt he was protecting the agency's good name? Or what if he was ordered to do it by someone even higher up the food chain?"

"Such as?"

"That's what I'm asking. Who would have had the clout to make Pegg do something like that?"

"C'mon, Mike, that's a bit of a stretch."

"Humour me."

Ramsden exhaled noisily. "Only members of the intelligence committee, or COBRA representatives, or the Home Office, or the PM's office would dare to interfere. We *do* have a certain amount of autonomy because of the nature of the beast. It wouldn't do to be a pawn in a political game, even if there is an acceptable level of oversight. The idea being that individuals can't use our resources for their own agenda."

"Why is it then," Devon said, "I can't shake the feeling that that's precisely what could have happened here? Is your investigation extending outside MI6?"

"No way! Christ, I'd have to get my ducks firmly in a row before taking a potshot at any of that little grouping. As far as I'm concerned we stick with inside the building until we can go no further."

Devon could see nothing to gain in pursuing the point. He decided to change tack. "Did you or your people know about Sonia and Christopher Hayden being transferred to the custody of *LonWash*?"

"Of course we knew. We've taken over the SO19 investigation into the attacks on them, so naturally we were informed about the changes in security. Where the hell is this leading?"

Devon told him about the attacks on his convoys. He omitted mention of using a helicopter, reporting only that an assault had been repelled and that the Haydens were safe and well. "Someone leaked the transfer information, and I aim to find out who."

Ramsden bristled. "It didn't come from here. You can rule that out of your thinking straight away."

"I'm glad to hear it, Peter, but do me a favour by running a double-check on anyone from MI6 who was privy to the transfer."

"You'll end up with the same answer, but if it will get you off my back I'll do what you ask."

An hour later, Commander John Hall was next on Devon's inquisition list. It was obvious from the outset that the SO19 man was still seething about losing custody of the Haydens. His anger was about to rise to a new level.

"Let me get this right, Mike. Your so-called watertight security was breached and you've got the nerve to come here suggesting we were the cause of the breach? Considering how we've been royally fucked-over to date, that really does take the biscuit."

Devon had explained about the pursuit of his decoy convoys. He'd been more open with Hall than with Ramsden, including giving details of the safe transfer by helicopter. He'd hoped it would help establish a better rapport, perhaps even eliminate the need for a slanging match. He was learning quickly that already-damaged feathers were more easily ruffled.

"Look at it from my side, Commander. I'm simply trying to piece together how the breach in security occurred. The only way I can protect this family is by eliminating any shortcomings, wherever that might take me. The obvious starting point is your department, since it was responsible for delivering the Haydens to us. How many of your people knew about the transfer? Is it possible any of them talked out of turn without realising it? Help me out here. This is about the Haydens. Isn't their safety the only thing that matters?"

"I know where you're going with this," Hall said in a quieter tone. "Yes, there must have been about twenty people among my various teams who knew we were forced to hand the Haydens over to you. But that's all they knew. Must I remind you that when I was at your offices, you refused to provide any details about when you intended to relocate the family. With hindsight, I'm glad you didn't tell me, otherwise I'd be in your frame for passing on details to the very people my department is working its collective butt off to apprehend. Doesn't that seem even the least bit contradictory?"

"Yes, I agree it does," Devon conceded. "There are two parts to this. Part one is the transfer from you to us. That's my starting point, finding out who knew and whether there was any chance they had some hand in part two, however unlikely. As you say, part two is down to us. It was my decision on the date and time of relocation, a random choice that somehow became known to the assailants. I need to eliminate all possible leaks from part one so that I can home on the second part. Do you see where I'm coming from?"

"It's a bit convoluted, but I'm getting there," Hall smiled, though he quickly became serious again. "I'll quiz my team. Me alone. You'll just have to trust me on that, even though I can tell you the answer already. Your leak didn't come from SO19, which leaves you with just two possible avenues to explore."

"And what might they be?" Devon asked rhetorically.

"The first is an obvious one. Your own organisation."

"And the second?"

"The man who ordered us to transfer the Haydens into your custody."

Chapter 19

THE HONDA BIKER was doing what he always did when he needed to de-stress. Wrapped in oily overalls, he was rebuilding a 1972 Ironhead 900cc V-twin engine on a vintage Harley Davidson Sportster he'd picked up for a song over a decade ago and was still working on its restoration. It was a labour of love, something that helped him find a degree of equilibrium when events went into a nosedive.

He needed the distraction now more than ever. He'd been suckered on the transfer of the Hayden family. There was no other way to describe it. He'd chosen the wrong convoy to pursue, chased shadows up and down a motorway, and been forced to watch his opponents take to the air in a fancy helicopter and jet.

What rankled most was that for the past twelve hours he'd failed to make contact with his employer. That had never happened before. It usually took no more than two calls to the burner phones to initiate a response. Not this time. Something was wrong. Not knowing the man's name, or his location, left only one option, a contingency he was reluctant to engage until he'd recovered his composure.

Hence the current burst of activity on the Harley. A few more hours at this, and he would get his thoughts into proper order. If his first contact was out of commission, he needed to convince his boss's bosses that he could deliver, despite what had happened. He didn't get the impression these were the type of men to forgive easily.

Whoever they were, they were not to be taken lightly. They'd used him for a number of high-profile jobs, and had ordered him to co-operate fully with the mysterious middleman on this latest assignment. Their default orders were simple: never make direct contact except as a last resort.

This felt like a last resort to the biker.

His name was Todd Hamilton, a moody loner who'd been kicked out of the Parachute Regiment's elite Third Battalion after one cock-up too many. He'd earned his prized maroon beret after training at Catterick in North Yorkshire, but had gradually rebelled against the unit's tight code of discipline, often getting involved in brawls in local pubs where he'd been too willing to brandish his service-issue Glock 17, the army's replacement sidearm for the long-standing Browning L9.

After being drummed out of service, Hamilton found a new career as a paid enforcer for several London gangs. He had quickly graduated to contract killings, becoming an independent operator when he'd realised the opportunities and riches were almost limitless. Someone always seemed to want to permanently remove a competitor or an enemy.

It was during that period that he'd entered the twilight world of his new benefactors. He hadn't liked taking orders, or being treated like dog turd, but the money was great. For one thing, it helped fund his urge to travel the world in style, not to mention his love of motorbikes.

Hamilton shook aside the memories and attacked his engine-cleaning routine with more gusto. He was so caught up in the moment that he failed to register the sound of footsteps coming from the side door of the garage.

Dave Millward and Mark Jennings pointed their weapons directly at Hamilton's head. "So, you're the competition who's been giving us all this grief? And there was me thinking we were dealing with a pro," Millward said with a snarl of disgust.

Hamilton spun around to face the intruders. He was genuinely perplexed. He didn't know these men, much less understand why they were threatening him. The idea that they could be here as a result of something from his past life as a gangland enforcer was the only thing that made sense, but even then the chances of that were remote. It had to be something else.

When he spoke, there was no trace of fear in his voice. He'd faced down too many thugs to let a few guns worry him. Then again, there was something about the cruel eyes of his visitors. He needed to tread lightly. "I don't know what this is about. Are you sure you've come to the right place?"

"That's your first mistake, right there," Millward responded. "Don't go thinking you can engage us in conversation in the hope we'll drop our guard. Your name's Todd Hamilton, you're currently contracted to kill the Hayden family, and yes we've come to the right place."

A hard slap across the face with a wet towel would have had a similar impact as the words Hamilton had just heard. There was nothing to be gained by denial. "So what has that to do with you guys? It's obvious you're not police, and you sure as hell are no friends of the family, otherwise I'd have known about you. What does that leave us with?"

Millward walked across the garage floor and sat on an upturned crate, his weapon held rock steady as he faced Hamilton from a gap of two yards. Jennings meanwhile edged his way around the other side until he stood immediately behind their captive, who was still kneeling beside the rebuilt bike engine.

"It leaves us with too many cooks spoiling the broth," Millward said. "That was *our* contract until you muscled in. I don't like competition, so I'm here to declutter the playing field." The threat was obvious.

The penny dropped for Hamilton. "You're the guys that shot up the hospital! Look, I don't know what went wrong, but I got a call offering me the contract and it was not something I could turn down. You'd do the same thing in my place. Shouldn't you be taking this up with the guy who hired you?"

"Already taken care of. In case you didn't know, our mutual paymaster was a sleazeball by the name of Rudi Valentine. He won't be hiring and firing any more, not with the rather large hole I left in his skull where his brain used to be."

It was the first time Hamilton had heard the name of his assignment broker. These guys were a jump ahead of him, but did they know the whole picture? "If this Valentine is out of commission, what do you gain by continuing to worry about the contract? If you haven't been paid, then surely you've cut off your money supply? Why would you do that?"

Millward's affability changed completely. His thin smile transformed into a tight lip-curl that bared his teeth, and give a glimpse of the anger bubbling below the surface. "You calling me stupid? I got paid in full, with a nice little bonus on top, before I stiffed that weasel, but there are still a few loose ends to be tied up."

"Such as?" The shaky words betrayed Hamilton's growing concern for his predicament.

"Valentine had bosses and I'm not going to spend the rest of my life looking over my shoulder for them. The way I see it, the job needs to be finished. Who knows, these people might want other jobs done in the future. Being a practical man leaves me with no option other than to see this through to the end."

Hamilton saw an opening. "I know about Valentine's bosses, or at least I know how to get in touch with them. Why not agree to work together and maybe get these people off both our backs. It's got to be worth a try?"

"No chance! I don't need you. I've got a team of five top men, more than enough to deal with this. At the moment you're nothing more than a distraction."

"Are you sure about that?" Hamilton responded. "I'm guessing that with Valentine out of the picture, you're as much in the dark as I am about how to locate the Haydens. The security firm that took them has them spirited away from London, and the only chance we have of getting a location is making a phone call. The people I'm talking about seem to have an inside track on what's happening."

"What if they don't know the location?"

"I overhead some things through a parabolic mic at Stansted airfield. It was a bit garbled, but I think there's a clue there."

Millward rocked back and forth on the crate, using up a few seconds to get his thoughts in order. "If, and I mean if, we agree to tie in with you, it's on the strict understanding that

I'm in charge. You take your orders from me, and you do exactly what I tell you to do."

"Seems logical to me," Hamilton agreed.

"Okay," Millward said, "make the call."

George Roper didn't seem surprised at the news of the demise of Rudi Valentine. He listened intently to Hamilton's precise report, shocked only by the revelation that two of his independent contractors had somehow been brought together. Far from being concerned by the turn of events, he immediately saw the opportunity to finally put this matter to rest.

He would have to exert further pressure on the Home Secretary to uncover the Haydens' new hideout, although even he might not be able to get the information. The use of a private security firm complicated the situation, probably because it disconnected the information pipeline into Charles Manning's office. That being the case, it was perhaps fortuitous the contractors were pooling their resources.

He readily agreed to the new arrangements, and even threw in a bonus sweetener for all parties concerned.

Roper disconnected the call and looked out through a window across the Boston skyline. His mind had already turned from events in London to more pressing matters on this side of the Atlantic.

Chapter 20

ALAN DOYLE HAD faced many dangers in a distinguished career as a special forces operative and counter-terrorism agent. He'd stared down the barrels of a lot of weapons, walked into fist fights with the odds stacked against him, and had lost his right arm in a ferocious gun battle that many men would have run away from. But running wasn't in Doyle's nature.

Until now.

Standing in the arrivals lounge at O'Hare International, Doyle badly wanted a way out. The knot in his stomach tightened with each passing minute, and he could feel perspiration on his forehead, despite the airport's generous air-condition system. He'd never before felt so nervous about confronting any situation. Facing the future in-laws was an entirely new experience.

"There they are!" Chelsea beamed.

Doyle lifted his head reluctantly to follow the direction of her pointing arm. A petite woman, dressed in light-blue jeans and a maroon sweatshirt, pushed through the crowd, letting go of the arm of a tall man, who trailed in her wake. He was easily Doyle's height, with a shock of white hair, almost hidden by a black Stetson perched at a jaunty angle on his oversized head. He had the bearing of a military man, a confident, alert stride that befitted the five-star general he once was.

Stan and Barbara Horgan hugged their daughter in a display of genuine affection and warmth. The long absence from their only child had taken a toll on their emotions, and neither was afraid to let it show. There was a lot of kissing, a few tears, and a large measure of suffocation in the way they squeezed Chelsea to their bosoms.

Doyle took in the scene with delight. He envied the family

bond, remembering the times when his own parents had welcomed his homecomings from one tour of duty or another. Sadly, he would never get the chance to experience those again.

He felt like an interloper and shuffled uncomfortably from one foot to the other, all the while subconsciously turning his prosthetic arm as much out of view as he could manage.

Retired General Stan Horgan drew apart from the three-way embrace and strode towards Doyle, his features suddenly taking on a frown as he spotted Doyle's outstretched left hand. "Son," he said in a booming voice, "I'm sure glad to meet you at last, but I would be proud and honoured to shake you by your other hand. I know you're pretty adept with it, so let's get it front and centre where it belongs."

Doyle's whole demeanour changed. The knots untangled, the nerves dissipated, and the sweat seemed to dry on his skin. "Thank you, sir, it's a pleasure to meet you. I hope you don't feel I'm intruding."

Horgan stopped his vigorous handshake and stared into Doyle's eyes. "Two things we gotta get clear right off the bat. You don't call me sir, or General. The name's Stan. The other thing is that if my daughter says you're good enough for her, then it's a damn sure thing that you're more than good enough for me. There's no such thing as intruding here; hell, I feel as if you're part of the family already."

Doyle was lost for words. The cold dread of just a few minutes ago was replaced by a warm glow that quickly spread over his entire body. Stan Horgan packed a pretty emotional wallop.

"Stanley! What are you saying to that young man?" Chelsea's mother pushed between the two men, feigning a pained expression. "I hope he's not been trying to terrorise you like the over-protective father he's always been? You pay him no mind."

With that, she reached up, threw her arms around Doyle's neck, and hugged him. "Welcome to Chicago, Alan. My, you're just as ruggedly handsome as Chelsea said you were."

"Mom!"

Doyle grinned. "Nice to meet you ma'am. I've seen plenty of pictures of you, but now in the flesh I can tell where your daughter gets her stunning looks from."

Barbara gushed. "Oh my, you Brits have a way with the honey words, but I warn you, young man, drop the *ma'am* or you and me will have a problem. Now, I'm sure you're both tired and hungry. Hope you like home-cooking, Alan?"

"Thought you'd never ask, Barbara."

The evening was an unqualified success. Doyle couldn't remember the last time he'd tasted chicken that good. "That's the proper corn-fed breeding they get here," Barbara had told him, delighted by his appetite, particularly when he asked for second helpings of her apple pie dessert.

General Horgan waited for a break in the after-dinner conversation. "If you ladies don't mind, I'll take Alan into the study to show off my war-game boards." Chelsea had already warned Doyle about her father's collection of reconstructed scenes from some of America's most famous battles.

To Doyle's surprise, the General ignored the displays and motioned him to sit in one of two large armchairs in a less-cluttered part of the room. "I want to talk about my daughter. I know what she does for a living, and I know she's damn good at it. I'm an extremely proud father, Alan, but fathers worry about their daughters. I want to know someone's watching out for her. Are you that man?"

Doyle could see the mix of love and concern etched into the old soldier's face. "I'll level with you, Stan, as honestly as I can. Chelsea is better than good, in fact she's probably the best agent I've ever worked with, outside my boss, Mike Devon, and that's saying something. She's cool under the most intense situations. Never takes risks, but neither does she shy away from anything. She has reflexes like a cat, and the heart of a lion, and I guess by now you realise that I'm in love with her. I'd never let anything happen to her, though if you need to know the truth, she's saved my bacon a lot more times than the other way around. I won't try to fool you by saying that what we do isn't dangerous. You know what goes on, but what you have to realise is that your daughter is probably more equipped for the job than even you can imagine. I can't stop you worrying, but I can tell you to sleep easier because of her ability to stay one step ahead. She's that good."

Horgan's eyes misted over. "I'm betting you don't usually talk at such lengths. I guess I hit a sweet spot when I asked you to discuss my daughter. Yes, I can see, you really do love her deeply."

"Can't hide the fact, and I don't want to, Stan. I want to spend the rest of my life with her."

"Wait just a doggone minute! Are you asking for my daughter's hand in marriage?"

Doyle flushed. "Yessir, my parents brought me up to be respectful of tradition. Dad always told me a man should never to ask a girl for her hand until he'd squared it with her father."

"Quite right," Horgan teased. "And tell me, have you asked for her hand before telling me this?"

"I'm afraid so, sir," Doyle responded sheepishly. "In my defence, I have to admit I didn't believe she'd accept a shipwreck like me. I'd have felt pretty stupid asking you, and then being turned down by Chelsea."

Horgan roared with laughter. "And did she accept?"

"To my surprise, she said yes."

"Comes as no surprise to me. You're a better man than I think you realise. I'd be real honoured to have you as a son in-in-law."

The two men stood and shook hands formally before embracing. The General stepped back suddenly, as if remembering something. "What if I'd said no?"

"You want an honest answer?"

"Is there any other kind?"

"In that case," said Doyle, "I'd have to tell you I'd have went ahead and married her without your permission."

Horgan roared with laughter, crossed the room to a small drinks counter, and yelled at the top of his voice for his wife and daughter to join them. "This calls for a celebration!"

Chapter 21

THE DU REUA superyacht bobbed gently at its berth in Boston Haven, an exclusive marina nestled in one of America's most historic waterfronts. The site of Samuel Adams' notorious Tea Party of December 1773 was less than a stone's throw from the quadruple-decked *Spirit of Enterprise*, a thirty-million-dollar superstructure which was virtually a fixture in this playground of the rich. The owners paid their harbour dues annually in advance, maintained a permanent full-time crew of six, and ventured beyond the breakwater for little more than a few weeks at a time.

The colossal costs were mere tax write-offs for George Roper and Giles Grimand. By their reckoning, the availability of a flexible base on America's lucrative north-eastern quadrant was a price worth paying. It served as a corporate venue – on those occasions when opulence and overtness earned a few extra brownie points – or as a private meeting place, when discretion required more clandestine surroundings.

There were other reasons for having such potent ocean-going transportation.

On those occasions when the *Spirit of Enterprise* slipped her moorings and moved out of the shelter of Massachusetts Bay, it was usually for activities unrelated to her stated intentions of pleasure-cruising or deep-sea fishing. Picking up contraband or illegal aliens often topped the shopping lists, depending on the demands of the owners' various "*shareholders.*"

The yacht made use of a ship-to-shore Marenco helicopter, or an underwater hatch for launching a manned submersible, to make collections from trawlers beyond the three-mile international boundary. The US Coast Guard rarely paid much attention to the infrequent comings and goings of one of the seaboard's most respected resident crafts.

A package picked up during a daytime voyage the previous month was the reason Roper and Grimand were entertaining two guests in the yacht's stateroom shortly after five o'clock on a Saturday afternoon.

Mehdi Naybet and Marouen Badri shifted uncomfortably on the large, leather settee that wrapped around almost the entire perimeter of the spacious lounge. The curtains were drawn, the lighting subdued, and the atmosphere crackled with tension. It was the Tunisians' first face-to-face meeting with the men who had been effectively running their lives for the past three years.

Naybet and Badri knew them to be highly-influential, ruthless and dangerous people. They'd always insisted on anonymity, so why the need for this meeting? The fear shared by the two London gangsters was almost palpable.

"I see you gentlemen look less than relaxed," Roper intoned with an air of condescension. "There's no need for alarm, particularly if you followed our instructions precisely. Did you switch hotels and check you weren't followed here?"

"Yes, yes, just as you asked," Naybet responded nervously.

"Excellent. I knew I could trust you to do things right. In fact, our trust in you is such that we've decided to bring you in from the cold. We want you to become part of our inner sanctum and to share in the greater bounties that your efforts have helped to secure. What do you say to that?"

The two men were speechless. They exchanged glances, clearly unsure how to respond. Could this be really true? What had they done to deserve the honour? Naybet finally found his voice. "I...we...don't know what to say. This is a great blessing. We will not let you down."

Roper waved the comment aside and opened a map on a table, pointing to the city of Quincy in Boston's southern suburbs. "A package was delivered to a warehouse here two weeks ago. It contains a rather large non-fission bomb that must be detonated two days from now. The blast will cause devastation over a radius of a few hundred yards, although we have planned that casualties will be kept to a minimum. This is a sprawling, largely-abandoned industrial estate, so we can expect the death toll to be no more than a few dozen."

"Why not relocate the bomb to an area which will guarantee greater results?" Naybet's question was designed to demonstrate his willingness to participate in mass genocide.

"The intention here is not merely to cause death and destruction, but also to spread fear and uncertainty. For that reason, we have also included a small amount of the Sarin chemical in the explosive compound. Again, it is not enough to have any lasting impact, but its very presence will strike terror into the hearts of the American people."

Naybet looked bewildered. "I don't understand. You want to detonate a bomb, but you don't want it to be really bad? Why would we do this? What's to be gained?"

Roper bent forward and extracted a large aluminium case from below his chair. He thumped it on the table, and left it sealed while he spoke. "Despite what Homeland Security will imagine, this is not a terrorist attack, but an economic one. The repercussions will cause panic and fear, leading to all manner of reactions, such as the plummeting of stocks and shares, increases in security budgets, fresh purchases of weapons, and the onset of new draconian measures against certain middle-eastern factions. All of these will be to our benefit, simply because we've aligned our interests to profit from the ensuing mayhem."

"If I may?" Grimand interrupted. Roper nodded at his partner to continue the briefing.

"We have two Arab friends currently babysitting the package. Your job is to travel to the site, arm the bomb, and hightail it out of there. The arming mechanism has been set with a false twelve-hour display, which will make our babysitters think they have more time than they'll need to make their own exit. The idea is that the bomb will detonate while they are still on location, leaving investigators with lots of evidence about the perpetrators."

Grimand hoisted the case and waved it in front of the Tunisians. "This contains maps and diagrams of three other bombs, supposedly located around the Boston and Chicago areas. There are also details of similar devices in four vague locations in various parts of England, most notably around the Greater London area."

"You mean we're going to detonate eight bombs?" Naybet asked incredulously.

"No, you idiot," Grimand snarled. "There's only one bomb; the maps are a ruse. Remember what we said about fear being more effective than reality? We'll have the authorities blundering around looking for things that aren't there, while we sit back and reap the rewards."

He pushed the case across the table towards Naybet. "This has been specially reinforced, although it is important you place it below the surface in one of the building's internal storm-drain ducts to protect it from the full effects of the blast. Our engineers tell us it should survive intact."

"One more thing," Grimand said earnestly. "You must remain on site until exactly midnight tomorrow. Don't leave earlier than that, otherwise it will appear suspicious to our Arab minders. Tell them you must leave to get final instructions, but that you will return to transport them away from the site. In reality, you will be aboard a flight to London by the time the explosion occurs. We want you back in England to help with the next phase of the operation."

Roper and Grimand watched the Tunisians as they walked across the marina jetty thirty minutes later. The time had been spent putting final polishes to the plan, whilst at the same time assuring their guests of their importance in the upcoming chain of events.

It was all a charade.

The timing mechanism on the bomb was indeed false. It would detonate much earlier than Naybet and Badri were led to believe. The two men were not needed back in London. Their usefulness had almost ended.

The real plan called for their body parts to be found among what was left of the warehouse in Boston.

Chapter 22

FOUR MORE PAIRS of eyes tracked Naybet and Badri across the marina's network of boardwalks. Doyle and Horgan had flown into Logan just before noon, meeting up with *LonWash* US agents Don Hill and Marta Tessler in the foyer of the Courtyard Hotel in Copley Square. To everyone's surprise, the targets had done nothing of note during the time they'd been under surveillance, although by late afternoon they had eventually surfaced from their room.

A number of taxi switches had put the watchers on full alert. When the Tunisians had finally entered the marina complex, Doyle sensed something big was in the air. It became imperative to discover who the pair were meeting.

Two hours later, Doyle studied his quarry emerging from the main courtyard where they hailed yet another taxi. He prodded Hill. "You and Tessler stay on site and find out everything you can about the *Spirit of Enterprise*. Use your phone to get pictures of anyone in the vicinity and contact the Washington office for a full work-up on ownership, plus all recorded movements of that vessel over the past six months. We'll take the car and follow our two friends. I'd particularly like to know what's in that case they're carrying."

Hill and Tessler climbed out of the agency's Chevrolet Suburban and disappeared into the shadows. Doyle waited until the taxi left the marina complex before he eased the SUV forward and settled into the early evening traffic on South Market Street, running parallel to the Massachusetts Turnpike. They were heading back to downtown Boston.

This time there was no taxi-hopping. The Tunisians made straight for their hotel, stopping briefly in the foyer to collect a room key before stepping into an elevator. Horgan, who had been dropped at the front entrance, made her way across the concourse to watch the display panel light up for a stoppage on the sixth floor.

She scanned for a vantage point and settled for a small snug area to the right of the main door. After pulling up a seat, she ordered coffee and sandwiches and waited for Doyle, who was trying to find a quick-exit parking spot. He joined her within five minutes.

"We could be in for a long wait," she told him. "We can't sit about here all night."

"I agree. We'll give it an hour or so, after which we'll have to think about taking a suite here."

She punched him lightly on the thigh. "Is that all you can think about! Just because we had to sleep in separate rooms at my parents' house, doesn't mean I can't wait to jump between the sheets with you."

He laughed loudly. "It *was* rather quaint and old-fashioned of your mum, but I liked her sense of propriety. In fact, I liked everything about your parents. I'm sorry the visit was so short - can't wait to return to Chicago as soon as things are wrapped up here."

"Do you really mean that?"

"Course I do. Last night was the most fun I can remember in a long time. Your old man is a mine of information and stories and, boy, can he drink!"

She snuggled closer to him. "Are you going to tell me what you and my dad talked about in the study?"

"That should remain strictly between two men, but if you must know, he warned me that you can be stubborn and headstrong, and it wouldn't do any harm to take you over my knee every so often."

"In your dreams, buster."

The playful mood was broken by the arrival of a waiter. After he'd deposited the coffee and sandwiches, and left them alone again, Horgan's expression suddenly turned serious. "Alan, are you sure about everything? Do you really want to get married? If you have any doubts, I want to know about them now, rather than later."

"What's brought this on? For the record, there are no doubts, no second thoughts, no chance of you getting outta my clutches. You're stuck with me, girl, and that's just the way I want it."

She leaned across and kissed him. "That suits me just fine, Mr Doyle."

"Ditto, Mrs Doyle. Hey, I like the sound of that."

They were so wrapped up in the moment that they almost missed Naybet and Badri crossing the foyer and exiting through the revolving entrance door.

"Jesus, they're on the move," Doyle whispered urgently. He flung a handful of dollar bills on the table, looked longingly at the untouched coffee and sandwiches, and sprang from his seat. "Watch where they go while I get the car."

Naybet felt a growing sense of unease as the hire car bumped across uneven ground in the centre of the Quincy industrial estate. Something was nagging at the back of his mind. It was almost within touch, but he couldn't bring it forward. Usually great at ordering his thoughts, it rankled that whatever was there was staying stubbornly elusive.

He switched attention to the rows of rundown buildings, many of which were stripped bare of the ubiquitous corrugated sheets that framed the skeletons of girders before the days of depression and falling productivity had taken their toll on a once-thriving manufacturing sector. Here and there, some smaller units were still in use - judging by a handful of parked cars - and weak interior lighting spilling out onto weed-covered concrete forecourts. Poor sods! Lucky to keep their heads above water; unlucky to be in the wrong place at the wrong time.

Naybet's gaze fell on a sorry-looking structure standing forlornly near the western boundary of the site. Faded lettering across a double door, which someone had once painted a hideous shade of green, told him it was the building he was looking for. He rolled the car to a stop beside a small commercial van, and climbed out to survey the surroundings.

A thin, dark-skinned man emerged from the side door. His hair was thick with grease, his clothes resembled cast-offs from a jumble sale, and his overall demeanour was one of apathy. He didn't look the type to be trusted with guarding such a valuable commodity. Then again, he was perhaps exactly the right kind of ask-no-questions downbeat that was required.

Naybet and Badri brushed past the minder and entered the warehouse, making their way immediately to a large crate in the centre of the deserted floor. They carefully jimmied open the top of the box and explained everything they knew about the weapon. The greaser and his friend shrugged off the revelation about the dangerous package. Being paid was all that mattered.

"I'm going to arm the device with a thirty-six-hour delay," Naybet told them. "After that, we will leave and return tomorrow evening with the rest of your money. We will all be well away from the area by the time the explosion takes place."

His comment produced more shrugs of indifference. If only they knew? He shook his head at the stupidity of the Arabs, and bent down to search for the command box on the device. Almost immediately he jumped backwards.

"The redhead! That's what I was trying to remember."

"What are you talking about?" Badri demanded.

Naybet tugged a Browning pistol from his shoulder holster. "We were followed! I saw a redhead with a man back in the lobby of the hotel. They were seated at a table with a plate of sandwiches, yet when we drove out of the car park, there she was, standing on the steps, pretending not to notice us. How could I have been so stupid?"

"Why did you notice this? There were a lot of people in the area at the time. Are you sure it's not your imagination?"

"Don't be a fool, Marouen. She was a most striking woman. I naturally looked at her in the hotel. She was like a model; how could one forget? But why would she just leave her table without eating and be standing outside when we left? I tell you we must have picked up a tail."

"What are we going to do?"

Naybet asked the Arabs to show him a rear exit before

ordering them to remain beside the crate. "Come, Marouen, let's see if we can catch a few intruders."

Doyle had switched off the car lights and rolled to a stop beside an abandoned building. The target vehicle had come to a rest beside a workshop less than five-hundred yards away. "We'll have to go on foot from here."

Horgan racked her MP5 and followed him across waste ground. It took them almost twenty minutes to weave their way through the shadows, careful to protect their silhouettes from the background of a strong moon. Fifty yards from the building they were faced with open ground. Nothing for it, but to get on their bellies and crawl the rest of the way.

Horgan heard it first. It was a shuffling sound, too close to miss. Footsteps. No doubt about it. She rolled onto her back, aiming the machine pistol towards two shapes emerging from the rear of the unit. There was no safety catch. She was good to go.

She never got the chance.

The first bullet sliced across the left side of her temple. The next two were high on her chest, one mercifully caught by her Kevlar vest, the other deflecting past it to gouge through the top of her shoulder. She groaned weakly, rolled over twice, and came to stop under a fine red mist that sprinkled her body.

"Noooooo!" Doyle screamed. He tore his eyes away from Horgan, leapt to his feet, and charged the two shapes. His weapon was on full auto. There was no thought for his own safety. Ignoring a volley of incoming rounds, his hand tight on the trigger, he watched two shapes pirouette in the shadows. By the time the magazine clicked on empty, Doyle was looking down at the mangled remains of two men. Chunks of flesh were torn from their faces and torsos, but the sight didn't stop Doyle from ramming in a fresh magazine and criss-crossing the bodies with another full-auto burst.

He stood, dazed for a moment, almost reluctant to look back at Chelsea. Finally, he shook off the stupor and raced to her side. There was blood everywhere. He fell to the ground, cradled her head in his lap, and emitted a loud, pitiful roar.

Chapter 23

"I've got an email from dad!"

All heads in the manor house lounge turned towards the excited youngster. Devon, who had returned to Bishop's Stortford earlier that morning, was the first to react to the outburst, rising from his seat to rush to the small desk where Christopher Hayden was staring agog at his laptop screen. Half-way there, Devon saw a sudden transformation in the youth's features.

Christopher's shoulders drooped, the life went out of his eyes, and tears started flowing. He looked plaintively around the room. "I'm sorry....I thought.....I thought he was alive. It's just a goodbye message... it's not fair."

Sonia Hayden ran to her son and hugged him, her eyes darting from the screen to meet Devon's steady gaze. "What's this all about? How could anyone do something so cruel?"

Devon glanced at the first few lines of the message and understood immediately what they meant. He touched Christopher on the shoulder. "Somehow your dad figured out a way of contacting you should something untoward happen to him. I know it's not easy, but you need to read what he has to say. It's something we'll have to take a detailed look at later, but for now it's personal to you. We'll leave you and your mum to go through it in your own time."

He nodded at Cheadle and Hunt, seated in the corner of the room in their capacity as full-time minders, and the trio quickly left the lounge. The men paced in silence, their steps echoing off the wooden floor to the accompaniment of a loud tick-tock beat from a grandfather clock. Finally, after fifteen minutes, the door re-opened and Sonia beckoned Devon to join her.

As he stepped into the room he noticed the smudged mascara marks on her face, though she did her best to hide the obvious distress. Christopher had moved away from the desk and was staring out through a window, his hands locked behind his head, his elbows shielding his face. There was a lot Devon wanted to say to comfort the boy, but now was not the time. He drew up a seat at the desk, tapped the touchpad on the laptop, and began reading the message.

Dearest Chris

I know this will come as a shock to you and I'm sorry for having to put you through it. You're getting this message because I'm no longer around, a situation I knew might happen, which was why I tried to keep you and your mum out of it. That didn't mean I didn't love you. There hasn't been a moment when you haven't been in my thoughts. I'm sorry for all the missed moments, for all those times when you've made me proud, even if I wasn't there to see you score the winning goal in the semi-final of the Universities' Cup. Oh yes, I know about that, and about the great results you've achieved in your exams, and all the other things you've done as you've grown into the fine young man I knew you'd become.

I wish the last two years had been different. If only I hadn't stumbled on things I was not meant to see! I was let down by so-called friends and colleagues, and as a result things became extremely dangerous. I could not risk the safety or you or your mum. I had to get away to try to get my life back together. Obviously I failed. Don't grieve for me. I had a great innings and my conscience is clear.

Tell your mum I always loved and cherished her. She deserved better. Be strong for her and look after her. I promise you, things will get better.

Remember how we used to play those games on the computer? I could never get the better of you when it came to navigating those weird machines in the skies. I think it was because you always came up with ways to block me out, like that time you devised a 24-character password that even I couldn't break – and I was supposed to be the computer genius in the family. I hope you revisit that old game and remember the good times.

Take care, Chris. Have a wonderful life and always be your own man. With love. Dad

Devon finished the message and scanned through it a

second time before he eased away from the desk. It was only then he realised Christopher had moved from the window and was watching him closely.

"My dad was a great man, Mr Devon. You have to find out what happened to him. These people can't be allowed to get away with what they did to him."

"Don't worry, they'll get what's coming to them. Now, I have to get this message to Tim Halloran, if only to find out how your dad managed to hide it and organise transmission direct to your inbox without, it seems, anyone being able to discover it. He wouldn't have taken any risks with you being exposed to his enemies."

Devon tapped the youth on the shoulder and walked out of the room to the sanctuary of the hallway. He pulled his sat phone from a jacket pocket, hit the keys, and was immediately connected with Halloran.

"What's up, Mike?"

Devon explained what had just happened and offered to forward the e-mail.

"No need for that. I've already set up an RDC on Christopher's laptop, but you need to ask him if it's okay for me to log on. I don't want him thinking I can do this whenever I want, so I built in a permissions window requiring his password."

"What's an RDC?"

"Remote Desktop Connection. There's an icon for it on the top right of the screen. I'll hold while you talk to Christopher."

Devon returned to the lounge and updated Christopher on the conversation with Halloran. Several minutes later, Halloran's invisible hand swept the cursor across the screen, opening sub-directories and scrolling through lines of coding faster than Devon's eyes could follow. He watched fascinated as command prompts layered on top of each other, more lines of type cascaded down the screen, and small data boxes were opened and stacked in vertical columns to the right of the text area.

The relentless process continued for another half-hour before the cursor finally stopped blinking. The screen froze and nothing happened for several minutes. Then everything went black before Halloran's face filled the screen.

"Hi guys, I'm using a spook's version of Skype. I want you both to hear what I've got to say, after which Christopher and me have got some work to do."

"Fire away," Devon responded. "Sonia's here too and will be listening to everything, in case you need her input."

"Great, the more the merrier. First up, Matthew appears to have used a dozen proxy servers to get this message to Christopher. There's no way these can be tracked, but at this point that's not important. He must have constructed the email with a command-sensitive breaker, which basically means it could never have been sent if he kept refreshing the instructions on a periodic basis, say very five days. When this wasn't done, the delivery instructions would have activated immediately. That's why it popped into your inbox today, Christopher."

"I was hoping," Christopher murmured sadly, "that he might have included some information about what's going on, and why he became a target."

"The obvious answer is that he couldn't trust the Ethernet. Despite all his precautions, he knew there was always a chance someone might stumble on it, for example by using grab-all software that's extremely random and impossible to safeguard against."

"So," Devon interrupted, "we appear to be no farther along in tracking whatever Matthew was working on?"

Halloran smiled. "Maybe yes, and maybe no. I've re-read the message several times and I think there's a clue that only his son will be able to solve. The part that discusses the game and the use of a password is a strange reference. What does it mean to you, Christopher?"

"It was just a silly game. I devised a password that included several dingbat characters instead of the usual letters and numbers. Dad had to admit defeat after running it through MI6's best decryption software. When I finally revealed it to him, he accused me of cheating, though he did congratulate me for thinking outside the box. That was a favourite expression of his."

"And do you still remember that password?"

"Of course," Christopher beamed, "but I don't see how it helps with anything."

Halloran's head disappeared off screen as he leaned away from his monitor. He returned holding a piece of paper. "This might be a long shot. I'm guessing the word *skies* in your dad's email is actually a deliberate misnomer for the word *clouds*. What if he stored something in a cloud account and pinned his hopes on you finding it?"

"That's a bit of a stretch even for you, Tim," Devon said sceptically.

"No, no," Christopher yelled. "I remember now! The game that dad said was machines in the skies was actually called *Pilots of the Clouds.* You're right, Tim, you're right!"

"Okay," Halloran responded, "this is the way I see it. There are literally dozens of Cloud storage facilities on the market. We're going to go through each one, enter a user name familiar to you and your dad, and insert that password of yours. It will be a lengthy process, though the boys here will help to speed things up by queueing the various accounts. We'll use your laptop remotely to ping the various Cloud alternatives onto your desktop. You enter the details, and we keep moving through the list until we get a hit. Are you up for it, Christopher?"

"You bet I am."

"Before we start, will you tell my boss beside you that this is a matter for us techies? We won't need him for a few hours."

Devon threw up his hands in mock surrender. "I get the message. I'll leave the computer geniuses to their work."

He was still smiling when he walked through the house and out to the front steps. An afternoon sun was doing its best to burn away a stubborn canopy of cirrus, and a light breeze ruffled the tops of the manor's perimeter trees. It was a day for picnicking, or walking the dog, or chilling out with a good book. His mobile phone chirped as if to remind him of the forlornness of hope.

The caller id displayed the name of *LonWash* senior

American agent, Don Hill.

"What's up, Don?"

Devon listened intently, his sense of wellbeing suddenly shattered by the words echoing in the handset.

Chapter 24

IT WAS THE longest twelve hours of Alan Doyle's life. Befuddled by shock and incomprehension, he had simply shut himself off from everything that was happening in the cramped ICU wing of Massachusetts General Hospital. People came and went in a blur of movement. Conversations were distorted into lines of gibberish. Doyle blanked them all out.

The only thing he could focus on was that his girl was in a theatre fighting for her life, and no-one was giving her any chance of winning. It should be him in there, instead of her. Why did she have to be the one who was cut down? Why wasn't he more alert to the dangers of approaching that building? How was he ever going to face Chelsea's parents?

He didn't have long to wait. Just as an orderly pulled back curtains to admit the first rays of daylight, Stan and Barbara Horgan rushed into the room. He stood awkwardly to meet them, his eyes refusing to lift from a small stain on the carpet that had held him transfixed for the better part of the last hour.

"Oh, Alan, this is terrible, what's the news? How's my baby?" Her words were garbled. It was only then Doyle realised she'd grabbed him in a tight embrace.

He pulled away, staring into watery-green eyes that reminded him so much of Chelsea, "They don't know...she's still in theatre. It's been a long time. It's all my fault."

Stan Horgan stepped forward and planted a firm hand on Doyle's shoulder. "Son, there are a lot of reasons why this happened, but one of them is not you. It's not going to help Chelsea, or us, if you stand around here taking the blame and feeling sorry for yourself. I believe in Almighty God; I believe He has a plan for all of us. I believe He will do what's best for Chelsea, though I've got to say He and I will have words if He doesn't do the right thing."

"Stan! Don't blaspheme."

"Just calling it as it is, darling. He'd better be watching over our little girl. That's all I'm saying." Tears welled up in the corner of his eyes.

Doyle needed to break the mood. His eyes turned to Hill and Tessler, who'd shown up several hours after calling an ambulance and staying at the scene to brief Homeland Security agents. They'd already reported to Doyle that two Arabs had been found cowering inside the warehouse, and that the bomb had been made safe. A follow-up search of the area had uncovered an aluminium briefcase, which contained details of other targets in both America and England.

Doyle introduced the agents to the Horgans, who shook hands warmly, especially after hearing how quickly the pair had got first responders to their daughter's aid.

The group settled into seats and lapsed into a brooding silence. There was a sudden commotion in the corridor, and all eyes turned to three men entering the room with all the grace and style of an elephant in a china shop. Dressed in comically-matching black suits, and each sporting spiral wires attached to earpods, there was no mistaking their identity. The man in the centre strode up to Hill. "Where's Doyle?"

Doyle was already on his feet before Hill responded. "Now's not a good time," was all he could think of saying.

Three Department of Homeland Security badges were waved in his face. The senior man spoke again. "There's never a good time, so right now, this is *your* time. You need to come with us to answer a lot of questions."

"Yeah, in your dreams, pal!"

"You don't have a choice. This is a matter of national security, and right now I have to find out how much you're compromising that security. You know, we can do this the easy way or the hard way."

Doyle moved nose-tight to the DHS agent. "Believe me, you don't want the hard way. I could put you three jokers in the casualty area of this hospital quicker than a ventriloquist puts words in his dummy. You really don't want to go down that road."

The two men stared hard at each other. Neither looked like backing down. The tension dragged on for several seconds before Stan Horgan leapt to his feet.

"This is not the time or place, agent whatever-your-name-is. My daughter is down the corridor fighting for her life, and this man is her fiancé. She needs him here; we need him here. I am retired General......"

"I know who you are, sir, but it doesn't make any difference."

Horgan found himself smiling despite his mood. "I doubt very much that you know anything about me, son. If you did, you would know that one phone call from me will end this nonsense, and by that I mean you will be ordered out of here by a man who will not take too kindly to the manner in which you have presented yourself this morning. Now, I suggest you take a moment to reflect. Why don't you and Mr Doyle have a brief chat outside so that any misunderstandings can be cleared up? But mind you don't keep him too long."

Hill and Tessler accompanied Doyle and the three agents out to a car park adjoining the main hospital building. The group found themselves standing beside a black Ford Crown Victoria, the default pursuit vehicle for numerous law-enforcement agencies. The DHS spokesman finally introduced himself as Robert T Younger, and fished a pack of cigarettes from a pocket of his immaculately-pressed suit.

Doyle declined the offer, but immediately changed his mind. He had given them up ten years ago, and had thought little about the habit ever since. Right now, however, he needed something to ease the tension. He also could have made a serious impression on a bottle of brandy, but that was one road he was not going down again. He sucked in a lungful of nicotine, grateful for the hit to his frayed system, and turned to face Younger. "Why don't you tell me what was in the briefcase?"

"Whoa, steady on," Younger held up his hands. "That's a

big back-to-front approach. Why don't you tell me how you came to be tracking a terrorist bomb, and why my office wasn't alerted before it almost exploded? We could have been looking at a major disaster, with no thanks to your interference."

Doyle bit a lip and fought to keep his emotions under control. He wanted to get this over with as quickly as possible. It was time for a soft approach. "There was no interference on our part. This started out as a simple job of tracking two London gangsters with no idea where it would take us. We followed them from a meeting on a yacht at Boston Haven to the industrial estate where they suddenly started shooting. If I'd had the foggiest notion they had a bomb, I wouldn't have gone in blind."

"And you had no idea of any terrorist connection?"

"There was a tenuous connection," Doyle admitted. "Their names came up in the investigation of the incident in Nice last month. We established a link between the Tunisians and the transfer of money into an account which could have been accessed by the man responsible for what happened in Nice. There were a lot of ifs and buts, and we were simply trying to connect the dots."

"Maybe we could have helped?" Younger suggested.

"I don't see how. All we had was two run-of-the-mill gangsters with a lot of money to throw around. We needed to find out whose money it was and where next they were going to throw it. It was an early-stage intelligence-gathering operation. There was nothing to suggest otherwise."

"And yet," Younger muttered, "it turned out to be much more than you thought."

"I see Homeland Security's twenty-twenty aftersight is as sharp as ever. Have you anything meaningful to say, or do you intend to stand there all day stating the bleedin' obvious?"

Younger made a point of throwing his cigarette butt on the ground and stamping it out in disgust. "Yeah, maybe if we'd been heading this up, there would be two terrorists still alive to tell us the big picture, not to mention there wouldn't be an agent at death's door inside this hospital."

Doyle lost it. The mention of Chelsea in such a casual fashion was a no-go area. It was time for a hard approach. He grabbed the lapels of Younger's jacket and slammed him against the Crown Vic. The other two Homeland agents reached behind their backs for holstered weapons, but Hill and Tessler beat them to it. The sight of matching Glock 22s made them slowly raise their arms.

Doyle locked his prosthetic arm under Younger's chin, cutting his air supply. "Are you talking about the same DHS that your own federal paymasters have criticised for mission-critical failures across all sectors, including corruption in your border security divisions and failure to inspect less than one per cent of USA chemical facilities? And didn't I read that your much-vaunted cybersecurity programme was such a monumental cock-up that you ended up being breached by third-level hackers? Yeah, I'm going to take a lesson on how to do things right by a bunch of incompetents."

"Just so we're clear," Doyle continued, "whatever way you slice and dice it, we've presented you guys with your biggest coup for years. While you were sitting on your asses, we tracked a mega-bomb into your backyard, prevented a catastrophic detonation, and left you telling the American public what wonderful guys you are. But we know different, don't we Bob? Any more gung-ho shit from you will send my people into overdrive. They'd like nothing better than setting the record straight."

Doyle released his grip and watched Younger gasp for breath. He nodded at Hill and Tessler to lower their weapons, and waited until Younger regained his composure. When he spoke again, the anger had left his voice. "We have a lot to share with you, including the background of the Tunisians, and the name of the yacht they were visiting. In the meantime, make sure we have copies of everything that was found in the suitcase. I'll leave you to sort out the details with Don and Marta."

Younger rasped his response. "Fuck you, Doyle. I don't need any favours from someone who thinks they can piss in *our* backyard and walk away without consequences. You haven't heard the last of this."

"You've had my offer." Without waiting for an answer he turned on his heels and walked away. He stopped abruptly twenty yards from the group, and looked back at Younger. "One more thing. The next time you talk about that girl inside the hospital, make sure you do so with all the respect and admiration she deserves."

He had almost reached the hospital entrance when General Horgan barged through the revolving door. "Alan, they're out of theatre and the surgeon wants to talk to the family."

The surgeon was a thin, bespectacled man, whose mop of unruly grey hair, framed a dark face etched with lines of age and stress. He was slumped back on a chair, gulping water from a plastic cup, and looking as though he might pass out at any moment. The rigours of twelve hours in theatre were plain to see. He didn't rise when Doyle and Stan Horgan entered the waiting room, but he nodded briefly at Barbara in an adjacent chair and sat upright.

"My name is Dr Patel and I wish I had better news for you. The patient has been stabilised and is being brought to a recovery room. However, I must warn you that she is far from being out of the woods, and might have long-term brain damage if she survives. At the moment, the chances of that happening are no better than fifty-fifty."

Barbara burst into tears. "Is my girl going to die, Doctor?"

"I'm afraid, Mrs Horgan, I can't answer that with any certainty. What I *can* tell you is that we've given her every chance, but her injury is such that it is really too early to say. The wound to her head resulted in gouging of the right parietal bone, which is a durable structure, but there's a gap that serves as a passageway for blood vessels and nerves, and this was also damaged. It's known as the *parietal foramen* and it houses some of the body's motor neurone capabilities. It was this which gave us most concern and which must now be monitored."

"How... how long will that take?" Doyle asked in a faltering voice.

"I wish I could put a timeframe on it for you. Unfortunately, we will have to react to things from here on. We can't anticipate anything in advance, so we must wait for the body to provide signals that things are either right or wrong. She will be hooked up to machines that will do this job for us."

"When can we see her?" Barbara asked plaintively.

Dr Patel shook his head. "I'm sorry. She must be completely isolated. You can view her through the ward window, but we cannot risk any undue activity around her. I'm sure you understand. There is one piece of good news I can share with you. The world's pre-eminent consultant on brain injuries is flying into Boston later today to review her case."

The news staggered Barbara. "How did that come about?"

"Apparently it was arranged during the night by your daughter's employer, Sir John Sandford. It seems he tracked down Mr Thomas Fotheringdale in London and arranged everything in less than an hour. I will be glad to have Mr Fotheringdale's support. He comes with an impressive reputation."

Doyle mouthed a silent thanks to the *LonWash* creator.

Chapter 25

GENERAL SIR JOHN Sandford had endured the kind of night he hoped to never have. The news that one of his agents had fallen in the line of *LonWash* duty was not something he'd wanted to hear, doubly so when it was Chelsea Horgan, a young woman he'd grown to admire and cherish, and who couldn't have meant more to him had she been his daughter.

Rustling up old schoolmate Tommy Fotheringdale, and getting him VIP clearance on the next available flight to Boston was the least he could do to make sure Chelsea had the best possible attention. Never mind that Tommy had warned him of the unpredictability of brain injuries, and that he should prepare himself for the worst, it was enough to know he was doing everything possible. It had never crossed his mind to do less.

Sandford had sprung into action as soon as he'd received Devon's report of the shooting. Shortly after securing Fotheringdale's services, he'd hurried across to the *LonWash* offices, as much to offer moral support to his team as to be in situ for any breaking news from Boston. He'd spent several hours doing the exact opposite. usually pacing the corridors and offices, getting in the way, and generally putting everyone on edge. He didn't seem to notice.

It was a much-depleted team because of the guard duties at the training centre in Bishop's Stortford, but everyone else had made their way to Charterhouse Street to wait anxiously for updates. By early afternoon the next day, the call finally came through from Boston. Allowing for the five-hour difference in time zones, Chelsea had been wheeled out of theatre at daybreak. She was hanging in there. She was still fighting the fight. That was good enough for Sandford.

He smiled at Devon, just as an Iridium satellite phone pulsed on a desk beside them. Devon grabbed the handset and spoke urgently. "Alan, it's great to hear from you. How are you holding up?" It was the first time the pair had spoken since the shoot-out at the warehouse. All previous contact had been made by Don Hill.

"Not good, Mike. I can't bear the thought of losing her. What'll I do if she doesn't pull through?"

Devon could hear the melancholy in every syllable. "We're a long way from there, buddy. She'll get the best treatment money can buy. I know it's easy for me to say, but you've got to hang tough, if only for Chelsea's sake. If there's anything you need, you just have to ask."

"I know you mean well, Mike, but they're just words. The doctors are saying she mightn't pull through and, even if she does, she could be a vegetable. She wouldn't want that, and I couldn't watch her existing in some parallel world. God forgive me, but I'd rather they take her now than leaving her to face a fate like that. Am I...am I being selfish?"

The last few words tailed off to a whisper. Devon ached for his friend's predicament. Part of him wanted to rush out to Boston to be at his side. He knew it wouldn't make a difference; it might even be counter-productive given the frailty of Doyle's emotions. The last thing anyone needed was to turn the days ahead into some sort of premature wake. Nonetheless, he had to offer something to ease Doyle's pain, though at that moment he couldn't find the words.

It was Doyle who rapidly changed the subject. "I had no alternative but to kill those fuckers. They had it coming for what they did to Chelsea. I don't know if I could have taken them alive; maybe I didn't try hard enough. I have to admit, Mike, I wasn't thinking of the bigger picture when I turned them into mincemeat."

"You did the right thing, Alan. We both know things can't always end the way we want them to. Who's to say we could have got any information from them? Anyway, there's more than enough to work on from your surveillance of the yacht to what was discovered at the warehouse. Take a back seat and let Hill and Tessler tie up the loose ends over there while you concentrate on staying with Chelsea."

It took a few seconds for Doyle to respond. "I didn't figure it any other way. Besides, I'm not much good for anything else at the moment. By the way, there's a Homeland Security asshole, by the name of Younger, who's intent on making life difficult for us. Hill and Tessler might need a bit of help to stay away from the shitstorm he's trying to create around *LonWash*."

"General Sandford's here beside me. I'm sure he can make a few calls."

"Hey, Mike, will you tell the Old Man I'm grateful for everything he's done. Sending that brain consultant has dared us all to hope that Chelsea will pull.... that she will not.... you know what I mean, Mike."

The line went dead.

Devon stared at the handset, knowing his friend had disconnected rather than allow an inevitable bout of crying to be overheard. The thought of the big, brash ex-soldier being reduced to a state of helplessness was almost unbearable. For the second time that day, Devon fought the urge to jump on a plane.

Christopher Hayden's enthusiasm to track down his father's potential Cloud account had dissipated rapidly after more than twenty failed attempts. Each time a new service was accessed, he had tried a combination of usernames followed by the secret password, but all he got in return was a succession of log-in failures. They were quickly running out of providers his dad might have used.

A site called *Dreamworld Storage* was number twenty-one in what was becoming a fruitless search. Christopher hovered the cursor over the username window and glanced down at a list of names he thought his father might use.

Mhayden5
MattHay5
MattChris5
ChrisMatt5
MattChris5

MattSonia5
ChrisSonia5

The list ran to over a hundred possibilities. The numeral 5 was used first because it was his father's favourite number, though of course Chris had to substitute it with other numbers to make sure he was covering all permutations. In quickly became obvious he was looking for a needle in a cyber haystack.

But he ploughed manfully on. The *Dreamworld* site was proving just as elusive as all the others. Christopher was on automatic pilot when he entered *MyMattAndSonia5* in the familiar first line of the log-in screen, before pasting the copied password string into the second line. He hit the enter button and was already consulting his list for the next possible username when a musical chime made him lift his head from his scribbled notes.

Welcome back MyMattandSonia5! Press any key to continue.

Christopher almost fell off his chair. He recovered his composure and used his index finger to hit the keyboard with a lot more force than he intended. The screen changed to a menu format that displayed a list of stored files. There was just one. The information showed it was a PDF file, last accessed barely a week ago, and was sized at just over nine thousand kilobytes. Whatever it contained, it was one hell of a document!

Eager to see what was there, Christopher used the laptop's trackpad to hover the cursor over the file name. Suddenly, the screen froze and a webcam feed showed Tim Halloran's beaming face in the top right-hand corner.

"You've done it! Well done, Christopher. Don't jump in just yet. We're going to run a few diagnostics at this end to make sure nobody's piggybacking the account. It's a pretty remote possibility, but I'm not taking any chances at this stage. Give me five minutes, after which you can open the file and see what's there."

"I understand, Tim, but please hurry. This could finally tell us what dad was up to."

Christopher sat for a few moments watching the frozen screen, not quite believing that a lot of answers were now within his grasp. He stood up to ease the muscles in his back and walked across to a bay window overlooking the front lawns of the Bishop's Stortford estate.

At that moment his face was framed in the crosshairs of a Leupold sniper's scope. It was the same piece of kit that had zeroed in on his father seconds before his death.

Chapter 26

THE FINGER MOVED inside the oval steel ring, crooking its way around the trigger of the Remington 700 rifle. Christopher Hayden's face was fixed unwaveringly in the sight. All it needed was a few ounces of pressure to send the 7.62mm round to its target. *Time you followed in your father's footsteps, you little creep*, Todd Hamilton whispered as he relaxed his muscles and prepared to take the shot.

The scope suddenly went blank. One moment he was staring at his victim, the next he was looking at a pink-coloured barrier that cut off the scene at the big manor house. Hamilton shifted his head away from the rubber-rimmed eyepiece and saw his companion's hand across the front of the Leupold scope. "What the fuck are you doing?" he mouthed.

Dave Millward leaned close to Hamilton's ear. "Are you fuckin' insane? We came here to get the lie of the land, not to take the first shot at anything that moves. I told you to bring the scope, not the whole kit. Stand down now, or I'll stand you down permanently." To emphasise the point, Millward pushed the tip of a Tanto boot knife into the soft tissue covering Hamilton's carotid artery.

The sniper lowered the rifle gingerly to the ground and turned to face Millward. "It was just as easy to carry the full rifle case, and anyway you never know when you get lucky. I had a clean shot. That was the Hayden kid standing at the window."

Millward, conscious of guards patrolling the perimeter of the grounds, tried to keep his voice low, despite his mounting anger. "And just what would that have achieved? Even if you'd made the shot, this place would be crawling with armed men within seconds, never mind there's still the mother to account for. We take them both at once, and only after we've prepared a proper plan of attack. If you've got a problem with that, just remember there's always another way to deal with your stupidity."

Hamilton was sick of this fucker's threats, but right now there was nothing he could do about it. "You're the boss. We'll do it your way, but just so you know, I'd have made the shot as easy as shelling peas."

Millward shook his ahead and slid the scope from the barrel mount. He used it to sweep the scene, noting possible points of entry, and mentally calculating the time required for getting from the perimeter to the sides of the house. It would have to be done in darkness, probably on their bellies in full camouflage to avoid the huge arc lights mounted on poles at strategic locations. He needed to carry out a second recce to see the full effects of the lights, and map any blind spots or shadowed areas. He decided to return later that evening.

They'd stumbled on the *LonWash* training centre by sheer dumb luck. The garbled words Hamilton had picked up through his parabolic mic at Stanstead airfield had led them to Bishop's Stortford, the only possible location that made any sense from the single word *Stortford* overheard by Hamilton.

After spending a day touring the town, the group had drawn a blank, despite chatting to scores of residents under the pretence of having an interview at a building owned by *LonWash Securities*. No-one, it seemed, had ever heard of the organisation. They had walked the town for hours looking at business nameplates in the hope of discovering a potential safehouse.

Finally, the group had headed out into the country in different directions in three cars. Millward had insisted Hamilton ride in the backseat of his vehicle, which was driven by Mark Jennings. He'd wanted to keep a close eye on the new addition to the team, still undecided whether or not they actually needed him.

Having Hamilton close turned out to be the best thing that could have happened.

Four miles outside the town boundary, on a country road

that seemed bereft of anything other than the odd isolated cottage, Hamilton had suddenly jumped forward and pointed to a Bell 407 helicopter rising above the treeline about a mile ahead of them. "That's the same chopper I saw at Stanstead! They've got to be around here somewhere."

Ten minutes later, Jennings had drifted the SUV slowly past the entrance to some sort of large estate, probably a common enough sight in rural England. What had made this place stand out was a steel barrier across the entrance road, a guard hut beside one of the stone pillars, and way too many rent-a-cop-looking bodies pacing up and down the long twisting driveway.

Millward knew he'd found what he was looking for.

He'd left Jennings at an off-the-road copse which screened the SUV from the sight of any passers-by. He and Hamilton had walked the estate perimeter until they'd reached a small service road that came to a dead-end against a ten-foot-high barbed wire fence. After skirting along the fence for several hundred yards they'd found a small treeline gap that offered a view of a manor house.

Millward traversed the scope one last time. The ex-military strategist in him bristled at the numerous flaws in security. For a start, the trees and bushes should have been uprooted along the entire perimeter, making sure there were no vantage points such as the one he currently enjoyed. He'd have put in a solid wall, mounted with razor wire, pressure plates and cameras. There should have been dog patrols, random vehicle checks on approach roads, and the use of drones to warn off even the most determined raider. On top of all that, he would have installed mirrored glass to make sure snipers couldn't pick their targets through unprotected windows.

The *LonWash* crew didn't strike him as amateurs in anything they did. He could only guess this was a last-minute arrangement, probably because someone reasoned that an out-of-the-way country conference retreat was as good a place as any for a stopgap safehouse. He had to admit it was an ideal location, one that he never would have discovered had it not been for an odd combination of events.

Despite very long odds, the fact was that he *had* found the place.

And he was going to make them pay for their mistake.

Shortly after 2am, Millward stepped out of the car and returned to the perimeter vantage point, using night-vision goggles to pick his way through the undergrowth. This time he was on his own. He was in for a long night.

He couldn't risk the vehicle remaining undetected in the copse throughout the night, so he'd ordered Jennings to return to their base at a town-centre hotel. A pick-up rendezvous was arranged for 7am.

Typically, with a five-hour stakeout stretching ahead, the heavens decided to open their unforgiving arms, dumping an incessant deluge over the bleak countryside. If nothing else, the driving rain and heavy skies blotted out any chances of his silhouette being picked up by the bright moonlight that had been a feature of previous evenings.

Millward had come prepared. He was draped in a large waterproofed ghillie blanket which he fashioned into a makeshift tent by tying off two ends against the branches of overhanging trees. He settled into the hide and used night-vision binoculars to sweep the estate in a slow, methodical action designed to divide the area into a series of grids.

Surprisingly, the area was not awash with lights. The large pole-mounted arcs were not turned on, the driveway lanterns were strangely muted, and only the occasional yellow wash could be seen from some of the windows in the main house. Not exactly what one could call high-visibility security! Maybe that was the point, Millward reasoned. Maybe the idea was not to draw attention to the estate. Keep it understated until such time as the merest hint of danger manifested itself. No doubt the place would then suddenly light up like Oxford Street on Christmas Eve!

It was precisely for this reason Millward had chosen an all-night vigil. He needed to see the nuances of the estate. Were there hourly drills? How did the inhabitants react to vehicles arriving in the wee small hours? Were the arcs sequenced to suddenly blare on at set intervals. What were the guard patterns?

Speaking of guards, where the hell were they? He stopped his grid search to jerk the binoculars across all parts of the grounds. Nothing. No perimeter patrols, no telltale shadows of entrenched look-out stations, no sign of life at all. He swivelled suddenly to look towards the main entrance guard house. From his vantage point he could see only a corner of the wooden outpost, but again there were no lights, and no movements that he could discern.

What the fuck was going on?

Millward felt a rising apprehension. His first thought was that the bastards had upped stakes and moved elsewhere. Easily done, especially with a chopper at their disposal. It was the oldest and surest trick in the book. Keep shifting locations. Keep the enemy on the back foot. Always stay one step ahead. Was that what was happening here?

He forced himself to relax. *Don't get ahead of yourself.* He still had more than four hours to kill. It could be that all the security was concentrated within the house. In a perverse way, it seemed to make sense. Why waste shoe leather when all they had to do was sit tight behind darkened windows and wait for intruders to show themselves? With the right number of people, all using NVGs, they could monitor the entire grounds from the comfort of the house.

He trained his scope on the windows, scanning for the slightest movement. For the most part, the curtains were open and no shadows appeared to lurk within. After thirty minutes, his eyes were sore and his patience was wearing thin. His only option might be to breach the perimeter and move closer to the building.

Suddenly a bright light filled his vision and forced him to drop the binoculars. He rubbed his eyes and squinted at the source of the disturbance. A single light mounted on the right-side gable wall illuminated a small area of no more than fifty yards, picking up the details of flower beds and rose bushes.

It also picked up the shape of a fox scurrying across the lawn.

Motion sensor lights, tripped by the nightime scavenger! He quickly fumbled for the binoculars, and aimed it back at the building, careful to angle it away from the glare. There! Two figures were standing at a second-storey window checking out the source of the disturbance. Fully dressed in dark suits and each cradling a compact sub-machine pistol, they watched for a moment as the fox bolted towards the safety of the perimeter foliage. Satisfied there was no danger, the figures retreated into the blackness of the room, just as the sensor light switched off.

Millward mouthed a silent thank you to the furry interloper. Its presence had revealed there were no pressure pads, at least not in that section of the grounds, otherwise its presence would have been detected before the sensor lights caught the motion. He settled back into his hide, knowing the game was still on. He also now knew exactly how to get at his two targets.

Twenty-four hours from now, he would put his plan into action.

Chapter 27

UTTER DISBELIEF! There was no other way to describe the look that passed between Devon and General Sandford. They each had a copy of the Matthew Hayden manuscript, and had spent a frantic hour leafing noisily through the single sheets of paper scattered on separate desks. Every time they thought they'd seen enough, there was always one more surprise waiting on the next page.

"Are my old eyes deceiving me, or is this the work of a fantasist?" The General finally broke the silence.

"I've got to admit," Devon responded, "I've seen some conspiracy theories in my time but this is right out there ahead of anything I've ever come across. I'm almost waiting for mention of aliens inhabiting the waxwork figures at Madame Tussauds, or five-headed dogs roaming the streets of Whitechapel. If I didn't know Hayden was a seriously-brilliant information analyst, or if he hadn't provided some irrefutable evidence to support his allegations, I'd have said this was the work of a delusional mind. If half of what he has put in here is remotely accurate, we're looking at something that has caused untold misery for this country."

"Yes," the General intoned, "unfortunately much of what he says has a chilling authenticity about it. We're talking about the loss of shipbuilding contracts to other nations, interference in our steel manufacturing industry, manipulation of tendering for major airplane manufacture projects and public sector road and rail schemes which were all grabbed by bidders from outside the UK. The loss to our economy from this section alone must run into the tens of billions. And that's not the worst of what Hayden uncovered, not by a long way."

"I take it you're referring to the potential links to terrorists?"

"You bet I am," Sandford snapped angrily. "Some of these allegations go back years. Funding for the London bombings of 2005 is just the tip of the iceberg. What about the mysterious leaks concerning our troops being supplied with shoddy equipment in Iraq – revelations, which at the time, forced the MoD to order fresh requisitions from machine and arms manufacturers? We now know how that happened. Hayden has documented phone calls and inter-office emails. Christ, he's even named names!"

Sandford paused to wave another batch of papers in the air. "Did you see what he uncovered about the so-called irrefutable evidence of Saddam's weapons of mass destruction? Listen to these text message extracts." He read aloud from one sheet of paper:

From Willywonka1 to BrerRabbit3: Time's running out – Downing Street wants confirmation of WMDs and they don't care how you arrange it.
From BrerRabbit3 to Willywonka1: Relax, everything's in hand. Small amounts of detectable materials have been moved on site. There are enough trace elements to make them concerned. Co-ordinates will be flashed to our usual sources.

The General snorted. "Do you see who Hayden alleges are the real names behind Willy Wonka and Brer Rabbit? These guys are still senior Whitehall officials. I meet them twice weekly with their pearly-white smiles and demurring attitudes, shuffling about as though they are nothing more than small cogs in the big machine. Yet, between them, they helped to perpetrate the most monstrous con ever foisted upon the British people. By the time I've finished with them, they'll wish they'd never been born."

Devon understood and shared the Old Man's anger. "It does seem as if someone has been leading us up the garden path for a long time, but this goes far beyond two Civil Servants. It's going to take days, or even weeks, to fully understand the scope of activities covered by Hayden's work, not to mention assembling a full list of everyone who was involved. At least now we know why the poor bastard was drummed out of MI6 and found himself in the crosshairs. The thing that's nagging most at me is why his colleagues didn't stand by him. What was the extent of the complicity within MI6?"

The General lifted a bundle that he'd earlier set to one side. It was topped by a single A4 sheet with a one-line heading in a 36-point Bodoni typeface that screamed from the page:

THE PAY-OFFS!

Below this was a short personal message from Hayden: *I have tried to follow the money trail. The following pages demonstrate that the actions I have catalogued were not about idealisms or misplaced loyalties, or even blind stupidity. This was greed on a vast scale, and I can prove it.*

The General shook his head. "Maybe this provides an answer to your question, Mike. This is the most damning section of them all. I don't know how he managed it, but Hayden has somehow obtained details of bank statements, money-transfer transactions, and decidedly dodgy receipts and payments in the name of some of the most influential men in the country. He's tried to overlay a lot of these around the times of significant events. Sometimes it looks like conjecture, or stumbling in the dark, but I've got to say it smacks of little more than a trail of pay-offs to those who abetted the various abominations that were committed."

"Did you happen to notice the one name that keeps recurring?"

"Sadly, Mike, it was something I hoped never to see. Our Home Secretary, Charles Manning, seems to have had his snout in the trough more than anyone else. This is filthy treachery, the worst kind of treason imaginable, coming from a person who has been entrusted with the nation's secrets and welfare, but who seems to have abandoned public service in the interests of feathering his own considerable nest. It was most likely he who yanked the MI6 chains that flushed Hayden down the toilet."

"What are you going to do about it, General?"

"I need to speak urgently to the PM. There's an emergency COBRA committee meeting later this morning to deal with the threat of bombs unearthed by the maps found in Boston. This will have everyone on high alert for days, and I'll be damned if Manning will be included in the discussions. We'll need to play it cool, however. Manning's too much of a lightweight to be the brains behind these events, and we can't spook the others until we get them firmly in our sights. We might need to let him run loose for a while."

Devon shot him a look of amazement. "You can't be serious! At the very least, let me mount a round-the-clock surveillance on him. It shouldn't be a problem finding out who he associates with."

"No, back off for now. This will be the PM's call. Besides, you'll have enough on your plate helping to find the location of these bombs. Put all your resources against this single objective until you hear back from me."

Charles Manning returned unexpectedly to his country estate in mid-afternoon. The two resident security guards hadn't been notified in advance and had to scramble quickly from the television games room to meet the limo at the front entrance. Manning ignored their attempts at conversation, stormed in to his library, and noisily slammed the door behind him. He clearly wanted no interruptions.

He flopped onto the large pedestal chair and opened a locked drawer in his writing desk. He fished out a mobile phone which had just one number secured in its contacts folder. While he waited for the call to connect, he lifted a Mont Blanc pen and absent-mindedly began doodling on a desktop jotter pad which was already covered with weird curls, swirls and boxes that bore no resemblance to known geometric shapes. It was a nervous habit, one that he needed to indulge in now more than ever.

A gruff voice interrupted his trance. "Why are you calling?"

Manning recognised George Roper's polished tone. "Something's wrong, Roper, you've got to get me out."

"Calm down, man, and tell me what's going on."

"They're on to me, that's what's going on. I was sent packing from a COBRA meeting this morning, ostensibly to take the PM's place at a bullshit lunch meeting with city bigwigs. I'm the Home Secretary, for God's sake; I should have been at the security briefing to learn what we're doing about these bomb threats. Instead they wanted me out of the way. They know something, or at least they suspect something, and that's why I was dumped. I'm not sticking around here to find out what they have on me. This thing with the Haydens must have uncovered something. I told you to get rid of them!"

Roper's voice lost its mellowness. "Listen to me, you tub of lard. You'll sit tight until I tell you otherwise. The Haydens have been tracked down to a place in Bishop's Stortford. That's one problem that will go away very soon. Now, what were you told about the COBRA meeting before you were ditched?"

Manning tried to compose himself. "Apparently, Homeland Security stumbled across a bomb at a warehouse in Boston. They were able to disarm it, and in a follow-up operation they found maps and diagrams of other devices planted at locations in both America and the UK. These were passed on to MI5 and, as you can imagine, there is a red-flag security alert to deal with the crisis. That was what I was supposed to be a part of."

"That's excellent news, Charles! You're probably better off out of it for now. I'll ring you if I need any further updates."

Before Manning could respond, the line went dead.

Roper glared disdainfully at the mobile phone and turned to face Giles Grimand. "That spineless prick is looking for an easy way out. At least he was able to confirm there's a hell of a furore being raised about what happened at Boston. I don't know how the authorities got to the bomb before it exploded, but the effects are just the same as they would have been had it detonated. We wanted to create panic by the very threat of other bombs, and now it seems we have succeeded."

Grimand flashed his partner a wide-eyed stare. "I don't see how you can be so confident. The bomb didn't explode, no-one's running for cover, and our gamble with stocks and shares could fail cataclysmically."

"Don't you see, Giles? The Boston bomb was all we could manage to put together. The intention was to create the impression there are others still out there. In hindsight, the fact they discovered it before detonation probably works better to our advantage. There's more plausibility this way because they think they know what they're looking for in the shape of the packaging and the manner in which it was stored. Our false trail will have them scurrying about like headless chickens, so much so that when the news is finally released we can be assured of the kind of market volatility we need."

"When will that be?" There was little enthusiasm in Grimand's voice.

"If the newshounds don't soon get full wind of the story we have people standing by to make some anonymous tip-offs to the main media outlets. And don't forget, there's no longer any real benefits in issuing DA-notices against the press, not in this day of social media. We'll make sure Facebook and all the other platforms are frantic with alarmist speculation. Our share and investment activities should pay immediate dividends when the panic sets in. I'd guess, as a conservative estimate, we should see a tidy profit of around thirty to forty million."

"Aren't you forgetting a couple of things? First, the authorities didn't just stumble into that warehouse. They must have been watching our Tunisian friends, which means we might also be on their radar. If you add in the fact that Manning appears to have been compromised, I'd say there's a fair chance of a net closing in on us. It's maybe time we disappeared for a while."

Roper rubbed his chin. "I think you could be right. What say we up stakes and head off on an early Christmas holiday to the Bahamas?"

His mobile phone chirped again. He stared at the small

window and recognised the caller as the sniper, Todd Hamilton. He quickly pressed the answer button. "Tell me you have some good news about the Haydens."

Hamilton didn't reply immediately, and when he did his voice was faltering. "Everything is set for the early hours of tomorrow morning. That gung-ho bastard, Millward, wants to go in with all guns blazing, so I didn't see any need for me to stick around."

"I thought I told you to join forces," Roper yelled.

"Look, I had the kid in my sights last night, but Millward wouldn't let me take the shot. He said he wanted all or nothing. There's no room for me in the middle of a firefight; it's not my thing. He and his mate Jennings went on a reconnaissance mission last night, so I slipped away from the rest of the group and returned to my own base."

Instead of facing an angry retort, Hamilton was surprised by Roper's response.

"Maybe you're right, my friend. You do your best work from a safe distance. As it so happens, this turn of events might be quite fortuitous. I have some other matters I need you to take care of. These will pay a bigger bonus than the hit on the Haydens. Are you interested?

"Tell me what you want me to do."

Chapter 28

IT WAS THE LAST thing Commander John Hall needed right now. His entire SO19 division had been placed on full operational alert, a euphemism for cancelled leave and twenty-four-hour shifts. It was a blot-everything-else-out command that left no room for doubting the urgency in tracking four dirty bombs that were supposedly planted in the heart of London.

The intel passed on from Homeland Security in Boston looked rock solid. They'd managed somehow to locate and defuse a device, apparently one of many designed to showcase the latest terror capabilities on both sides of the Atlantic, and nobody was getting any sleep until all bombs were accounted for.

Hall was as agitated by the imminent threat as anyone, probably more so, and yet his emotions were being torn straight down the middle. What lousy timing! The encrypted email alerts had landed on his desk within a matter of minutes of getting a breakthrough in the hunt for the gunmen who'd shot up Rosemund Hospital and killed three of his officers.

DNA taken from some of the dead crew had launched a trail of cross-referencing against known associates, lists that quickly grew into a who's who of ex-military drop-outs and well-travelled mercenaries. There was a small army of them, men who either couldn't hack it in uniform or who couldn't wait to grab the riches of private contracting. Running all of them to ground would have been a frightening prospect, if not for the fact that two names jumped out in each of the individual lists.

Dave Millward and Mark Jennings.

The common denominators. The pair most likely to have been part of the attack on the hospital. Two scumbags that

Hall desperately wanted to get his hands on.

And now this! Hamstrung from proceeding any further because of a threat he couldn't ignore, he knew every second wasted increased the chances of losing their trail, perhaps forever. Was that something he could live with? And what if they resurfaced somewhere down the line to murder Sonia and Christopher Hayden?

His mind was made up. He would have to divert precious resources into a hunt for Millward and Jennings. He would need at least eight officers, practically a quarter of his frontline operatives, a sizeable hole that was bound to be noticed sooner rather than later. He convinced himself he could argue a direct link between the two cases. Call it a copper's hunch that the fugitive duo was somehow connected to the terrorist threat. He knew it was tenuous at best, and certainly not enough to prevent that fat-fuck Home Secretary from taking disciplinary action. *Let the chips fall where they may*, he decided.

Two hours later an SO19 utility vehicle burst into the grounds of Dave Millward's country house at Surrey. The four occupants were armed to the teeth, although one look at the deserted house and grounds told them there was no-one around. They quickly gained access to the building and finished a room-by-room search within twenty minutes. It was as they expected. Empty.

The address was not listed in Millward's name and had been tracked down only after checking known aliases and cross-referencing property databases and bank records. He'd covered his tracks well, but not enough to escape the forensic scrutiny applied by the SO19 computer boffins.

Six miles away, in a housing estate near Ealing, a second squad of officers, also drew a blank at the known home of Mark Jennings. Neighbours didn't appear surprised by the police presence and were happy to share what little they knew about the taciturn loner. He was described as a short-fused bully who disappeared for days on end and refused to engage in any social interactions. They were always glad to see the back of him, such as lately when he hadn't been spotted around the area. The speculation was that he must have a second house somewhere else, or maybe some woman was stupid enough to let herself be taken in by the obnoxious creature.

The news that his teams had come up empty-handed reached Commander Hall on location at one of the bomb-search sites. He ordered an immediate Vehicle Identification Number search on cars registered to Millward and Jennings, knowing that if they were still in the country they could be tracked within a matter of minutes.

The first query was easily answered. Millward's Audi A8L 3-litre TDi was still parked in the garage at the Surrey estate, where officers were going through its Sat Nav history for details of recent movements. At the very least they would discover what he'd been up to during the past week.

It took less than another five minutes to track a Toyota Rav4 utility vehicle belonging to Jennings. Using SO19's own AVL system, the Automatic Vehicle Location software pinged the car at a location in Bishop's Stortford, a commuter-belt area which Hall considered an odd choice for a hideaway.

Gotcha, you bastard!

Hall spent several minutes stomping around a car park near the bomb search site, trying to figure out his next move. One thing was for certain; he couldn't stay here, not when he was so close to getting his quarry. His mind made up, he handed over command to his deputy, ordered his two mobile units to meet him at a junction on the M11 motorway, and made a frantic dash for his squad car. Before turning the ignition switch he suddenly remembered one important detail. A phone call later, he was on his way, content that the AVL was maintaining a live feed on the movements of the Toyota Rav4.

"Whataya mean he disappeared?"

Jennings looked Millward in the eye. "It's just like I said. By the time I got back to the hotel after dropping you off for your surveillance stint, the spineless bastard had upped stakes and left. None of the others noticed he'd gone."

They'd travelled less than a mile from the pick-up at the *LonWash* retreat when Jennings broke the news of Todd Hamilton's desertion. "Ask me, he's no great loss, not unless you'd already factored in the need for a sniper on the job."

"As a matter of fact, I hadn't," Millward admitted. "It's the principle of the thing. To tell the truth, I was going to make sure Hamilton was one of the casualties, but I don't like the idea of him on the loose and us not knowing what he's up to. You know me, there's a place for everything and everything has to be in its place."

Jennings smiled. "So what has that analytical brain of yours conjured up for us?"

"Shock and awe, my friend, shock and awe."

The Rav4 pulled out of the country lane and eased its way into the main traffic stream heading towards Bishop's Stortford. Jennings settled the vehicle into a steady fifty-miles-per-hour cruise and glanced across at his passenger. "I'm waiting."

"Don't be so impatient," Millward teased. "We're going in with everything we've got. That's RPGs for the front and rear doors, as many grenades as we can carry, and full auto from everyone when we get inside. There's no telling the strength of the opposition, so we deal with whatever we come up against. I'd guess a minimum of six or eight minders, but it could be as high as twenty."

"What about security? They're hardly going to let us waltz through the front gates and drive unchallenged to the front door?"

Millward smacked his friend on the knee. "That's the beauty of it, Mark. There are no perimeter or ground patrols, they don't use the security lighting, and they don't seem to carry out random checks for intruders. They appear to be content to sit behind their walls and wait for whatever comes at them. I intend to throw more at them than they can possibly hope to deal with."

"It can't be as easy as that?"

Millward's mood turned sombre. "No, I'm not saying it'll be easy. We'll have a lot of belly-crawling to do along areas I've mapped out as weak points. That should get us into position to hit them from three sides, with less than thirty seconds allocated for primary breaches. If all goes to plan, we'll be among them before they know we're there. I'm going to grab a few hours' kip and run through a full mock-up with the team this afternoon."

The remainder of the journey was completed in silence. It was only when the car pulled into the park at the rear of their hotel that Millward spoke again. "One more thing. Grab us a rented van, a big Transit, or such like. I don't want to use your car on the job. We'll keep it stashed here as a changeover and getaway."

Chapter 29

SECURITY WAS as good as Alfie Cheadle could make it. He'd covered all the obvious bases, dealt with the weaknesses that were left, and then spent more time than he wanted to in dreaming up responses to unlikely scenarios, the unforeseen combination of events that could propel intruders straight into the heart of the protection cordon before he'd had a chance to work out how the hell they got there.

But no matter what he did, there was a gnawing doubt that he was coming up short. This wasn't a chess board where pieces could be moved around or sacrificed to protect the king. This was a dangerous, in-your-face real life offence and defence struggle that didn't conform to rules, and usually ended up with one side wiped out and the other claiming the spoils of war.

As a soldier, it was a game Cheadle was used to playing. However, this was no battlefield, and the stakes were a lot higher than any he'd ever previously dealt with. This was not a tactical operation, with one side trying to outmanoeuvre the other. He was not looking to win brownie points by toe-to-toe heroics, or killing the enemy, or winning the high ground. His sole responsibility was keeping Sonia and Christopher Hayden alive. If that meant running for cover, that's what he'd do.

His defensive position was a strong one. Not perfect, but a lot better than he could have hoped for. The estate had a lot going for it – plenty of good open spaces where intruders could be detected at an early stage – and the main house was full of rooms and corridors where he could move the Haydens away from trouble if the outer defences were breached.

And yet, there were flaws. Still too many imponderables if an attack was large enough and determined enough. It was why Cheadle was constantly on edge.

More so in the last twenty-four hours. Young Hayden had been making great recovery strides from his stab wound, and had insisted on getting some fresh air and exercise. Reading his father's email journal had rejuvenated the lad, almost to the point where Cheadle half-expected him to set off running through the front gates in pursuit of the men who'd brought about the family's misery.

A small walled compound to the left of the house provided ideal cover for Chris and his mother to spend as much time outdoors as they wanted. The structure was tall enough to shield them from a sniper attack, which was a moot point since Cheadle stepped up boundary patrols in that area when the Haydens were out and about.

Chris seemed to find solace and anger in equal measure every time he turned a page of his dad's revelations. The more he read, the more he became absorbed by his father's thirst for justice, and the obstacles he'd had to face. These were not the incoherent ramblings of a madman, as he and his mother were led to believe. No, this was a cogent, painstaking, brilliantly-incisive investigation that looked like the work of scores of operatives rather than just the determination of one man working under intense pressure while facing the rejection of his colleagues.

Cheadle had watched a myriad of emotions pass through the young man's body. Tears and frowns gave way to a new-found radiance as pride forced life and colour back into the pallid shell. A slumped and pitiful look was replaced by a sparkle of new vigour that months of medical care could never have hoped to achieve. Chris Hayden was being transformed into the kind of man his father must have been.

And that brought with it a whole new dimension of problems for Cheadle.

He'd read the Hayden manuscript and fully understood why powerful forces were in play to prevent the possibility of the information being made public. These people were not to know that Matthew Hayden had already figured out a way of getting past their attempts at silencing him. As far as they were concerned, the matter could not rest until all links to

Hayden were severed forever.

At that moment, however, the bigger picture didn't concern Cheadle. That was a matter for Devon and General Sandford. Right now, all he needed to concentrate on was keeping Sonia and Christopher out of harm's way.

From the get-go, he'd agreed with Devon that the estate's resident trainees would be used only for daytime patrols – a highly visible show of strength that would hopefully act as a deterrent against incursions. They were stood down at nightfall, purely on the basis that they were not sufficiently experienced to deal with professional mercenaries, men who would welcome the chance to silently snuff out raw opposition under the blanket of darkness.

Eight trainees were on a nightly rota to keep watch from the windows of the main house. The remainder were confined to their own quarters, under the charge of an experienced instructor, and warned to remain there, no matter what was going down. The trainees in the house allowed Cheadle to share shifts with Terry Hunt, Jim Cross and Dan Gosling, meaning that at least two of them were posted outside the Haydens' bedroom door at all times.

In the absence of a stronger force, it was as good as he could do in the circumstances.

As another day turned into early dusk, Cheadle stared across the grounds from a first-floor window, and hoped it would be enough.

Dave Millward was a careful planner. Despite his earlier flippancy about *shock and awe* tactics, he had meticulously sculpted a military operation for getting to the Haydens. He'd drawn precise maps and diagrams, and spent three hours going over the details with his team. The timings for each phase were drilled down to within a matter of seconds. There was no margin for error. Each man knew what was expected of him.

A black Ford Transit van was picked up from a local rental yard in late afternoon. It was a typical workhorse vehicle, with a rear cab length of ten feet, no-windows, and ample space to accommodate eight men and their equipment. They'd left it in the hotel car park until darkness, taking their time to transfer their belongings in thirty-minute intervals so as not to raise suspicions. The colour had been chosen to make it difficult to detect in the copse of trees near the *LonWash* estate. As an added precaution, once on site, the front and tail lights would be masked to prevent reflections being picked up by passing vehicles.

The group wolfed down sandwiches and gulped pots of coffee in Millward's room while he took them through the plan. Alcohol was banned, so too were mobiles, which had been stripped of batteries and sim cards. He handed around small comms sets and checked that the connections to a central unit were working. "As soon as we leave the Transit, these are the only means of communication. No chatter, keep things on mission, and unless you see anything out of the ordinary, stay silent until you hear my five-second countdown command."

Seven heads nodded in agreement. "Okay," Millward continued, "here's a recap. Two groups of three at the rear and right side of the house. The left side's a bust because of a walled area that must be a garden or play area that will cause too much bother to consider. Mark and I will go through the front door two seconds after the RPG blasts the hell out of the rear entrance. Before that, the group on the right side will shatter the ground-floor windows with MP5s and toss in two grenades at each opening. Remember, the grenades must be away before we start into the house. I don't want to get concussion waves because you bastards are late with your deliveries."

There was a chorus of nervous chuckles before he waved for silence. "We leave here as planned. I want to be on site at least an hour before we move in. After that, we'll make our way across the estate, an inch at a time if need be, just as long as we all get into position at precisely 0200. I don't need to remind anyone that whatever we come across, we deal with it. The mission parameter is that if it moves, shoot it."

Fifty minutes south of the hotel, two SO19 vehicles hurtled along the M11. Commander Hall was in the front passenger seat of the lead car, his attention torn between receiving regular updates from what was proving to be a fruitless search of four bomb sites, and his growing anticipation of what he'd find at the location where the Automatic Vehicle Location signal was pinging Jennings' car. According to the latest message from HQ, the vehicle was still immobile, apparently at the rear of a hotel in the centre of Bishop's Stortford.

The bastard is either lying low, or planning some other skulduggery.

Hall hoped it was the latter, particularly if Millward was there as well. What better way to catch the pair of them than *in flagrante delicto,* so to speak? Either way, whoever was there was going down. Hard.

He had considered contacting Devon to let him know about the progress made in cornering the villains responsible for the hospital attack against the Haydens. He'd quickly dismissed the notion, rationalising that Devon had made it clear the Haydens were *his* responsibility. Hall was kept out of the loop as far as information-sharing on where the Haydens were being sequestered. Well, two can play at that game.

He would have acted differently had he known that he was closer to the family than he could have imagined.

Chapter 30

IT WAS RARE for Devon to disagree with General Sandford's reasoning. The idea of leaving things to decision-making by the Prime Minister was one of those times when the potential for chain-of-command procrastination was too great a risk. Every minute wasted sitting on their hands was a minute gained for the rats to scurry for cover. The Hayden dossier had unmasked not only the Home Secretary, but a several other senior ministers in a variety of key department posts. If he'd learned anything, it was that politicians were adept at covering each other's backs. And when push came to shove, the PM was - first and foremost - a politician.

The Old Man should have let *LonWash* loose to round up Manning and all the other named traitors. To hell with digging deeper! There was already enough here to burn the bastards and force them to fill in any blanks that were left. Get them into interrogation rooms, drain them dry, and dump the file, pink ribbons and all, on the desk at Downing Street. That way, there'd be no wriggle room, no favours, no early retirements, no cover ups.

Part of him understood the need for caution. The shitstorm would shake public confidence to the core, perhaps undermining forever the fragile trust that existed between the legislative guardians and the people who put them in power. Nobody really believed it was a perfect system, but if at least it appeared to be working, everybody was content to go along with it.

Would it survive the scandals brought about by the Hayden disclosures? What would happen to Britain's reputation around the world, particularly now in the middle of increasingly hostile Brexit negotiations with her European counterparts? *Whoa! That's way too much highbrow stuff. Stick with what you know. Get your head out of the clouds.*

The thought made Devon grin and relax for the first time in several hours. The General would sort it; he always did. It was now seven o'clock and he needed to phone Emma to tell her he would be pulling an all-nighter. His entire tech team were running down a string of leads provided by the Hayden manuscript, and he needed to be here to help piece together any new discoveries. Check, verify, add, follow the trails, build the cases. Get it right.

His satphone jumped on the desktop. So too did Devon's heart rate. Alan Doyle was ringing from America, obviously with news of Chelsea Horgan, but what was he going to say? Devon hit the answer button, but didn't speak. He waited for Doyle to set the mood.

"Mike, are you there? Chelsea's going to make it! She's come back to me! Mike, she smiled at me!"

The relief Devon felt was matched only by his joy over his friend's animated excitement. "That's great, Alan. What happened."

"She just suddenly opened her eyes and smiled. She recognised me. She looked around the room, saw her mom and dad, frowned at all the gadgets hooked up to her and went back to sleep."

"Is she going to be alright?"

"Course she is! She's just having another nap. The doctors say she'll be like that for another few days, but the signs are all good."

Devon waited for his friend's burst of emotion to die down. "I have to ask, Alan, what are they saying about the long-term prognosis? Are there going to be any.....any, you know, complications, or such like?"

"Stop pussyfooting around, Mike. If you mean is she going to be brain-damaged, the answer is no. The consultant says the fact that she regained consciousness under her own steam in such a short period, and because she demonstrated such spacial awareness, whatever the fuck that means, the chances are there is little likelihood of permanent disability. He wants more time to assess her, blah, blah, but I told him the answer already. She's beaten this, and she'll continue to beat it. He's a nice guy, by the way. Tell the General thanks for sending him."

Just then, Devon's door opened and Sandford strode into the room.

"You're never going to believe it, Alan, but the Old Man has just arrived. He'll be delighted to hear the news." Devon cupped his hand over the console and told the General what was going on.

Sandford's eyes lit up. "I can't tell you how happy I am to hear that. Tell Doyle that whatever she needs, she gets. He's to stay there with her and make sure everything is done properly over the next few weeks. I know my old friend, Tommy Fotheringdale, will put her on the road to full recovery. Didn't I tell you he was the world's best consultant surgeon?"

"Are you still there, Alan?"

"It's okay, Mike, I heard every word. Just so you and the General know; I'll be staying here for quite some time. I'm not leaving until she's fit to travel with me, even if that means a few months. I hope you're good with that?"

"Don't be silly, you big chump! Of course we're good with that. I'll get the General to arrange a transfer of funds into your bank to cover your expenses and anything else that crops up. Start with a new wardrobe – knowing you, there's probably only one change of clothes in that holdall you brought with you."

"You know me too well, buddy. Thanks for everything. I'll keep you updated."

Devon cut the connection and stared at the General who had slumped into a chair, his face a mixture of relief and concern. "What's up, sir?"

"It's been a hard day, Mike, I don't mind telling you. This news has perked me up no end. Good of you to mention some funds for Doyle. I'll see to it he has more than he needs."

"There's something else, General. I can tell."

Sandford straightened in his seat. "Yes, perhaps we need to get back to business. The COBRA committee went into overdrive this afternoon, without the Home Secretary, of course, although the best guess is that these bomb maps might be hoaxes. We can't take a chance, however, so every agency has been mobilised to come up with an answer. The thing is, no matter what way it goes, there's bound to be a massive fallout of confidence in financial sectors, which judging by past episodes catalogued by Hayden, might be the real intention behind the threats."

"Speaking of Hayden," Devon said without enthusiasm, "what's the PM's take on the revelations?"

"I sense a lack of certitude in your question. As it happens, he was apoplectic with rage at Manning's treachery. After banishing him from the COBRA meeting, he cleared his diary for the afternoon and spent hours discussing with me what we should do about the erstwhile Home Secretary."

"Did you say erstwhile?"

"Yes, there's no possibility of him continuing in position. Statements are being drawn up even as we speak. A new appointment will be made tomorrow morning."

"So Manning just gets to walk away?"

"My dear boy, whatever give you that idea? No, you will accompany me to Manning's house where he will sign his resignation before being brought back here to *LonWash* headquarters. To all intents and purposes, he'll be recuperating from an illness over the next few days while you question him on everything he knows. That'll take him out of the public eye long enough to decide what to do with him, although I think the PM has already made up his mind on that score. There'll be no cover up."

Devon puffed out his cheeks. "That comes as a surprise. I thought Downing Street would try to put a lid on this."

"It's not always perfect, Mike, but it usually works out. The PM's a straight-batter and he wants Manning to pay for his crimes."

"So, when do we pick him up?"

"Get your coat, we're leaving now."

Ninety minutes later, Devon rolled the Range Rover to a stop in front of locked gates at Charles Manning's country estate. A Metropolitan Police Special Protection Officer stepped out of the shadows from a side entrance, and approached the passenger side of the vehicle. He had earlier received a call about the visit and told not to alert Manning.

General Sandford depressed the car window and showed his credentials. "Is he still in situ?"

"Yes, sir, he's in the library. It's the first door to your right as you step into the foyer. I've left the main door unlocked."

Manning was seated at his centrepiece desk when Sandford and Devon barged into the library. A solitary desk lamp threw their shadows across the ceiling to merge with the shape of a large conifer tree, the outlines of which were projected by a weak moon through an uncurtained set of patio doors.

Manning's reaction to their entrance bordered on the farcical. He jerked heavily in his seat, reached forward to fumble with the lamp in an attempt to plunge the room into darkness, and then pushed back hard towards the patio escape route. His chair upended, sending him plunging to the carpet, his feet pumping for traction in mid-air.

He wriggled off his back and used the desk for leverage to haul himself into a kneeling position. Tears started flowing freely as he looked pleadingly at Sandford. "I know why you're here, General. I guessed as much when they froze me out of the meeting today. I'm innocent....I was duped....I'll pay everything back. Please, you've got to help me."

Devon walked around the desk, grabbed Manning under the armpits and marched him across the room to an armchair. He threw him backwards into the seat, pulled out his Sig P226, and made a show of racking the slide. "Not another fucking word, you piece of shit."

Sandford ambled across the room and made a pretence of calming Devon's anger. "Come now, Mike, let's not cheat the courts out of their pound of flesh. I'll take great pleasure in watching our former Home Secretary squirm from the dock during weeks and months of what will undoubtedly be a show trial. And just think of all those years he'll spend sharing a small cell with men who'll make his every waking moment a living hell? Isn't that much better than a quick bullet to the brain?"

"Please, General, I can tell you things. I can be a great help. Surely we can cut a deal?"

Before Sandford had a chance to respond, the dynamics in the room suddenly changed. Devon was aware of the faintest of tinkling sounds, followed by a short pop, followed by Manning's head disappearing behind a haze of blood spray."

Chapter 31

DEVON PROCESSED the scene in real time. There was no shock delay, no frozen moment of inertia; he knew what had happened the instant it happened. He dived immediately at Sandford's legs and wrestled him to the floor, away from the sniper's line-of-sight through the patio doors, the only possible route for an assassin's bullet. A small hole and a spiderwebbed crack halfway up one of the doors confirmed the obvious.

Devon crawled across the room and swiped the lamp off the desk, cutting down the chances of the gunman adding to his kill tally. "Stay down, General, don't move a muscle," he yelled before loosing off three rounds at the nearest door.

He waited for the glass to disintegrate and sprinted for the gap. He dived through the opening, ran down three concrete steps and tuck-rolled into a kneeling position in the centre of a small lawn. He aimed another three-round burst towards a shadowy hedge he judged to be close to the sniper's vantage point, and was up and running again before the noise had subsided.

It was a full-out, committed charge, which left him praying there were no hidden, immovable objects, such as concrete posts, to bring him to a shuddering stop. At the last moment, he dipped his right shoulder, closed his eyes, and went for it. He felt foliage brushing hard against his body as his momentum slowed, but he managed to keep going until suddenly he was out the other side.

He opened his eyes and adjusted to the new surroundings. He was in a large field, rising ahead of him in a steep slope that climbed towards a four-strand wire fence running across the plateau. A big sycamore tree stood sentry on the left of the ridge, and directly across from it – at a distance of no more than twenty feet – he spotted the silhouette of a figure running in a zig-zag pattern in an attempt to offer as difficult a target as possible.

Devon was seventy yards away, almost twice the effective range of his handgun, and had no notion of wasting valuable ammo. He bowed his head and sprinted up the incline, settling into an easy rhythm despite the harshness of the ground. The area was rutted with the hoof prints of cattle and grassy clumps that would have slowed the progress of anyone but a trained cross-country athlete. Days spent on treks across the forbidden landscape of the Brecon Beacons in Wales were something he was suddenly grateful for as his feet glided across the surface in a stamina-sapping surge that took him to the crest in just under twelve seconds.

Despite the heroics of a fast ascent, he already knew he was too late. The deep, throaty roar of a motorcycle blasted through the night air somewhere off to his left. The high-rev din gave way to the steady staccato beat of a machine finding traction and speeding off into the distance. He was just in time to watch it burst through an open gate and glide across the surface of a country lane that would soon link with the main road to London.

He watched it disappear from view before reluctantly heading back to the Manning house. At the bottom of the field he met the police protection officer, kneeling against the hedge with his weapon trained on the approaching figure.

"Put it away, Sergeant, the bastard's gone. Get out an APB for a motorcyclist on a big works machine, probably anything up to a 750cc job, judging by the signature noise. Get roadblocks thrown up all around London, and tell them to stop everything on two wheels. Do not, I repeat, do not, provide any information about what happened here. Make the call under the pretence of a known terrorist seen in the area."

A look of annoyance crossed the policeman's face. "I've already had the lecture from General Sandford. You know, we *are* trained to be discreet, especially when something as big as this goes down. Apparently, as far as the Met is concerned, I've just been seconded to act as the General's personal bodyguard and will be incommunicado for several days."

Devon smiled. "Welcome to the team, Sergeant. Just so you know, there was no offence intended."

"None taken, sir."

General Sandford was on the phone when Devon stepped back through the shattered patio door. He noticed the Old Man's overcoat was draped over Manning's corpse, concealing the grisly gap where half a head had once been. Blood pooled out from below the coat, and splatter patterns could be seen on a wall and bookcase directly behind where Manning had been standing.

The desk lamp had been restored to its former position and a twenty-bulbed chandelier bathed the library in a harsh glare. Everywhere he looked, the place reeked of money and indulgence. One wall was covered by library shelves stacked with titles in ornate Morocco bindings; another was devoted to watercolours that looked expensive even to an untrained eye. There were ceramicware vases, china sculptures, and solid silver trinkets that seemed to take up every available inch of space in what many people would consider a collector's heaven. Devon thought of the manner in which the owner had earned the cash to afford the haul and, for a moment, felt like taking a hammer to the sleazy horde.

"That was the PM," Sandford announced as he set the house phone back in its cradle. "We've got to lock this down until he figures a way of releasing the news. It wouldn't do to have Joe Public thinking there's an assassin at large picking off our top people, even if – to quote the vernacular - he was a scumbag of the first magnitude. We might have to settle for a heart attack brought on by the strain of office. It's not that Manning deserves a whitewash, but there's a bigger picture to consider."

"How are we going to keep a lid on it?"

"You might consider this a poisoned chalice, Mike, but everything's being dumped in the lap of *LonWash*. We will not be alerting the Metropolitan Police or the City Coroner, unless something forces our hand. For the moment, we'll store the body under a John Doe and concentrate on finding out what secrets are held within this house. You get started on a search while I organise transport for the deceased."

Devon understood the dilemmas caused by Manning's death and was content to operate on the basis that a news blackout was necessary because of an ongoing investigation. It was an overused cliché by police authorities the world over, but one that provided much-needed breathing space. It was time he intended to use to the full.

The obvious starting point was the large desk, a neatly-kept surface which supported only the bare essentials – a lamp, a paperweight, a neat row of pens on both sides of a deskpad, and the ubiquitous computer and keyboard combo, without which no self-respecting office could do without.

He decided to leave the computer for Tim Halloran and his boys and turned his attention to the desk drawers, three either side of the chair space. As expected, they were locked, a situation quickly remedied by a Tanto knife strapped to a compact leg holster. The top drawer on the left contained just one single item, a cheap mobile phone that looked out of place among Manning's other possessions. Devon pocketed it quickly, careful to ensure he didn't trigger any alerts before Halloran delved into its little secrets. This was a 'burn' phone, if ever he saw one.

The rest of the drawers produced disappointingly little. A neat stack of House of Commons headed notepaper and envelopes, sundry bits of office paraphernalia, such as paper clips and post-it blocks, and another assortment of pens. No personal wallets or files, no damning scraps of correspondence, nothing to suggest that the owner led a double life on the scale that Manning had. There had to be files somewhere!

His eyes dropped to the deskpad, a discoloured pink blotting sheet held in place by leather corner-grips. It was covered in squiggles and doodles of every shape, a poor testament to the supposedly sharp mind of the author. Devon smiled at the banality of it all.

A second later, his smile disappeared.

In the top right corner of the pad, there were several lines of scrawled writing inside a heavy circle. It took Devon a few heartbeats to decipher the words, and when he did, his blood ran cold.

The Haydens tracked down to Bishop's Stortford!!!

Chapter 32

COUNTDOWN MINUS TEN. Millward made a final sweep of the upstairs windows, confident the stealthy approach of his team had gone unnoticed. Fifteen minutes earlier, he'd sweated over the movement of curtains before realising it was caused by nothing more sinister than nightime breezes whistling through an open window. The occupants of the house were blissfully ignorant of what awaited them. The assault was a go.

When the eight men entered the grounds shortly after midnight, they'd found things exactly as Millward said they would. A heavily-veiled moon had obligingly cast dark shadows over the lines of entry which had been precisely marked on the team leader's maps. The tall arc lights were switched off, the house was in darkness, and a thin mist hung across the damp ground, making progress a lot easier than the raiders could have hoped for.

The perfect conditions hadn't made Millward any less cautious. The order to advance in ten-yard segments remained unaltered. Crawl, stop, wait, move. The rest periods were no less than three minutes each. Remain still, blend in, be invisible.

The men were dressed head-to-toe in black combat fatigues to match the black satchels strapped to their backs. NVGs were strictly forbidden because of the small, telltale green dot that illuminated the corner of the scopes when they were powered up. They were nothing more than pinpricks, but they produced anomalies that could be spotted by careful watchers.

The face of each man was streaked with broad camouflage crayon lines which were crudely applied over stubbles and beards, and ran from forehead to neck where they disappeared below a black scarf, the standard dress code to hide throat mics and comms wires.

Their advance was typical of a Special Forces operation. They used knees and elbows for propulsion, and cradled MP5 machine pistols in the crooks of their arms. It was a slow, laborious, yet impressively-disciplined approach that took them to their various holding positions less than fifty yards from the main house well within the allotted time.

Twenty minutes elapsed while Millward studied and re-studied the target. Finally, he pushed back his jacket cuff and looked at the large wristwatch. Just ten seconds remained.

He flicked a switch on his comms unit, paused for a few more seconds, and then spoke urgently.

Five seconds on my mark......

Four

Three

Two

One

Go, go, go...

Millward watched as three figures materialised to his right. They charged forward, triggering the sensor light at that part of the building. One of the men peppered the console with a sustained burst that knocked it off its mounting and plunged the area back into darkness. The other two opened fire on two ground-floor windows, and raced to a stop beside the brickwork. They each fished out two hand grenades from the pockets of their combat trousers, tossing them through the shattered windows. They waited several moments after the explosions had died down before jumping through the windows and disappearing from view. The man who'd shattered the sensor light followed close behind one of his colleagues.

Millward then heard a louder explosion to the rear of the property. His second team had disintegrated the back door with an RPG, and would now be making their way into the interior. As if to confirm his thoughts, the sound of gunfire echoed from that part of the building. His men were shooting on the run, although as yet he could hear no return fire.

He nodded at Jennings who was kneeling beside him with

an RPG already hoisted on his shoulder. He heard the whoosh and followed the vapour trail across the lawn to the front door, which disintegrated in a maelstrom of matchsticks and flying debris. Jennings dropped the launcher onto the grass and joined Millward in a mad dash across the lawn. They pushed through the dust and smoke which filled the gap where the door had been, before dropping to their knees on a tiled floor covered in debris. Both men trained their weapons on a stairway immediately ahead of them.

All raiders were now in position. But where the hell was the opposition?

Commander John Hall paced across the car park of the Bishop's Stortford hotel and aimed a frustrated kick at one of the Rav4 tyres. "Where the hell are they? Why leave their vehicle here?"

The four heavily-armed SO19 officers shrugged in unison, each as disappointed as their team leader at the absence of action and waste of adrenalin resulting from a fruitless search for the car owner, Jennings, and his sidekick Millward. One thing they'd learned from hotel staff was that not only were the pair guests of the hotel, they had also been seen in the company of six other men who'd registered at different times during the previous few days. None of them had checked out, but neither had they been around since early evening.

A search of their rooms revealed nothing, other than a mess of coffee cups and half-eaten sandwiches. A painstaking check of drawers, suitcases, and wastepaper baskets yielded no clues to what they men had been up to, or where they were headed. For the moment, they'd dropped out of sight, but why?

Knowing the background of his targets, Hall was under no illusion about the significance of eight men spending time holed up in a local hotel. This was no convention of insurance brokers or sales reps. They were here for a reason, and that reason had to be tied in with Sonia and Christopher Hayden.

It was now after midnight, and Hall was becoming frantic. "Wait a minute!" he yelled and grabbed one of his men by the arm. "Get back onto the AVL boys and find out if this car went anywhere after arriving at the hotel. I want to know everything about its movements and I want to know now!"

He didn't have long to wait. The policeman spoke quietly into his car radio before turning to face Hall. "It has only left this location twice in the last twenty-four hours, and on both occasions, it travelled back and forward to the same location. We have a general area about five miles outside town.

"What are we waiting for? Mount up and let's see what the bastards are up."

He needed to cover the hotel, but was reluctant to deplete his force. Instinct told him that where they were headed would require as many men as he could muster. In the end, he was forced to leave one officer behind with instructions to radio in for back-up. It was a futile gesture. He knew support wouldn't arrive on time.

It took less than five minutes for the assault teams from the rear and right side of the building to clear the downstairs rooms. And they weren't subtle about the way they went about it. Door locks and hinges were blown off by sustained machine-pistol fire, grenades were thrown into each room, and the interiors were thoroughly hosed before moving to the next target. So far they'd met with no opposition.

Millward and Jennings waited impatiently at the foot of the stairs for the completion of the first stage of the operation. It hadn't surprised the former that the occupants had chosen to hole up on the first floor – it was an obvious choice from a defensive standpoint – although he'd expected at least one downstairs watchman. He looked up through the gloom and wondered what kind of reception awaited the unwary.

When the rest of the team reached the hallway, and fanned out in a semi-circle, he aimed a pencil torch in a slow sweep of each step in the stairwell, checking for tripwires or carpet bulges that might betray hidden pressure plates. The area looked clean.

He counted fourteen steps, a solid wall to the right and a handrail on the left that guarded against the dropdown to the hall. The top step disappeared into a landing area, with corridors running off to either side, providing ideal blind spots for a counter-attack in the event that anyone was stupid enough to contemplate a headlong rush.

Millward was a lot more circumspect than that. He hand-signalled two of his team to start advancing, while the rest kept their weapons trained on the landing above. The two men climbed three stairs, pulled the pins on grenades, and tossed them at the entrances to both corridors. They dropped on their bellies, waited four seconds after the explosions, and crawled forward another three steps, before releasing a second pair of grenades. They repeated the exercise twice more. The higher they reached on the stairway, the farther they were able to toss the grenades into the darkened corridors.

The damage to the upstairs had to be extensive. Millward half-expected to see part of the area collapsing, or at least the floor dropping through some gaping holes left by the explosions. But it was an old building, fashioned out of reinforced concrete and oak timbers that were made to withstand a century of whatever the elements could throw at it. There were heavy creaking groans, but nothing to suggest the structure was about to cave in.

The air was laden with dust as Millward ordered two men to remain in the foyer while the rest moved up the stairs. He took point on the right side, stepped onto the landing, and triggered a full magazine of 9mm parabellums into the gloom of the corridor. As soon as the MP5 bolt clicked on empty, he knelt to replace the magazine, allowing the second man in line to reach over and continue the attack.

The team to the left, with Jennings taking the lead role, executed the same manoeuvre. The whole area reeked of cordite, and echoed with the hammering of gunfire. It was a withering barrage that was not survivable for anyone foolish enough to be anywhere within the twin funnels of death.

The gunmen waited patiently for the noise to settle, allowing their vision to adjust to the murky interior whilst listening for any signs of the opposition. Millward used his torch to pick out three separate doorways, one on the left of the corridor, the other two evenly spaced along the right wall. Despite the damage caused to the area by the grenades, all doors were intact and firmly shut.

He turned and flashed the torch to get the attention of the second team. He mouthed at Jennings that he had three doors and would begin the third phase in five seconds. Jennings nodded, confirming he faced a similar situation in the second corridor.

"Now!" Millward yelled and all six gunmen headed off down their respective passageways.

Access to the rooms was achieved in the same way as the ground-floor clearance operation. Door surrounds were shattered by MP5 bursts, grenades were tossed in, and the interiors swept with volleyfire designed to dispose of any occupants.

Millward's team completed the sweep of the three rooms to the right of the landing without encountering any opposition. He cursed and crunched his way across the shell-laden corridor to join Jennings and his men at the left side of the upper floor. They had still one more room to clear.

"They have to be in there," Millward whispered into his friend's ear and signalled four men to take up station either side of the door while he knelt and gingerly tried the handle. To his amazement, it depressed fully, allowing the door to swing slowly open. Two team members pulled the pins on flashbang grenades and threw them into the room. The three-second delay provided the raiders with enough time to cover their ears and shut their eyes to minimise the intended disorientating effects of the devices.

They moved quickly in teams of three, fanning out to left and right, and laying down a blanket of fire that cut swathes of damage across a wide area. Furniture splintered, ornaments were sent flying in miniscule pieces, and small feathers danced in the air from shredded pillows and cushions.

Millward paid particular attention to fitted furniture along one wall. There were six closed doors, some covered by full-length mirrors, behind which gunmen could be lurking among the usual clothes and paraphernalia accumulated in wardrobe spaces. He peppered the area, sending shards of glass leaping into the air and punching holes from bottom to top of the flimsy laminated wood. By the time he finished, the area resembled a giant mural colander.

The firing stopped, the echoes receded, and realisation dawned. There was no-one here. The entire ground- and upper-floor areas were deserted. There was nobody in residence.

"We've been fuckin' had," Millward announced with resignation.

Chapter 33

SEVEN PEOPLE huddled in a basement two floors below where Millward and his team were gathered. It was more of a wine cellar than a basement, though over the years the bottle racks had been emptied and the area turned into a store for the kind of discarded clutter more commonly found in attics and outhouses.

Alfie Cheadle was grateful for the rusted fridges, washing machines, and countless boxes of junk that littered the concrete floor. They provided decent cover, but not enough, he had to admit, to ward off a sustained attack, particularly one that included grenades on the scale he'd heard in the rooms above.

The cellar ran for almost half the length of the house, before ending abruptly against a solid wall that must have been part of the original building before an annex was added later. It was rectangular in shape, measuring forty paces by thirty with foundation concrete struts dotted at various intervals. There was only one way in and one way out, via twelve stone steps which reached to the ground-floor kitchen. The entrance was cleverly concealed, more for aesthetic reasons than a desire for subterfuge. The door was panelled to match the kitchen décor of beechwood and ceramic tiling that covered the walls in a half-and-half mixture, and although the handle was recessed it was easily detectable with little more than a cursory scan of the area.

Cheadle knew it was only a matter of time before the raiders found their hiding place. Over the past hour he'd done his best to make it as secure as possible, moving Sonia and Christopher Hayden and their nurse to the farthest recess of the cellar and surrounding them with the sturdiest barriers he could find.

Between them and the entrance he'd fashioned two

defensive hides, one he shared with Terry Hunt, the other for Jim Cross and Dan Gosling. Each man had an MP5 with three spare magazines, a Glock 22 with two spares, and a combat knife in the unlikely event things got to the last resort of hand-to-hand fighting.

The ace up his sleeve came in the shape of four small bricks of Semtex. These had been moulded into position at intervals on the stairs, and were controlled by remote detonators shared out between each hide. Anyone coming down those steps was in for a nasty surprise.

It was the best he could do in the circumstances. The urgent phone call from Devon had provided little time for anything else. He recalled the terse conversation.

"Alfie, no time for details. Prepare for an imminent attack...I repeat.... imminent. Get everyone down to the basement. Do not engage. Expect heavy forces. Priority one is protection of our assets. I'm on my way with support. Good luck."

Cheadle looked at his watch. That was seventy minutes ago. "Where are you, Mike?"

The Bell 407 GXP helicopter was in the middle of a maintenance go-over when the pilot received Devon's call. It had taken thirty-five minutes for the bits and pieces of the routine check to be refitted, followed by another twenty minutes of flight time from the airport to the estate grounds of the rural laneways of Bishops Stortford.

Devon was in a foul mood when he scrambled aboard, his anxiety heightened by an inability to contact Cheadle over the past ten minutes. He hoped it was because mobile and sat phone coverage was being blocked by the underground cellar, something he acknowledged should have been checked out before now. He tried not to think of other reasons why Cheadle was not responding.

The message he'd found on Manning's deskpad left no room for doubting that an assault would be made on the house. There was no way of knowing when Manning had scribbled the note, but it was obvious that once the location of the Haydens was known to the opposition it would be acted upon immediately. A period of time, say no more than a day, would be allotted for reconnaissance, which meant the attempt on the Haydens' lives had to come sometime soon, most likely under the cover of darkness. Every fibre of his body screamed that it would be tonight.

The helicopter was carving a path beneath the clouds at an altitude of 4,000 feet and an airspeed of sixty-five knots. The pilot estimated time of arrival at the *LonWash* estate within the next thirty minutes, a total gap of almost one and a half hours since Devon had first contacted Cheadle.

A Browning M2A1 fifty-calibre was primed and ready and lying at Devon's feet in the copter's rear compartment. The belt-fed heavy machine gun had a cyclic firing rate of over 500 rounds per minute, and was capable of providing air-to-ground support that would deter a large number of intruders. Its effective range took it outside the limit of the kind of portable weaponry likely to be used by the assailants, meaning the chopper could hover at a distance and allow Devon to pick off any unwelcome visitors.

If the site was not compromised by the time he reached his destination, Devon intended to land directly in front of the main building and join forces with Cheadle. They would leave a two-man team in the basement to guard the civilians while the rest took the fight to the enemy, supported by the power of the M2A1.

He'd ordered Cheadle to keep the grounds in darkness, reasoning that a sudden burst from the arc lights might force raiders into action before his people had the chance to reach the relative security of the basement. He hoped there was still time to use the lights to their advantage.

The pilot's voice erupted in his headset. "Four minutes to target."

Millward found the basement door. It was in the last place he expected it to be, though he guessed it made sense in the old upstairs-downstairs days when servants required access to all areas, particularly those which stored coal and potatoes and hanging pheasants and God knows what else in an era of class barriers and privilege.

He teased the door open and noticed the stone steps disappearing into the gloom below. He knew instantly he'd found his quarry. *Come out, come out, wherever you are!*

He turned and grinned at his team. "Let's not be too subtle about this. Toss in four flashbangs. This ends now."

He stood back to allow two of his men to move to the side of the door. This time there was no need to fling the grenades into the open space; they simply pulled the pins and let them bounce down the steps in a noisy clippity-clop beat that rang out in the hollowness of the area.

Millward slammed the door shut and rushed behind a service counter. The racket was deafening, each explosion rolling into the other in what seemed like a never-ending boom. A concussive wave tore the door off its hinges and ploughed a blast of compressed air over the room, before finding the point of least resistance – the large kitchen window that blew out in a maelstrom of shattered glass.

He waited ten seconds before jumping to his feet. "We'll do this in teams of three," he commanded, pointing a finger at the first attack trio. "You know the drill; shoot, advance, shoot. We'll bring up your rear."

Just as the first of his team entered the stairwell, he heard the sound of gunfire from the front of the house. "Abort, abort, all bodies to me. We need to find out what the fuck is going on."

The SO19 vehicle drove past the *LonWash* estate entrance for the third time. Commander Hall knew the AVL locator was accurate to within fifty feet - all well and good in an urban area with landmarks to help pinpoint precise spots, but out here in the country there was nothing other than fields and hedges from which to get a bearing.

One of the backseat passengers echoed Hall's own conclusion. "This must be the place. Why would a country yokel have closed gates and a sentry post? This looks like a safe-house setting to me."

Hall agreed. "The only thing that concerns me is why the place is in darkness. There are no lights in the driveway or in any of the buildings we can see. It's as if the place is totally deserted."

"Maybe that's the impression they're trying to create, sir?"

"Good point, Tomkins. Let's go to the end of the road again before doubling back to pay a visit to the house."

The dynamics in the police vehicle changed dramatically two minutes later.

"Stop!" There's something in the trees to our right."

The driver braked sharply, turned off the road, and killed the lights as he brought the car to a stop alongside a black Ford Transit van. All four occupants jumped to the ground and trained their weapons on the side and rear of the parked vehicle.

"Armed police! Step out with your hands raised."

Even as he uttered the command, Hall knew it was pointless. There were no shadows or noises coming from the interior, although his team still went through the standard protective procedures of confirming his guess. They released the safety catches on their machine pistols and shone Maglites into the interior. Nothing.

Hall walked around the vehicle, noting the black duct tape on the reflectors and knowing instantly what it signified. "Now, who would abandon this in the middle of nowhere and go to the trouble of protecting it from the glare of passing lights."

A loud explosion in the distance stopped any chance of a response from his men.

"What the fuck was that?"

He turned in the direction of the noise, only to be met by a second and then a third explosion. "Christ, it's like World War 3 has just started. It's coming from that house down the road.

Move. Move!"

It took only three minutes for the SO19 armoured vehicle to arrive at the *LonWash* gates. Hall had counted at least another three explosions, and a succession of machine-gun rat-a-tats that sounded like a fireworks display in the distance. The driver looked at the closed gates and glanced across at Hall.

"What are you waiting for?" Hall barked. Back up and ram the fuckers. We need to get in there."

The gates buckled apart under the impact of the heavy-duty vehicle, which twisted off line before the driver corrected the steering and sent it hurtling up the curved driveway, its lights on full beam.

Hall rattled off a string of instructions. "We need to be wary of what we'll find here. Remember, we must assume there are friendlies as well as hostiles, so make sure of your targets."

Fifty yards from the main door, two black-clad figures stepped through what appeared to be a gap and started firing. The SO19 driver braked to a halt and slid the vehicle into a sideways stop, as bullets pinged off the armour-plated body and toughened glass.

"Guess we know which ones aren't friendly," Hall said as he slid across the seats and followed his driver out the door.

Chapter 34

THE HELICOPTER arrived on station and settled into a hover, three hundred feet above the ground on the south-east quadrant of the estate. Devon pushed the heavy fifty-cal machine gun on its tripod towards the open door and sighted up the front lawn just as the SO19 vehicle burst through the gates and rocketed across the tarmacked drive.

The attack has started!

He swivelled the barrel to track ten yards ahead of the SUV, knowing it would plough straight into a five-inch-bullet storm as soon as he depressed the trigger. Even a short burst would have devastating consequences – quite simply the car and its occupants would be chewed up into unrecognisable pieces.

He was about to apply final pressure on the trigger when something struck him as odd. Why only one vehicle, if this was a go-for-broke assault? Surely a gamble of that type called for at least two cars in a pincer movement to divide the attention of opposing forces? Better still, why not lob in a few rockets from a safe distance and lay down a smokescreen before unleashing the Charge of the Light Brigade?

What the fuck was going on?

He moved his thumb away from the trigger plate as two figures emerged from the front of the house and began firing at the approaching vehicle. The big SUV slewed sideways and four figures jumped out on the driver's side, shielding themselves from the incoming barrage.

Devon was too far away to identify the gunmen or their targets. But one thing was obvious; Cheadle would not have sent his men outside the building in such a reckless fashion. He swivelled the M2AI and unleashed a short burst above the heads of the gunmen on the porch, intent on forcing them back under cover while he assessed precisely who they were.

Better to be safe than sorry.

He spoke urgently into the chopper's headset. "Take us down behind that vehicle. Keep me side-on to the men hiding behind it. If they make a false move, they're toast."

The Bell dropped slowly from its hover, the pitch changing as the pilot fought the increased vibrations. He tipped the rotors towards the stern to produce a reverse glide that took the machine fifty yards behind the SO19 vehicle before the struts touched the ground.

Devon kept a steady gaze on the four cowering figures. Their weapons were pointed downwards in a non-threatening gesture, and all used their arms to shield against the backdraft of air that kicked grass and dust particles into their faces. One of the men waved at Devon.

"Shit, I don't fucking believe it," Devon murmured, "what's *he* doing here?"

He jumped to the ground, took a quick look at the heavy machine gun, and decided to leave it. It would be too cumbersome under the new circumstances. He ordered the pilot to move to a safe distance and be ready for a recall signal at a moment's notice. As the machine rose and dipped and soared off into the distance, he turned his attention to Commander Hall.

"You'd better have a good reason for being here. I came within the blink of an eye of destroying this vehicle. I thought it was part of an assault on the estate."

Hall nodded his head. "Needless to say, I'm grateful you didn't. Look, explanations can wait until later. I know that Millward and his crew are inside the building and that there was a series of explosions within the last five minutes. We also heard a lot of gunfire, but that died down until those two bozos appeared on the steps."

Devon's mind went into overdrive. If Cheadle had reached the basement, they might still be there, although the news about explosions was worrying. He needed to come up with a plan. And fast.

"Okay, Hall, this is *my* operation. I could do with your help, but if you're not prepared to follow my orders, then stay the fuck out of my face. I have people holed up in the basement and I need to get to them before Millward discovers their whereabouts. It might already be too late."

"C'mon, Devon, this is not about the size of each other's dick. We're with you, so tell me what you want us to do."

Devon was grateful for not having to get involved in a slanging match. "Okay, can your men provide covering fire for you and me to get to the porch? Then I want them to move to the rear of the building, via the open ground to the right, and set up an ambush for anyone attempting to leave."

Hall nodded at his three officers, one of whom had already started crawling to the front of the vehicle. He remained on the ground, peering below the chassis, while his two colleagues jumped up and leaned across the car bonnet. All three started firing in unison.

Devon and Hall waited at the rear of the vehicle. As soon as the first volley of shots rained down on the porch, they sprinted across the lawn, heading for the darkest portion of the wall nearest the remains of the front door. The firing from the SO19 men stopped abruptly, and Devon pulled a pin on a fragmentation grenade. "Why don't we give these bastards a taste of their own medicine?"

Millward, and the five men with him in the kitchen, froze at the noise of the heavy machine-gun fire. If there was one thing guaranteed to put the frighteners on even the most committed soldier it was the introduction of artillery they couldn't hope to match. The sound of a helicopter was another dimension altogether.

"They've got us boxed in!" Jennings screamed. "My guess is that the SAS has just joined the party. We need to exfil, and we need to do it now."

Millward shrugged his shoulders in resignation. "I have to admit, I didn't see this coming, and we sure as hell can't do a Butch and Sundance number on whatever's out there. Mark and I will provide support to the two sentries at the front while you four slip out the back. Good luck, it's been a pleasure working with you."

The four men singled out by Millward shared a look of admiration at his sacrifice. A rear exit offered a better-than-evens chance of survival, whereas a stand-off against superior forces at the front of the building was a one-way ticket to a funeral. They mumbled their thanks and goodbyes and took up position at the kitchen door to await the start of hostilities, which Millward promised would happen within the next three minutes.

The hallway leading from the kitchen was strewn with the debris from the earlier RPG attack on the front door, and the crunch of combat boots alerted the watchers to their presence. Both men had somehow survived the fifty-cal attack and were crouched at either end of the doorway, grateful to see their leader.

Millward spoke softly. "Hold here while we work our way to the side. The rest of the team are coming through shortly to support you. Don't worry, we'll get out of this jam."

He tugged at Jennings' sleeve and led the way into a second, smaller corridor running to the left side of the building."

"Where are we going?"

"There's a walled compound at this side of the house. If we can find a door leading to that area, it will shield us from the eyes of the enemy. It's our best chance for escape."

"What about the others?"

"Don't be so fucking naïve, Mark. We can't all get out. Hopefully, the rest will provide enough distraction for you and me to leg it. Unless, of course, you have a better idea."

Jennings glanced back towards the door sentries and then at the passage leading to the kitchen. "Naw, you're right. Let's go."

Devon's grenade killed the two sentries before they had a chance to react. He waited the standard five seconds after the blast before rushing through the gap and spraying the area to his right, relying on Hall to do the same on the left. Both men knelt in the rubble and changed magazines on their MP5s, their antennae on maximum alert. They heard movement at the rear of the building.

Devon pointed towards a corridor. "The entrance to the basement is down there, through the kitchen. I'll take point, but shoot only if you have to. I don't want to risk hitting any of our team who might be in there guarding the door."

As he started forward, he called out. "Alfie, it's Mike, are you there? Can you hear me?"

Silence.

He rushed into the kitchen, and scrambled behind a serving counter, leaving space for Hall to hunker beside him. He noticed the splintered basement door and crawled across to the opening. "Alfie, where the fuck are you? Is anyone down there?"

Silence.

Dust and smoke billowed from below, a sure sign the area had suffered an explosion within the past ten minutes. Had anyone survived? He tried to fight back against the dread mounting in his gut.

"Mike, Mike, is that you?"

The plaintive voice was barely audible in the recesses of the cellar, but Devon recognised Cheadle's Yorkshire burr.

"Thank God to hear you, Alfie. Is everyone alright?"

"We're a bit deaf, and a whole lot shook up, but other than that, we're fine. I'll take everyone up top."

"No," Devon yelled more harshly than he intended. "We're still not clear here. You and Cross come on out to help the mop-up, but leave Hunt and Gosling as guards. There are still a lot of people unaccounted for."

The sound of gunfire in the grounds beyond the kitchen confirmed his statement. The sporadic fire continued for several minutes before the area fell back into silence. Hall's SO19 radios were still working and he hit the transmit button.

Echo one niner seven, this is Charlie Bravo, report. Over

Charlie Bravo, this is Echo one niner seven. Four Tangos bolted from the rear of the house. We have three confirmed dead, and one surrender. Over.

Copy that, Echo one niner seven, are the two main players among them? Over.

Negative, Charlie Bravo. Over.

"Dammit!" Hall mouthed in Devon's direction.

"What is it?" Devon asked.

"Millward and Jennings are still on the loose. According to staff in the hotel where this lot were holed up, there were eight in the party. Looks like the main rats have jumped ship."

Just then Cheadle and Cross emerged through the gloom of the stairs, their faces and clothes plastered with dust. Devon stepped forward and patted each of them on the shoulder. "Good to see you both. Glad we got here in time."

Cheadle walked forward to the kitchen sink, turned on the tap, and gulped mouthfuls for water from cupped hands. "Look, Mike, they can't stay down there. The place is stifling. We need to bring them up."

Devon looked around the kitchen. "Okay, this will be the main defensive area. Alfie, go get them while we prepare to tie this place down tighter than a cork in a bottle. The birds have probably flown, but I'm taking no chances."

He asked Hall to bring his team into the house for a briefing on what could be done to locate Millward and Jennings. If the pair had escaped the grounds, they'd have a considerable head start in getting clear of the area. He needed the helicopter back on site, although it wouldn't be much use until daylight. In the meantime, he ordered Cross to switch on the arc lights to illuminate the grounds.

Sonia and Christopher Hayden were supporting each other as they walked, coughing and spluttering, into the room. Despite their ordeal, Devon detected a steely resolve in their eyes.

"Sonia, I'm sorry this had to happen. There was an unforgiveable leak, which has now been plugged, although that's hardly any consolation after what you've been put through."

"Don't apologise, Mike. We're just glad you got here on time, but I *do* need to know when this thing is going to end."

"Soon, Sonia, soon. I promise."

Chapter 35

MILLWARD AND JENNINGS made it over the compound wall as the grenade exploded near the front of the building. They knew the men they'd left guarding the entrance had been disposed of in the most summary way possible. Rapid gunfire to their right told them the rest of their team were faring no better.

The other side of the wall led to an open field, which stretched to a small forest five hundred yards away. They needed to make the treeline before lights started blazing and the area became awash with searchers. They still had darkness on their side, but if they were caught in the open it was game over. Millward punched Jennings on the arm and set off at a blistering pace, half-expecting to catch a bullet long before they reached cover.

But there were no searchlights and no bullets.

They crashed into the undergrowth and dropped on their bellies, each sucking in a lungful of air as they fought against the effects of their exertions. Although they took pride in their physical conditioning, it'd been a long time since either of them had been forced into a full-tilt, life or death race on the scale they'd just endured.

Millward's emotions were all over the place. Where had the cavalry come from? Had they been suckered into a corner? Were the Haydens even in residence? They had been there two nights ago when that clown Todd Hamilton had held the kid in the crosshairs of his sniper scope, but that didn't mean they hadn't been moved in the meantime. None of it made any sense.

He'd been convinced his quarry was hiding in the basement. If only they'd been able to use frags instead of flash-bangs, his job would be over, but they'd expended their lethal grenades during the needless clearance of the other rooms. In the end, it didn't matter whether the Haydens were alive or dead. He was finished with them. Fuck professional pride, and fuck the faceless men who cowered behind telephones and issued orders without caring a damn about the risks.

He needed to get out of the country. He and Jennings could lie low in a villa he'd purchased under one of his aliases several years ago in Marbella. It would be impossible to track them there, and he had enough cash stashed away in various safety deposit boxes across Europe for them to be able to live like kings for a long time. Maybe a few years down the line they could pick up the threads and launch a new enterprise. There were always people in need of their particular skill-set.

But first they had to get out of the woods, and then out of the county, and then out of England.

Easier said than done.

"What?"

"Whataya mean what?"

"I thought you said something."

"Sorry, Mark, just thinking out loud. We're in a bit of a pickle, old friend. We can't go back to the van on the other side of the estate and your car is probably compromised back at the hotel. On top of that, we're stuck in the middle of nowhere, and come morning this place will be crawling with cops."

"And there's me thinking we're up shit creek."

Millward burst out laughing. "You're right. No sense hanging around here feeling sorry for ourselves. We need to see what's on the other side of these woods, maybe hijack a car, and find somewhere to lie low for a bit. I've a mate, Jimmy Madine, who owns a small yacht at Maldon Harbour, thirty-odd miles from here. He can ferry us across the channel to Belgium or France."

"And what are we going to do about money and travelling papers?"

"That'll be the least of our worries. I've a rainy-day stash in a holdall at Euston train station. Jimmy'll pick it up and after that, all I'll need is access to a computer to manage a few offshore accounts. A couple of days from now we'll be sunning ourselves in Marbella and wondering what all the fuss was about."

Devon surveyed the damage to the house and came to a decision. "It will take months to put this place back in order, so we've no option but to relocate the Haydens asap. I'll talk to the General to see if he has any suggestions. In the meantime, we need to find Millward and Jennings."

"Not so fast," Commander Hall boomed from the other side of the room. The big SO19 man looked as if he was spoiling for an argument. "The manhunt has nothing to do with you. These are my pigeons and if you had been more forthcoming about this little hideaway, things mightn't have got as far they did. I suggest you stick with protecting your charges a lot better than was the case here."

Devon bristled. "Go fuck yourself, Hall. We've been working against leaks at the highest levels since this operation started and I don't need clever-dick hindsight to remind me what could have happened."

"If you're still thinking my team had anything to do with these leaks, we're going to have a big problem moving forward. I'm not some twopence-ha'penny underling you can throw around to suit the level of self-importance you seem to place on this organisation of yours. I'm a senior ranking officer in the Metropolitan Police and from where I stand, you're nothing more than a civilian impeding the course of justice. I warn you now, I'm not prepared to stand on the sidelines any longer, no matter what level of political clout is standing behind you."

Part of Devon wanted to throttle the man. The other part held a grudging admiration for the way he stood his ground. And there was no getting around the fact that if Hall hadn't showed up when he did, the Haydens might not be sitting safe and well and drinking coffee in an adjoining room. He decided to lower the level of tension. "Just so you know, we've uncovered the leaks, and none of them pointed in your direction."

"Care to share?"

"I'm sorry, Commander Hall, but it's too early to know how far they reached. What I can say is that the safety of the Haydens has been made a lot easier by what we've discovered to date."

For a moment, it looked as though Hall was about to launch into another tirade. Instead, he walked to the nearest armchair and flopped down. "Obviously, I'm delighted to hear it, but it won't stop the Home Secretary from giving me one in the eye for being here. No matter what way you cut it, I disobeyed a direct order not to get involved in the Hayden investigation and I'll be lucky to save my pension when news gets out."

Devon thought briefly about how much he could share. In the end, he decided there were probably few men he could trust more than Hall. "You no longer have to worry about the Home Secretary."

Before Hall could respond, Devon closed the room door, drew up a seat beside the policeman, and told him everything.

General Sir John Sandford emerged from the rear entrance of Downing Street, crossed Horse Guards Road, and eased into his chauffeured staff car, a downplayed reference to a silver Rolls Royce Phantom that was the General's choice of runabout. He settled into the luxury leather seat, told the driver to head for the Shannon Club in Knightsbridge, and pondered the momentous events of the past few hours.

The Prime Minister had acted decisively at the news of Charles Manning's assassination. It was to be treated as a suicide, brought on by the pressures of mounting debts and personal torment. Certain well-placed journalists had already been briefed with veiled references to Manning's unnatural sexual proclivities and the likelihood that he was being blackmailed by several rent-boy clients. On balance, it had been decided, these revelations would play out much better than the spectre of assassination and treason.

Two junior ministers and three senior Civil Servants had

been unceremoniously dragged from their sleep and brought directly to Downing Street to face the PM's wrath. Their removal from office was as swift as it was brutal. They were given twelve hours to chronicle everything they knew about the schemes contained within the Hayden dossier. The PM demanded names, dates, and the mechanisms used to subvert government. Anything less than full accounts of their treachery would result in immediate ruin and lengthy incarceration. What he didn't tell them was that, irrespective of their confessions, these sanctions would not be taken off the table.

The General had been present during each of the dressing-downs, and had taken particular pleasure at the way in which the PM had left the men as little more than blubbering wrecks before waving them dismissively from his sight.

The absence of the men from their offices would be put down to a Government reshuffle caused by the death of the Home Secretary. It would be announced in time for the breakfast news on the main television channels.

Shortly after 6.00am, a telephone call to the Governor of the Bank of England completed the final part of the PM's strategy. An immediate freeze was put on twenty separate bank accounts, which were to be placed under forensic audits to track every individual transaction stretching back five years, with a proviso that any other dubious accounts discovered during the course of the investigation would also be frozen until the full trail of corruption was completely unravelled. It was agreed that the International Corruption Unit attached to the UK's National Crime Agency would take the lead role on completion of the Bank's large-scale trawl.

General Sandford watched the early-morning traffic blur though the window as the Phantom rolled past Harrods and turned towards the residential area that housed his club. He needed a brandy, a full English breakfast, and a long soak in the bath. The only thing missing was sleep, but that would have to wait. His satphone flashed in the console behind the driver's seat.

He leaned forward, punched a button, and spoke wearily.

"Mike, this can't be good news at this time of the morning."

He listened as Devon filled him in on what had happened at the *LonWash* estate. "I must say, it seems fortuitous that this fellow, Hall, showed up when he did. Do you trust him?"

"Implicitly, sir. In fact, I've clued him in on what happened to Manning. He's agreed to say nothing until an official version is decided."

"I trust your instincts, Mike and, as it turns out, there will shortly be a press statement announcing that Manning committed suicide. Let me tell you where we are."

After the General had finished detailing events at Downing Street, Devon brought him up to speed on the search for Millward and Jennings. "Hall contacted the Hertfordshire Constabulary as a matter of courtesy and they will be leading the manhunt. They've asked for Hall's team to support their efforts, although it's been made clear *we* should stay out of it."

"Quite right too. We've more pressing matters to deal with. There are still a lot of trails, other than financial ones, to be pursued. I want you and the team to find me every individual involved. We haven't cracked this yet, not by a long shot."

"I agree, General. We'll be heading back to London, but what will I do about the Haydens. They can't possibly stay here."

"No, and I won't risk a public place such as an hotel. I'll meet you at HQ shortly before noon to make arrangements for them to move into an altogether more suitable environment."

Chapter 36

THE TEMPERATURE had dipped below freezing point as Millward and Jennings scrabbled their way through thick undergrowth for more than two hours after leaving the surrounds of the *LonWash* estate. Grateful for their neoprene all-body thermal underwear, and warmed by the exertions of their flight, they were nonetheless on the brink of exhaustion when they finally broke clear of the forest. A weak sun was doing its best to climb above the horizon, providing sufficient light to show the fugitives what stretched ahead of them.

Millward liked what he saw. A vista of open fields, scattered housing, twinkling lights, and busy roads. *Welcome to civilisation!*

Traffic on the roads appeared to be moving normally, dispelling the fear that vehicle checkpoints were in place. In the distance, maybe three or four miles from where he stood, he could make out the familiar canopies of a garage forecourt, most likely a motorway service station, judging by the number of buildings and parked trucks. An ideal place to hitch a ride, or hijack the services of an unfortunate long-distance lorry driver.

Before leaving the cover of the trees they decided to dump their machine-pistols and remove all bulky items, including the last of the flash-bang canisters, from their combat trousers. They had already washed the camouflage markings from their faces at a small stream they'd stumbled across in the forest, and were confident they could avoid casual scrutiny, despite the mud on their clothes. They tucked their handguns into waistbands, exchanged let's-do-this nods, and set off at a crouching run through the first of the open fields.

An hour later, with daylight in full swing, they skirted the service area and scanned a full car park. Millward's eyes fell on a blue Scania cab hauling a forty-foot container draped in concertina-fold polyurethane side flaps, easier to access than solid-metal surrounds. He nudged Jennings, withdrew a serrated combat knife from a leg holster, and duck-walked between parked vehicles until he reached the side of the rig. He punched the knife into a fold in the side flaps, and easily sawed through two feet of the toughened fabric.

He pulled apart the opening and stuck his head into the gap. The compartment was filled with brown cardboard boxes, stacked floor to roof and secured by a series of straps hooked to guard rails. There appeared to be small walkway gaps in the freight, and he guessed there was probably a central aisle for ease of unloading.

He pulled free of the opening and signalled Jennings to join him. Five minutes later, they settled into a makeshift hide behind several rearranged boxes.

"Are you sure this is wise?" Jennings asked in an anxious tone. "We haven't a clue where this rig is going."

"Yeah, but we need to get well clear of the Bishop's Stortford area. Even though we haven't seen any yet, there's bound to be roadblocks, and the more distance we put between them and us the better chance we'll have of evading the bastards. We can take stock when we get to wherever we end up, and then we'll figure a way of reaching out to Jimmy Madine at Maldon Harbour."

A Hertfordshire detective constable stared disbelievingly at the CCTV screen as two men disappeared into a Scania goods trailer. The small control room at the rear of the Little Chef cafeteria had a single monitor split into eight squares showing various angles of the car park, with two squares reserved for the interior dining room. After three hours of scanning the sea of faces stopping for pie and chips, the staple diet even so early in the morning, the detective was on the edge of sleep when he'd spotted the unusual movement near a blue trailer, the longest in the car park.

His eyes constantly switched between the monitor and two large colour photographs he'd brought with him for the surveillance, and decided the figures were close enough in appearance for him to hit the panic button. In this case in wasn't a button, but an open radio link to a central operations centre at Basbow Lane in Bishop's Stortford.

The constable thought he'd grabbed the shitty straw when assignments had been handed out in the middle of the night. The higher echelons of command had decided to throw a three-hundred-and-sixty-degree ring around the *LonWash* estate by placing men at strategic locations within a five-mile radius. Rather than relying on roadblocks, the plan involved putting eyes on the ground at every house, building and vantage point where fugitives might be seen emerging from their forest retreat. A team from the 23rd SAS Regiment was due to be helicoptered to the centre of the forest to begin a search-and-find mission at 0900 hours.

The radio message from the detective went directly to a comms screening desk, which was manned by five operatives, and was immediately relayed to the man in charge, Chief Superintendent Richard Atkinson. The urgent tones of the caller left Atkinson in no doubt that they'd found their fugitives. He clicked his fingers to get the attention of Commander Hall at the opposite end of the room.

"Great work, Detective Constable," Atkinson barked effusively. "Are you sure they're still in place? Can you track down the driver of the truck? Is he part of the gang?"

The questions flowed quicker than the detective could answer them. Hall tuned into the excited voice of his Hertfordshire colleague and rushed forward, urging Atkinson to put the call on speaker. The man on the ground at the motorway service station was doing his best to keep his report on a professional level. Yes, the men were still in the truck. No, he hadn't yet located the driver. No, there was no telling if the driver was there because of some pre-arrangement.

Hall leaned forward and hit the mute button. "Tell your man to stand by, Chief Superintendent, I have an idea."

Thirty minutes into their cramped wait, Millward and Jennings were suddenly alerted by the banging of a door, followed by the roar of an engine.

"Looks like we're on the move," Millward said as the big rig shook and trundled forward. It swerved hard to the right, straightened and picked up speed. Wind whistled through the knife-slit in the canopy and the vehicle shuddered as it settled into what Millward guessed was a cruising speed of around seventy.

"The driver has had his breakfast and a fill-up of diesel so there should be no stopping for a while. If there are any roadblocks they'll come in the next half hour, otherwise we'll be well clear of the area. Even if we're stopped, we should be safe unless some cop gets too diligent about his duty. He'll not live to regret his nosiness."

Jennings removed the Glock 22 from his waistband and nodded agreement. "I'm with you. I'm not doing time, that's for sure. Can you see me cooped up in an eight-by-six room with your smelly feet for company, day in and day out? No sir, if they're thinking of taking Mark Jennings alive, they've got another think coming."

"Don't be such a fatalist," Millward teased. "We both know you've got the luck of the devil. Why do you think I've put up with you all these years? I figured out a long time ago that if I stand close enough some of that luck will rub off. Have to say, it seems to have worked out so far."

"Yeah, I've lost count of the times I've saved your sorry ass. Remember that incident at.........what the fuck was that?"

Both men were thrown forward as the truck came to a shuddering stop, its air brakes hissing an eerie beat that matched the screech of tyres. The rig wobbled and settled on its chassis, and suddenly there was nothing but silence.

Jennings jumped to his feet and racked his pistol. "It's a fucking roadblock. I knew this was getting too easy."

"For God's sake, Mark, keep quiet and settle down. It could be anything. Maybe there's an accident, or the driver overshot a turn-off...."

Millward's attempt at easing the tension was cut short by

a booming megaphone voice:

Attention, Dave Millward and Mark Jennings, this is the police. You're surrounded by armed officers. Throw out your weapons and exit the vehicle head first through the opening you made in the side of the trailer.

"How the fuck did they know that?"

Millward ignored the question and walked forward to the slit in the panel. The half-inch crack provided a limited view, but what he saw was enough to tell him he'd reached the end of the road, in more ways than one.

The decision to move the rig away from the crowded service station area had been taken after assessing the risk to scores of civilians using the area. At Hall's suggestion, the detective constable on site had tracked down the driver and convinced him to drive three miles down the motorway to a cordoned off area that was being prepared as an ambush collection point.

The policeman had accompanied the trucker on the journey and was amazed by the scene that greeted them. The southbound carriageway on which they were travelling was closed to all traffic, except for an outer lane which was kept clear for the arrival of the distinctive Scania rig. All northbound traffic had already been halted at a junction five miles farther down the route.

As the truck eased clear of the cordon, it entered a no-man's-land stretch of empty motorway that culminated in a tunnel of police vehicles lining both sides of the road. There had to be more than a hundred cars and twice as many policemen, most of whom were dressed in riot gear. They stood behind perspex shields and held an assortment of handguns in a manner which suggested they were keen to use them.

The cordon ended at a four-vehicle barrier which had brought the Scania rig to a sliding stop. The driver and his detective passenger immediately exited the cab and disappeared behind a wall of men, fronted by the unmistakable uniforms of an elite army group. The SAS had been diverted to the location!

There were twelve troopers, each cradling a C8 CQB carbine, the wicked-looking 10-inch-barrelled machine pistol that was the Regiment's weapon of choice for close quarter battle.

It was that sight that had made Millward realise there was no way out.

Time's up! Throw down your weapons.

As the seconds ticked by, the watchers heard voices, which steadily grew into shouts, and then became a full-blown argument. The SAS Captain had witnessed similar scenarios played out in previous tense stand-offs. When rats are cornered, they usually turn on each other before realising who their common enemy is. He knew things were about to come to a head, one way or another.

"Hold your fire, we're coming out."

Chapter 37

"THEY JUST GAVE UP?" Devon shook his head in disbelief. "Let me get this right; they walked in off the fields, climbed into the back of a lorry under CCTV surveillance, and then threw down their weapons when they were stopped at a roadblock?"

Commander John Hall was on the other end of the line and his voice betrayed the same shock as Devon's had. "Yep, that's it in a nutshell. Mind you, there was a lot of luck involved in spotting them at the service station, and the fact that we had an SAS troop surrounding the vehicle didn't leave them with too many options. It seems, however, that Jennings was all for shooting it out, but was eventually calmed down by Millward, who thought he could cut a deal."

"What was he offering?"

"A bit of a moot point really, Mike. When we got them back into a squad car, Millward looked for immunity in return for helping us to track down his employers. He offered to lead us to some real movers and shakers, but it was no dice as far as we were concerned."

"Why so, Commander?"

"Come on, Mike, you don't need me to remind you that three police officers were killed in that hospital shoot-out? That's a deal-breaker right there, never mind the bastard's repeated attempts to kill an innocent woman and her son. Trust me, there'll be no get-out-of-jail-cards for this duo."

Devon chose his words carefully. "Couldn't agree more, Commander, but is there any way you can string them along without actually offering immunity or reduced sentencing?"

"Naturally we'll give it a go, but Millward's not the type to start talking unless he has written guarantees. I think we can safely say that's a dead end."

It was what Devon expected to hear and he saw little point

in pressing the matter. "Yeah it's par for the course for Millward's type. Anyway, congratulations on a great bust, and thanks again for all your help, particularly at our training complex. If there's ever anything I can do for you, just holler."

Devon was about to ring off when he sensed something in the other man's momentary silence. "What is it, Commander?"

"I was.... was just wondering how Sonia and Christopher are doing? Any chance I could call and see them?"

"All things considered, they're doing great. We've relocated them and I want to keep them safe for a while without any visitors."

"I understand... will you tell them I said hi?"

The penny dropped for Devon. "Why don't you do that in person? I'll arrange something in the next day or so."

Devon returned to his study of the Hayden papers, still trying to get his head around Hall's personal interest in Sonia. Goodness knows, the woman had been through a lot, and could certainly be doing with a friend. *Go for it, Commander, and good luck to the both of you.*

He lifted a scanned copy of a series of handwritten notes and arrows, and re-read several lines that had caught his attention during an earlier run-through.

What's the American connection?

If Brer Rabbit3 is Rudi Valentine, who is pulling the strings in Boston? Is there a Brer Rabbit4?

Why did R and G travel to Boston on so many occasions? There are no records of any businesses tied to their names (not legitimate businesses anyway!) so what's their interest there? Who are they meeting?

Are R and G at the top of the pyramid?

Manning is connected to R and G, but who is their American political puppet? Could it be Senator Theodore Armstrong? Why does his name keep cropping up? Who he is working with?

Devon thumped the desk in annoyance. Who the hell were R and G? Why hadn't Hayden spelt out their names the same way he had with others? He quickly skimmed through more than thirty pages, but couldn't find any clue to the identity of the mysterious duo. Or maybe these weren't the initials of individuals. Maybe it was the name of a company? He resolved to get Halloran and the techies to mount an immediate search.

They had already reached a dead end with the name of Rudi Valentine. His body had been found in a top hotel and carried all the hallmarks of a professional hit. Despite hours scouring financial records, nothing had been found linking Valentine to Manning, or any of the other key players. In fact, the man's history was squeaky clean and wouldn't have been worth a second look were it not for Hayden's references to him. No wonder these bastards had flown under the radar for so long!

Maybe they'd do better with this Senator Armstrong? Hayden had seemed confident enough about wrongdoing to include his name among the roll of dishonour in the manuscript, so maybe he was worth a follow-up. Yes, he'd get *LonWash* American agents Don Hill and Marta Tessler to dig up what they could on the Senator. And he'd make sure they didn't bother Doyle with what they were doing. The big man had enough on his plate.

"Alan, will you please stop pacing up and down? You're making my head light."

"I'm sorry, darling," Doyle responded as he settled into the bedside seat and gingerly lifted Chelsea Horgan's hand. "You know me, I hate being cooped up."

"Oh, so you'd rather be somewhere else?" she said playfully.

"No, no, I just can't wait to get you out of this hospital, so that I can look after you properly. I'm no good at not being able to do anything."

"Alan, we both have to accept that it will be at least another week before they let me go, and even then, I'll not be much use for anything for a good while. You can't be my nursemaid on a twenty-four-seven basis. Mom and dad will pamper me at home, so why don't you head back to London for a while?"

"That's not an option," he scowled. "I'm not leaving here and that's my final word on the subject. You'll just have to get used to this ugly mug every time you wake up."

Horgan's reply was cut short by three visitors who marched into the room. Doyle followed her gaze. "What are you doing here? I thought I made it clear this ward is out of bounds."

Homeland Security agent Robert T Younger held up his hands in a gesture of apology. "Sorry for barging in, but I need to go over a few things with you. I'm glad to see you're doing well, Miss Horgan, and I promise not to intrude any further. Perhaps you wouldn't mind if I borrowed your...er... fiancé for a while."

Doyle leapt from the seat. "I told you before, Younger, I've nothing more to say to you people. Now, get the fuck outta here'" To emphasise the point, he pushed the DHS man hard against the door, and turned to stare menacingly at the other two agents who stepped forward to intervene.

"Alan, Alan, please don't...."

Horgan's faltering voice made him break off the confrontation and rush to her side. He knelt down and whispered in her ear. "I'm sorry, darling, but there's something about these jokers that makes me want to wipe the smug looks off their faces every time I see them."

She smiled at him. "I know their manners aren't exactly all they might be, but go with them and hear what they have to say. I could do with a few hours' sleep and you could do with some fresh air. Go and play, and be nice to the other kids."

He kissed her gently on the forehead, stood up to inhale a calming breath, and barged through the agents on his way to the corridor.

Thirty minutes later, the DHS Crown Victoria pulled into a rundown compound on the edge of an industrial complex and rolled to a stop beside a building with boarded-up windows surrounded by weed-infested gardens.

"Can't say I admire what passes for federal offices these days," Doyle said with more than a hint of disdain.

"It's one of our safe houses," Younger responded with curious pride. "Don't let the outside fool you; we have all the mod-cons, including some state-of-the-art surveillance recordings I want you to take a look at."

Doyle shrugged and climbed from the passenger seat. "Let's get this over with. I know you probably don't want my company any longer than I want yours, so if it's all the same to you, our business together will end after this."

He followed Younger through a dilapidated front door and into a lobby that was covered in dust and reeked of a dozen musty odours. Doyle's inner alarm screamed. Before he could react, he felt a pain on the right side of his head at the same time as his muscles turned to jelly. Suddenly, he pitched forward into blackness, oblivious to the three DHS agents smiling at each other.

He was also unaware of Younger's words to his two colleagues. "Well, he got that right. Our business together will soon be coming to an end."

Chapter 38

IT WAS EASY TO understand why people might be fooled by Senator Theodore Armstrong. He had one of those homely, favourite-uncle faces that generated trust and bonhomie in equal measures, and a persona that was enhanced by chubby cheeks with a painted-on permanent grin. Give him a white beard and a pair of spectacles and he'd make the ideal store Santa Claus.

But – if you knew where to look – there was a dark side to the four-term Senator from Maine. There were pointers to an alter ego that was a far cry from the aura that Armstrong liked to portray, and all of them would have made any parent think twice about letting their son or daughter bounce on the knee of this particular fraudster.

As Devon stared at the ten-by-eight colour photograph, he saw glimpses of the real Senator. Okay, he had to admit, the fact that he'd read Hayden's revelations about the conspiracies and pocket-lining shenanigans of the subject under scrutiny made it easier to look beyond the winning smile. The eyes were a giveaway; two elliptic pieces of obsidian untouched by the fakery around them. Hard, callous eyes that were windows into a soul without compassion, like a feral cat skulking in the bushes waiting to pounce on its next victim.

There was something unsettling about the wide rubbery lips, the bulbous nose, and the bushy eyebrows that could hardly be described as handsome, in much the same way as the red welt of a birthmark which covered most of the right side of a squat neck. The teeth were altogether too perfect, nothing more than two sets of unnaturally-white crowns and veneers that were as out of place as a small gold stud earring that glistened under the flash of a photographer's light.

It was all a sham, an attempt to mask the real being that

lurked below the surface. Devon could almost visualise the Senator's features transform into those of a snarling, petulant and dangerous animal at the first sign of someone rattling his cage.

And that was exactly what Devon intended to do.

But first, he needed a break. Sonia and Christopher Hayden were safely tucked up in General Sandford's Mayfair home, a location far more secure than any safe house and one the Old Man had insisted upon, particularly because these days he seemed to spend more time being pampered at his club. Agents Jim Cross and Dan Gosling had been delegated as full-time minders, and free access was granted to Commander John Hall, the obviously-smitten SO19 chief who had become a third watchdog for the Hayden family.

Millward and Jennings, and what remained of their gang, were safely behind bars and the Whitehall leaks had all been plugged, the most notable taken care of by the assassination of the Home Secretary. The job of unravelling the intricate web of deceit would be a long-haul exercise, likely lasting months, and was now the responsibility of the techies and financial muscle-boys, rather than Devon's frontline agents.

The potential bomb sites had turned out to be nothing more than an elaborate hoax, although nobody was standing down just yet. The Metropolitan Police intended to keep their threat alerts at the highest levels, meaning the souped-up presence of armed officers within the Greater London area would continue for some time.

The motorcycle sniper was a big outstanding wrinkle. Alfie Cheadle and Terry Hunt had been pulled off guard duty to lead the hunt for the gunman, and had already begun the painstaking search of CCTV footage from hundreds of cameras on the approach routes to London from the Home Secretary's country address. Sooner or later they'd get lucky.

All that remained – and it was the most important part of this sorry mess – was finding the people who had yanked everyone's chain. They had to be pretty influential figures to have put together such elaborate schemes, which had included subverting some heavy hitters at the centre of government. These shadowy figures were part of the long game, and would eventually be brought into the light only after the careful dissection of the Hayden dossier.

All in all, that left Devon with the prospect of time on his hands, a rare luxury he intended to make full use of. He'd already put the company's Dassault jet on standby for a trip to Boston, an opportunity for a pre-Christmas break for Emma and little Michael, and an excuse to catch up with Doyle and Horgan. Not surprisingly, Emma had jumped at the idea and was already busily packing more clothes than they would need for a week-long trip.

As Devon headed out the door, his satphone vibrated in a pouch clipped to his waistband. Caller ID showed the name of *LonWash* American agent Don Hill.

"Hi Mike, it's Don, just giving you an update on our research into Senator Armstrong."

"Good to hear from you. Anything interesting?"

"Honestly, I don't know where to start. This guy has his fingers in so many pies we've lost count of the corporations and charities he's mixed up in, and not all of them are whiter than white. There are rumours that he's in bed with all sorts of shady types, including organised-crime bosses, but everyone seems to be running scared of investigating what he gets up to. The word is that he's got Homeland Security in his back pocket, mainly because he's their mouthpiece for getting bigger and bigger shares of federal budgets."

Devon bristled at the news. "In other words, Don, an all-round scumbag?"

"Seems like, although we've got a lot more ferreting to do."

"Take your time on this one, Don. I don't want to spook the bastard. Be patient and make sure you cover your tracks. I want this dickhead to get the biggest shock of his life when we eventually confront him."

"Understood."

"One more thing, Don. I'm paying a surprise visit to Boston to drop in on Doyle. I kind of miss that ugly face, but don't tell him I said so, and don't let him know I'm coming. I want to surprise the big ape."

Hill chuckled down the line. "He'll be glad to see you, Mike. He keeps asking for things to do, but we're staying out of his way, just as you asked."

It took a long time and a lot of willpower for Doyle to claw through the black mist towards a faint light that shimmered on a spot far above him and seemingly out of reach. He ignored the pain and the silver asterisks that danced across his vision like an exploding roman candle intent on preventing his escape from whatever hellhole he'd been cast into. Finally, he forced open his eyes, immediately regretting the decision as a bright glare drilled into his brain and added one more layer of pain to the mother of all headaches.

A fluorescent tube dangled a few feet above his aching brain and for a moment he thought he was going through one of those out-of-body experiences where he was floating heavenward while his mortal remains were left to rot where he'd died. The flickering of three distinctive shadows and the sound of a voice told him he was still very much alive.

"Good to see you've decided to rejoin us, Mr Doyle, although I dare say you'll come to regret it."

He tried to move, but couldn't. He was lying on his back atop a long wooden bench, his arms folded underneath and bound with plasticuffs that dug deep into his wrists. His legs were encased in duct tape that pinioned him to the bench like a turkey wrapped up and ready for the oven.

He swivelled his head to catch sight of DHS agent Robert T Younger. "What the fuck's going on? How did I miss the part that we're not on the same side?"

Younger smirked. "Not so cocky now, Mr Doyle. I told you before that we can't have outsiders running amok in the middle of our well-ordered scheme of things and I now intend to get to the bottom of everything there is to know about your little operation."

"Christ, man, are you off your fucking head? We were on a routine surveillance of two Tunisians when we stumbled across a bomb at......"

His words were cut short by a blow to the solar plexus. It was a hard, vicious whack that drove the air from his lungs and brought the silver asterisks back onto the dance floor. He ignored the pain and concentrated on sucking hard to replenish his oxygen supply, at the same time as his fogged brain tried to work out what the hell was going on. He looked up through watery eyes and saw that Younger held a length of plastic hosepipe that whipped through the air as another blow landed.

"I'm not here to play games with you, Doyle, so cut out the bullshit about innocent surveillance and tell me what really brought you here. I have a nervous principal who needs to know if he's been compromised by some intelligence that you Brits have somehow managed to drag up. We both know this goes beyond a few scumbag Tunisians, and the sooner you start talking the sooner the pain stops."

He nodded at his two companions who walked into view carrying a bucket and a dirty towel. Doyle had seen the props too many times not to know what was in store. "I see Homeland Security's interrogation methods still haven't stretched beyond waterboarding. Nice of you to think about my thirst. I could do with a good drink."

Younger's face turned purple. "Keep it up, Brit, we'll see if you're still full of quips when we've finished. But first, a little taster to soften you up."

The hosepipe blurred through the air. Doyle felt his stomach, legs and feet catch fire under the merciless onslaught, which seemed to go on forever and which he knew was causing real damage to his muscles and bones. These bastards really meant business! Just as he was on the verge of unconsciousness, the attack halted, providing respite only for the pain to travel through his body and light a thousand touchpapers at the tips of frayed nerve-ends.

A damp towel smacked across his face, followed by a cascade of water that made him smack his lips tight and hold his breath. He knew how it worked. The stream would continue until he was forced to expel air and take in water that would fill his lungs unless the torturers knew exactly what they were doing. The trick was to simulate drowning without letting it actually happen. Go to the edge, remove the towel, let the victim breathe, and then start over again. And again. And again.

Thirty minutes later, Doyle sensed he was nearing the end. He couldn't take much more of this; better to gulp down the water and free himself from the agonies. *Fuck that! I'll not give these bastards the satisfaction.*

The pause between breaths was much longer this time. The interrogation was about to start. Right on cue, Younger's voice cut through the pain. "What do you know about Senator Armstrong? How did you know he had a planned meeting on the *Spirit of Enterprise* yacht at Boston Haven?"

Doyle was genuinely perplexed. What were they banging on about? Who the fuck was Senator Armstrong? He shook his head vigorously, not trusting his ability to say the words.

The towel went back on his face.

Chapter 39

THE DASSAULT FALCON 2000Ex settled into her cruise speed of 0.8 Mach at an altitude of thirty-nine thousand feet above the Atlantic, close to mid-point on the London to Boston flight path. It was still three hours from Logan International when a light flashed on the passenger cabin's Iridium ST3100 Aircell unit, an instant access link to all manner of satellite communications.

Devon had been watching his son Michael curled up fast asleep on a reclined executive seat when the sharp beep interrupted hopes of grabbing his own forty winks. He rose and walked forward to the console's push-button control pad, and waited a few seconds for wavy electronic lines on a monitor to morph into a screen shot of Don Hill, sitting red-eyed and grim-faced in front of a desktop PC camera.

He knew things had to be urgent for *Lonwash's* senior American operative to be making contact in this fashion. "What is it, Don?"

"Mike, we've got a situation here. Alan Doyle has gone missing. He left the hospital eight hours ago with three DHS agents and hasn't been seen since. I've tried contacting the local office, but they say they know nothing about any planned meeting and have refused to put me in direct contact with their people. I'm getting the run-around about classified information and the dangers of interrupting agents on assignment. The bottom line is that we haven't a clue where they are or what they're up to."

Devon felt the first stirrings of panic. He didn't like what he was hearing, more so because he knew Doyle would not have left Chelsea Horgan's side for that length of time unless.... The thought hung in the air. "How come we're only hearing about this now?"

Hill cleared his throat. "I spoke to Chelsea a short while

ago. She says she fell asleep for most of the afternoon and was awakened only by the visit of her parents. She immediately tried to contact Alan on his mobile, but got no answer and that's when she contacted me."

"Who did he leave the hospital with?"

"Chelsea says it was agent Robert T Younger and two other men whose names she never got. They were at the hospital before and said they wanted to go over a few things with Alan to clear up loose ends. Chelsea urged him to go to help take his mind off things but, as you can imagine, she's feeling guilty about what might have happened to him."

Devon could understand her trepidation. Something was badly off here, although for the life of him he couldn't put his finger on it. Surely, if Homeland Security wanted specific information, they could channel their requests back through London. He knew Doyle would stonewall their questions, so a mop-up interview was unlikely to last beyond the first cup of coffee, assuming they even offered him one. What were they after, and what was taking them eight hours to get it? The answers when they came were not what he wanted to contemplate.

"Mike, what do you want me to do?"

Devon's gears began to synchromesh. "Don, didn't you tell me that Senator Armstrong was in bed with Homeland Security?"

"Yes, but what's that...."

"What if Armstrong's using these DHS grunts to do his dirty work? Maybe he's figured out that what happened at the Boston warehouse is too close to home? Could be he wants to know if his name has come up in any fall-out from the discovery of a dirty bomb on his doorstep."

"But surely, Mike, DHS wouldn't let themselves be used in this way. It would be a bit of a reach for the Senator to expect them to do his bidding without them realising the wider implications."

"Not if these were rogue agents already on the Senator's payroll. If that's the case, I don't give Doyle much chance of getting out of whatever situation he's in. I've no doubt he walked into a trap that even with his considerable skills would be hard to handle on a three-to-one basis. We've got to find him and pray we're not too late."

"How do you figure on doing that?"

Devon paused to gather his thoughts. This was no time for protocols or niceties. He needed leverage – and he needed it fast. He barked out a list of orders, waiting impatiently for Hill to scribble notes on a pad in front of his monitor. When he finished going through a checklist, he broke communications and sagged into his chair, wondering if he'd ever see his friend alive again.

Emma's soft voice cut through the torment. The last time he looked his wife had been fast asleep and he hadn't realised she heard his conversation with Hill.

"Oh, my God, Mike, is Alan going to be alright? Why would they do this to him? Will you be able to get to him in time?"

"Truthfully, Em, I don't know. You heard what I asked Hill to do?"

"Yes."

"Are you okay to go along with everything?"

"Of course! You do whatever it takes to get Alan. Michael and I will be fine."

He looked at his watch. Still two hours to touchdown.

Doyle had no way of knowing how long he'd been unconscious. When he did resurface, all he knew was that the pains and aches were still there, his throat was constricted and burning from the endless coughing fits, and he could feel bile trying to force its way from his stomach into his esophagus. He was on his last reserves of energy and willpower.

A familiar monotonous drone echoed across the derelict room. "You're a tough bastard, Doyle, I'll give you that. But the time for heroics is over; why not do yourself a favour and come clean. This will all end as soon as you start co-operating."

Doyle spoke through chapped lips, his voice barely more

than a whisper. "Go fuck yourself."

"Have it your own way then. You must know by now that we can't let you live; we've come too far down the road for that, although I *can* offer you an alternative. Surely a bullet to the brain is better than going through these agonies? Start talking and this will be over, quicker than you can say Smith and Wesson."

"What do you want to know?"

"That's better! Has Senator Armstrong's name been implicated in any investigations? Why was your organisation looking into the Senator? What is it that you think he's done wrong?"

Doyle motioned with his eyes for Younger to lean closer. When the DHS agent's ear tilted towards Doyle's mouth he was tempted to bite a chunk off, figuring things couldn't get any worse than they already were. Instead, Doyle smiled and whispered. "We heard he was banging your old lady and picked up syphilis from all those other men she's been shacked up with while you and your limp dick are running around playing treason with a bunch of lowlifes. How's that for starters?"

Younger pushed away from the bench and hoisted the plastic tube, his lips curled in a murderous rage. Blow upon blow rained down with such force that one of them smashed through Doyle's prosthetic arm. It was an out-of-control assault that ended only when the DHS man inadvertently landed two heavy strikes across Doyle's temple.

Younger's colleagues rushed in to stop the onslaught. By that time, Doyle had already descended into a hole that was blacker and deeper than he could have ever imagined.

Devon carried his son down the steps of the jet and walked across the tarmac to two waiting *LonWash* SUVs. He introduced Emma to Don Hill and Marta Tessler, before carefully placing Michael across the back seat of one of the vehicles. The youngster was still thankfully fast asleep.

A US Customs and Border Protection agent moved from the shadows of an executive hangar and introduced himself to the new arrivals. He made a cursory inspection of the diplomatic papers Devon was entitled to carry with him, and then signalled that the group were free to leave via a separate airport off-road reserved for dignitaries. The arrangements had been prepared in advance by General Sandford back in London.

Devon kissed Emma and watched her climb in beside her son in the first SUV. "Tell Chelsea we'll bring him back safe."

"I know you will, Mike."

Tessler headed for the driver's door, but was stopped before she got halfway. Devon placed a hand on her shoulder. "Get them to the hospital safely and stay with them at all times."

"They'll be fine, Mike, I promise."

He watched the vehicle as it swept through the gates and barrelled along the one-lane exit road, waiting until it was lost in the distance before turning to Hill. "Did you get everything we need? Is Armstrong still in Boston?"

"Yes, we got a bit of luck there. He's hosting a late-night dinner party at one of the city's most exclusive restaurants. It's only due to start about now."

"How far are we from the location?"

"It'll take us about forty minutes to get across town. The traffic's relatively light, so we shouldn't run into any hold-ups."

"Good job, Don. What are we waiting for?"

Chapter 40

TODD HAMILTON'S EYES lingered on the Honda Fireblade for several minutes before he draped an oily tarpaulin over its sleek bodywork, knowing he'd probably looked at it for the final time. Thanks to London's all-pervasive CCTV cameras and traffic cam networks, the bike had become a liability, one he couldn't afford to take a gamble on. They were probably already out there, tracking his previous movements, and beating a path to his door. But he'd stay one step ahead, just as he'd always done.

He knew some lens or another could have picked him up during the initial motorway pursuit of the Hayden family from the *LonWash* offices at Charterhouse Street, and he could certainly have been spotted when that damned helicopter overflew his position at the airfield. What wasn't in doubt was that fucker who'd chased him across the fields after the Charles Manning assassination had clocked him and his bike making a getaway. The Honda simply had to go.

The lock-up room he was standing in was a back-up storage unit that couldn't be traced back to him. It was rented through an alias, paid for annually in advance, and was one of several hundred crammed into a four-acre site near Gatwick airport. When he'd arrived a few hours earlier, he'd bolted the door, turned on a flickering fluorescent light, and sat down at a dressing table that looked incongruous among the usual detritus of castaway machine parts, cardboard boxes and the general bric-a-brac of a hoarder.

He removed a handkerchief from his jacket pocket and began wiping dust off the dressing table mirror. Next, he opened a top drawer and removed a large brown envelope, the contents of which he spilled across the top of the table. Rooting through the small mound of papers, he selected one of a half-dozen passports and folded it open at the page that held his photograph. He'd changed somewhat from when the picture-booth print was taken, but knew it would take little effort to restore the look from the array of make-up and personal grooming kits stored in the other drawers.

He used a trimmer to reshape his hair and cut away his beard to the desired length of designer stubble, and finished by adding a pair of plain-glass, black-framed spectacles that matched those in the passport photo. Satisfied with the transformation, he stripped off his clothes, tore open one of the boxes, and dressed in new clothes that were vacuum-packed in neat layers. The dark blue suit, white shirt and rainbow tie fitted snugly over his frame, complementing the Gucci shoes and overcoat that looked as if they'd just been plucked from a shop-window mannequin.

Finally, he opened the bottom drawer, removed a walnut-brown leather suitcase, and began filling it with a number of items that didn't exactly gel with his new persona of a smart business executive. First in was a Smith & Wesson Model 41 pistol, plus two 12-round spare magazines, followed by two small bricks of C4 explosive with det cord and arming switch already moulded into the plasticine-type surface. A small combat knife was tucked into one of the suitcase folds, and an array of useless paperwork and files was crammed into all compartments. The contents would pass a routine inspection, but not much more than that.

His only regret was that he'd have to leave behind the Remington 700 rifle and scope. It would be good for only one of his two targets, and one would not be enough to trigger the quarter of a million payment that still awaited the successful elimination of Sonia and Christopher Hayden. It was not the sort of money he could afford to walk away from. He had a new life waiting for him in the South of France, and he'd need every penny to engineer a rebirth.

He'd heard the news that Millward and his gang had been captured in what the media had been told was a failed terrorist plot. He'd known from then that the Haydens were alive, and would most likely be returned to London. He'd pick up their trail somehow, and finish the job that had started with the bombing of the cottage in Yorkshire. His only point of reference was Charterhouse Street, the base of the security company responsible for safeguarding his targets.

The Bell helicopter settled on the rooftop pad at Charterhouse Street. *LonWash* agents Jim Cross and Dan Gosling stepped out, ushering the Haydens towards a small door cut into the building's southside façade, away from the prying eyes of workers in surrounding multi-storey office blocks.

The group descended two floors to the main control room and settled into seats around the conference table. Waiting for them was General Sir John Sandford, his smile a genuine display of relief. "I can't tell you how glad I am to see you've made it through what must have been a terrible ordeal. Please accept my apologies for the breaches in security, but rest assured you're safe now."

Sonia returned his smile. "We're grateful for everything you've done for us, General, but if it's all the same to you we'd like to return home and try to pick up the pieces of our lives."

"Quite so, Mrs Hayden. I understand fully your desire for some normality, although I have to tell you there are still some loose ends to be tied up. I don't intend to take any chances with your safety until we've finally buttoned down this thing for good, so I would ask you to be guests at my home in Mayfair for just another few days. I'll stay out of your hair to allow you and Christopher the chance of some privacy, after which I will do everything I can to see that your futures are taken care of."

Sonia frowned. "That's very good of you. I hope you would understand, however, that we have to learn to stand on our own two feet. No disrespect, General, but the sooner we get away from all of this, the better."

"Spoken like a real trooper," Sandford beamed. "Would you mind indulging an old man for just a while longer? Agents Cross and Gosling will go with you to Mayfair, and then we'll see about getting you back to your own den by the end of the week. Do we have a deal?"

Sonia looked across at her son, who was nodding his head in agreement. "Looks like you're stuck with us for a while longer."

General Sandford's Mayfair home was everything you'd expect in one of London's most desirable quarters. A three-story Victorian mansion, wedged into a crescent of similar buildings, it had stunning views of Hyde Park and the cluster of renowned hotels, including the Dorchester, which dotted the nearby golden mile of Park Lane.

Sonia stood admiring the view for just a moment before she turned on her heels and fixed the *LonWash* agents with a determined look. "I need to do some shopping, and I won't take no for an answer. Christopher and I could do with some new clothes, and other personal items, and I fully intend to march out of here to the nearest Primark store I can find."

Gosling glanced at Cross and both burst out laughing.

"What's so funny?" Sonia said tetchily.

"Forgive me, Mrs Hayden, but the General was one step ahead of you. He left instructions for us to take you to Harrods and to charge all items on his account. Looks like we've got a busy afternoon ahead of us."

Todd Hamilton sat in a hire car a hundred yards from the Sandford house. He'd got lucky with his surveillance of Charterhouse Street, watching the group leave from the basement garage barely an hour after he'd turned up. The faces of the Haydens could be clearly seen in the back of the vehicle.

He'd tailed the SUV to Mayfair and watched his targets enter one of the houses, a plum residence to be sure, but hardly a state-of-the-art safe area. He could simply march up to the door on some pretext or another, shoot whoever stood in his way, and get the hell out of there before anyone realised what had happened. He wouldn't even need the explosives, although he might set a few charges just for dramatic after-effect.

He opened the briefcase, removed the Smith & Wesson, and screwed a suppressor into the threaded barrel. Just as he was about to climb from his car, the door of the house opened and four figures descended the steps towards the parked SUV. Within minutes, they headed west, merging into traffic, and making it easy for him to follow.

Thirty minutes later, he watched incredulously as the vehicle drew to a stop at the pavement beside Harrods. A uniformed doorman walked forward, accepted the keys, and drove off to a nearby store car park, leaving the group eyeing the Christmas-dressed windows of one of the world's most iconic shops.

The fuckers are going shopping! This must be my lucky day!

Chapter 41

THE FOUR MINDERS were easy to spot as Devon walked into the restaurant lobby. They were typical caricatures of muscle sans brain, believing their bulk and menace was enough to dissuade anyone from venturing close to their domain. True to form, the ability to blend in and be subtle were not in the psyche of this particular quartet.

Devon couldn't understand why there were four of them. A United States Senator, no matter how powerful, didn't rate this level of protection, certainly not from the Secret Service who were usually charged with shadowing the more high-profile and vociferous members of Capitol Hill. Then again, Senator Theodore Armstrong could well afford his own private army, as much for the aura of importance they provided, as for guarding against any real danger.

It could be the minders might not all be attached to the Senator. The information Hill had received was that Armstrong was entertaining some friends, most likely other influential politicos who would rate their own security detail. There was only one way to find out.

Devon and Hill marched forward to a man standing behind a plinth near the entrance to a room marked *The Kennedy Kitchen*, a somewhat downmarket name in honour of one of Boston's most notable sons. The restaurant seating clerk looked up at the new arrivals. "Good evening, do you gentlemen have a reservation?"

"We're not here to eat," Devon told him forcibly. "I believe Senator Armstrong is dining this evening and I need to speak with him as a matter of urgency. Please be so good as to show me where I can find him."

The clerk shook his head. "I'm afraid that won't be possible. The Senator is in one of our private rooms and has asked not to be disturbed."

Devon beckoned the man to lean forward and whispered in his ear. "Trust me, the Senator will want to see me. I have urgent presidential briefing papers for him, and he won't take too kindly to any delay."

"Of course, sir. He's in the Lincoln Room at the bottom of the corridor." A shaky finger pointed Devon to a corridor behind where the minders were seated. One of them rose and bulled his way across the foyer.

"Just hang on there a minute feller. Where do you think you're going?"

There were only two ways that Devon could play this. He could stand and debate the issue, which would likely become a protracted shouting match with a goon who understood only his standing order of not allowing the Senator to be disturbed. Or there was always the more direct way.

Devon went for the latter. He met the minder halfway, in a classic example of the immovable object meeting an unstoppable force, and hammered a vicious punch into the man's kidneys. There was a soft grunt, a bulging of eyes, and a look of bewilderment as the immovable object dropped to his knees. The fight had well and truly gone out of him.

Hill stepped smartly up to the table where the other minders sat open-mouthed. He brushed aside the corner of his jacket, showing his hip holster and flashing a warning look. "Not your fight, gentlemen. Just sit tight and this will all be over soon." He mouthed an *I've-got-this* message to Devon and settled into a seat, his Glock pistol now resting below a serviette.

Devon left the foyer and made his way down a short corridor. He stopped beside a closed door, pasted on a false smile, and confidently pressed the handle, stepping into a room full of cigar smoke and loud laughter.

There were eight people present, all of them male, and most on the wrong side of seventy. The city's great and good, enjoying the fruits of their labours away from the common man. At the head of the table was the unmistakeable figure of Senator Theodore Armstrong, full of the joys of life and regaling his audience with some tall tale or other. The mask of civility slipped totally at the sight of an unwarranted intrusion. The voice, which a moment ago was full of warmth, was now coated in acid. "What's the meaning of this? How dare you intrude on a private party."

Devon tried for the most obsequious front he could muster. He needed to ratchet things down, figuring the best way to achieve this was to go directly to the man's vanity and sense of importance. "Forgive me, sir, but I have an urgent message from the President. He needs your input on a matter of national security and has asked me to deliver briefing notes for your eyes only before he contacts you."

To emphasise the point, Devon removed his Iridium satellite phone and held it aloft. "A direct line is already established to the White House. Perhaps there is somewhere we can go so that you can talk to the President?"

Armstrong's smile returned. "It seems the affairs of state must take precedence, gentlemen. Sometimes I wish I were back on my Vermont farm with nothing to worry about other than next season's new stock of stallions. But, as they say, duty calls." He pushed back his seat and nodded to a door on his right. "We'll use the manager's office. I'm sure he won't mind."

Devon waited until the office door was closed and Armstrong had eased his considerable bulk into the manager's chair. He walked behind the Senator and delivered a short knuckle-punch to the exposed neck, a blow intended to disorientate rather than incapacitate.

He then walked to the front of the desk, took out his Sig Sauer P226, and stared into the frightened watery eyes of his captive. "I'm not going to fuck around with you, Senator. A friend of mine is in trouble and I know you can help me track him down. The sooner you start talking, the better will be your chances of living through the night." To emphasise the point, he pushed the pistol against Armstrong's forehead, burrowing the snub-nosed suppressor into the folds of skin.

Armstrong wheezed for several seconds and tried to find

his voice. "Are you completely mad? I'm a United States Senator, under the full protection of federal authorities. You'll spend the rest of your days in Leavenworth for this unwarranted assault."

"Cut the crap, you tub of lard. We know all about you and your conniving money-making schemes. We have it all; the offshore bank accounts, the paperwork trail that shows you immersed in treasonable and terrorist acts, the ways in which you've manipulated government projects, your third-party Wall Street share-dealing escapades, and the misuse of federal agents to carry out your every whim. It took two years for a rather special and dedicated member of the Secret Intelligence Service back in London to run you to ground, but he got there in the end, even at the cost of his own life."

Devon was filling in the blanks with guesswork, but he was on a roll. "We know about your ties with financiers and industrialists and people like the British Home Secretary, a man I caught up to a few nights ago. You might have read about his apparent suicide, although we both now know differently." It seemed expedient to take credit for the death of Charles Manning, and judging by the look of terror on Armstrong's face, the message had got through.

"That's right, Senator, I'm here to clear house. The good news is that there's a get-out-of-jail-card, if you want it. This friend of mine is someone I badly want to see alive, much more than I want to see you dead. He's been held by your puppet Homeland Security agent, Robert T Younger, and all you need to do is make a phone call instructing him to back off."

The Senator's eyes flickered recognition at the mention of Younger's name. When he spoke, however, there was a renewed bullishness to his voice. "This is all fanciful nonsense! Even if what you say is true, how can I trust you to do what you say. You could still put a bullet into my brain, or release these so-called scraps of evidence you have. I must say, as a negotiator you've a lot to learn, son."

Devon stepped back from the desk and fired. A chunk of upholstery blew out from the top of the Senator's chair, sending the man pitching forward, holding his head as if to confirm it was still intact.

"How about this for negotiation? You've just had your final warning," Devon told him. "You're right about not being able to trust me, but what are the alternatives? If you don't do what I ask, I'll kill you here and now. If you stall any longer, and I find my friend dead, I'll come back and finish the job. Make the call and get me out of your hair. All I want to do is return to London and leave Uncle Sam to clear up his own mess. Sooner or later, you'll get what's coming to you. Right now, the choice is yours."

Devon could almost hear the cogs turning in Armstrong's brain. He was scared, sure, but he was also a formidable foe, a man used to always getting his own way. People like him didn't climb to the top of the tree without ruthlessly clambering over weaker souls. He needed time to come to the right decision. He needed to know he really *had* run out of options.

Time was a luxury Devon didn't have. He had to buy every second possible to give Doyle a fighting chance of surviving whatever ordeal he was currently undergoing, but killing the Senator would shut the door tight on any chances of finding his friend still alive.

Devon wanted to look at his watch; the temptation to hurry things along was too great, particularly when Armstrong appeared to be stonewalling. Despite the risk, he had to take a gamble.

"Time's up, Senator. Either you make the call, or I'll cut you a new hole just above the bridge of your nose. There's no wriggle room here."

Armstrong watched as Devon pointed the weapon at his forehead. It was not the misshapen tube that worried him. It was the cold hard eyes staring along the sight line. There was no doubting this man's resolve to kill him, but he'd be damned if he'd simply roll over. He let twenty seconds elapse before he responded, his voice laced with as much steely determination as he could muster. "You'll get your phone call, but only if I get two things in return."

Chapter 42

THERE'S NOTHING MODEST about Harrods department store. Located on Brompton Road in the heart of Knightsbridge, it describes itself as the world's most famous luxury sales outlet, with a catchy slogan to match its lofty aspirations. Its promise of *Omnia Omnibus Ubique* (all things for all people) means it needs every inch of one million square feet of retail space to house its vast collections of goods.

The problem for Todd Hamilton, as he pushed through the main door five minutes after the Hayden party had already entered the building, was guessing where they could possibly be among the three-hundred-odd separate departments within the six-storey building. It was a case of first finding the haystack, and then looking for the needle. More than two thousand shoppers were usually milling about the premises, even on "quiet" days and, with Christmas looming, there was no hope of anything other than a crushing throng.

A quick glance at the melee told him it would be a waste of time to start looking. The ground floor central aisle was jammed solid with people, each waiting their turn to divert towards individual display areas, or fight their way to the bank of elevators and escalators at both ends of the building.

The best option, he decided, would be to head for the car park, locate the SUV and attach a C4 bomb to its undercarriage. Job done. The only problem was that he had to rely on a simple timer switch, one that needed to be preset to a guesstimate of how long his victims would take to return to their vehicle. He had no means of wiring the unit to the car's ignition, or using a mercury tilt, or hiding in the shadows with his finger on a remote control. Without these luxuries, he was hamstrung.

He'd just have to go with the forlorn hope of tracking his quarry somewhere within this vast edifice. What he needed was another sprinkling of luck.

And he got it!

Sonia Hayden's blonde hair swayed above the heads on an escalator heading to the first floor. He recognised her immediately, noting with relief that the rest of her party were in tow, eyes fixed forward, oblivious to the danger lurking behind them. The quartet were smiling and talking, the excitement of shopping evident from their total lack of caution. This would be easier than he could have hoped for.

Hamilton shouldered his way through the crowd and stepped on the staircase, allowing its slow ascent to carry him upwards some twenty steps behind the Haydens. He was in no rush, and certainly didn't want to attract attention by trying to force his way closer to the group.

He stepped off at the top and walked down a lingerie aisle that kept him parallel with his targets. His fist closed around the butt of the Smith & Wesson, hidden in a generous pocket of his overcoat. A round was chambered, the safety off, and he was good to go. All it needed was to pick the right moment, which came a lot sooner than he expected.

Sonia stopped at a display rack for men's designer hoodies and held one in front of Christopher. The two minders, who were facing away from Hamilton, appeared intent on throwing in opinions of her choice, one even going so far as to lift another garment to make a comparison.

Hamilton moved into a small passageway and headed straight for Christopher Hayden. The pistol cleared the pocket and was held by his side as he stopped within ten feet of what he'd decided would be his first victim. It would all be over within a matter of seconds.

Alfie Cheadle emerged from the umpteenth fruitless search of an empty building during a morning spent chasing down tenuous leads from CCTV footage. Until four hours earlier, he hadn't realised how many fucking motorbikes used the streets of London for the daily commute of their owners, or whatever other reasons these helmeted jackasses threw their leg over a steel mustang. Personally, he could never see the attraction.

He tried to narrow the search down to the rough outline of machine size and colour he'd caught a glimpse of during the helicopter flyover at Stansted airport, but dividing thousands of potential hits by a factor of only three or four, still left a lot of possibilities. This was a wild goose chase, and then some.

"Let's head back to the office," he told Terry Hunt forlornly. "I'll check in to see where everybody is, and maybe take a fresh look at where we go from here. One thing's for certain, I'm not chasing down any more fucking motorbikes."

His first call went straight through to Dan Gosling. "Is everybody settling in alright?"

"Actually, Alfie, we're in the middle of Harrods, doing a bit of shopping."

Cheadle jumped forward on the seat. "What the fuck do you mean shopping? Are the Haydens with you?"

"Yes, we're...."

"Are you out of your mind? We still have at least one gunman on the loose, and you're parading our clients like staked-out goats. Get the fuck out of there now!"

"But General Sandford authorised the trip."

Cheadle bit hard on his lip. "With the greatest respect to General Sandford, this is the most idiotic thing I've ever heard. I'm ordering you now to clear the area and return to base! Can you hear me?"

The mobile connection cut abruptly, hardly surprising in a closed-in environment such as Harrods. But Cheadle couldn't help worrying that there was another explanation for the silence.

He thumped Hunt on the shoulder. "Get to Harrods now!

It took ten minutes of quick-fire driving for the *LonWash* Range Rover to punch its way through heavy afternoon traffic and slide to a halt in Brompton Road. The scene that greeted Cheadle was one he'd hoped not to see. "Christ, we're too late!"

People were running down the centre of the road, leaving a trail of discarded bags and packages in their wake, and screaming at the top of their voices. Behind them, hundreds more were attempting to wedge themselves free of the store's frontal exits, the pavement littered with bodies as men, women and children tripped, stumbled, and were crushed in the stampede.

Cheadle leapt from the vehicle and tried to make headway against the panicking tide of humanity, dropping one pace backwards for every two steps forward. He stared into confused and frightened faces, knowing it was useless to attempt to elicit information from any of the fleeing horde. Then he heard a woman yell. "There are gunmen in there. They're killing people."

The urgency in Cheadle's voice had made Dan Gosling swing his attention towards the blurred figures of shoppers in a circular sweep that stopped abruptly before he'd gone through one-eighty. There was something off about the well-dressed man approaching from the right.

The appearance of a gun in the man's right fist galvanised Gosling into action. It took a slow-motion nano-second for him to realise the weapon was pointed at the centre of Christopher Hayden's back. And that's the direction Gosling dived towards.

The nine-mil copper-jacketed bullet disintegrated Gosling's mobile phone and continued an unerring path through his chest and into his heart. He died long before his brain had the chance to transmit a pain signal. He pinwheeled backwards, taking Sonia and Christopher to the ground, and leaving a clear line of sight between the gunman and the second *LonWash* agent, Jim Cross.

Hamilton quickly adjusted his weapon to line up with Cross. It was a fast-action manoeuvre, typical of an accomplished operator, totally relaxed and at ease with the situation. There was no panic; no jerkiness. Just a cold-blooded, practised routine that had served him well throughout a life of violent crime. It should have been enough to get the job done.

Only this time it wasn't.

Cross had seen the alarm on his partner's face, and was already clearing his holster when the fatal shot struck home. By the time Gosling pitched to the ground, Cross had straight-armed his Glock 22, pointing it at the centre of the assassin's face. Their eyes met only briefly, but the image was lost in the explosion of gas and compression that sent Cross's bullet into Hamilton's left cheek. A follow-up insurance round through the middle of the forehead was nothing more than a training reflex.

Chapter 43

TEN MINUTES INTO a frantic drive across Boston, Devon was sweating profusely. He knew he was gambling with Doyle's life, although Senator Theodore Armstrong's ultimatum hadn't left much choice in the matter. Before giving up Doyle's location, the Senator had insisted on seeing all evidence gathered by the Matthew Hayden investigation. More than that, he wanted a five-minute head-start before texting the address. The only concession he'd agreed to was providing a general route, on the west side of the city, so that Devon could be as close as possible to the location when the message came through.

If it came through.

Devon had wasted five minutes contacting Tim Halloran in London to order an email transfer of a small section of the Hayden file direct to the Senator's smartphone. He'd refused point-blank to give anything other than the bare details of what had been uncovered about Armstrong's shady bank transfers and share dealings. "Take it or leave it, that's all you get. There's enough there for you to try to cover your back and warp any subsequent investigation. That's the only head-start I'm prepared to offer."

Armstrong pause for a moment before agreeing to the terms.

"One more thing," Devon said. "Even if you run, you can't hide. If I don't receive the location, or if my friend turns up dead, I'll hunt you down and kill you, no matter how long it takes."

The deal was not something Devon had wanted to do. However, Doyle's safety trumped any concerns about letting Armstrong go free.

As soon as the file transfer was received, Armstrong had got up and walked casually out of the restaurant, looking like a man who'd just busted the bank at Monte Carlo. His parting words were said with a sneer. "Wait until I've left and then head west. You'll get your location within five minutes."

It was now seven minutes since they'd seen the Senator's limousine disappear into the night. Devon and Hill were parked at a convenience garage, each staring intently at the dashboard mobile phone, willing it to flash into life. It remained stubbornly blank.

Five minutes after the agreed time, the phone finally chirped. Devon grabbed it, read the screen message, and shouted the address. Hill spun the wheels of the SUV on the loose gravel and accelerated through the light traffic onto the main road. "I think we're close to that location."

They found Doyle still tied to the bench, his head lying to one side above a small pool of blood on the dust-covered floor. The white face was covered in bruises, his shirt torn open to reveal vicious welts across his chest, and the prosthetic arm was bent at a crazy angle. It was a pitiful sight.

As Devon ran to his friend's side, it was easy to see what the interrogators had put him through. After kicking away a water bucket, sodden towels and plastic hosepipes, Devon knelt to check for a pulse. It was weak, but at least there was one.

"Call an ambulance!"

While Hill fidgeted with his mobile, Devon withdrew his Tanto knife from the leg sheath and began hacking through the plasticuffs. He cradled Doyle's head and lifted him into a seated position, trying to force air into the lungs by slapping his back and shouting encouragement.

"C'mon you big lug, come back to me!"

The eyelids flickered briefly to reveal a small opening. "Jesus, Mike, what are you...how did you get here."

Devon sighed with relief. "Take it easy."

"It was Homeland Security...Robert Younger...the bastard blindsided me."

"I know. We'll sort all that out later. Right now, we need to get you to hospital. Just lie back and relax."

Doyle forced a weak smile. "Do me a favour. Don't give me a drink; I've had enough water to last a lifetime."

With that, he lapsed back into unconsciousness.

Twelve hours later, Doyle was propped up in bed, sharing a ward with Chelsea Horgan, and demanding to be released. The senior doctor shook his head emphatically. "You have concussion, several cracked ribs, possible blood clots running through your veins, and a pair of lungs that need time to recover from being swamped with filthy water. I'd say you're lucky to be alive, so no more macho talk about throwing back the covers and marching out of here."

"I know you're trying to be careful, doc, but I feel great. Why not cut me some slack?"

"Don't answer him, doctor," Horgan said from the adjoining bed. "If he dares to leave this ward, I'll have to go after him, and who knows what damage that will do to me. I can't believe my fiancé could be so callous."

"Ah, Chelsea, that's not fair."

"Don't talk to me about fair, Alan Doyle," she chided. "I've been worried sick about you, and now you want to put me through all that again. Promise me you'll do what you're told."

"A lover's tiff, now that's what I call real therapy." Devon stepped into the room, followed closely by Emma, his son Michael, and agents Hill and Tessler. The group gathered around the two beds, as Devon shot an apologetic look at the doctor. "We promise not to stay long."

"Take all the time you need. I've other patients to see, and frankly I could do with a break from this one. I gather a replacement prosthetic is being sent out from London, so he can pass the time getting it into working order." He smiled as he hurried out of the room.

The small talk lasted fifteen minutes before Devon's face turned serious. "I think you both should know that Dan Gosling was shot and killed in London yesterday. The Old Man's taking it bad because he'd agreed to a shopping trip for the Haydens and that's when the hit took place."

"You're kidding," Doyle responded with sadness. "Good man, Dan, he didn't deserve that. Who did it?"

"We think it was the mysterious motorbike rider who was also responsible for Matthew Hayden's death. Thankfully Jim Cross nailed him and the Haydens are safe, although this thing just keeps stretching on and on. Can't help thinking we should have been more proactive."

"Nonsense, Mike, what else could we have done?"

"Maybe we lost a bit of focus," Devon said forlornly. "I think we forgot what we're about. Instead of playing investigators, we should have sanctioned everyone we came across, and made sure there was nobody around to give any more orders. I think it's time to go back to basics."

"Do you mean Senator Theodore Armstrong?"

"Just one on a long list. I let that bastard run in order to get the information on your whereabouts. As far as I'm concerned, that particular deal is now off."

Don Hill pushed forward. "The thing I don't understand is that the night we mounted surveillance on the yacht, there were only two people who left the area, and Senator Armstrong was not one of them. We have to now wonder just who those two gents were."

"Didn't you get photos, as we agreed?" There was an unexpected harshness to Devon's voice.

"The thing is, Mike, I turned those over to that Homeland Security jerk, Younger, so that he could run them through facial rec, although what are the chances that he actually did so?"

"Do you still have copies?"

"Yes, everything is automatically saved to my Cloud account."

"Rush them to Halloran in London. I want priority on finding these jokers."

General Sir John Sandford looked a broken man, hunched as he was over the boardroom table at *LonWash* headquarters in Charterhouse Street, and refusing eye contact with the men and women who walked in and out of the room. Guilt over the death of Dan Gosling pressed on his chest like an anvil, the weight of which he believed he thoroughly deserved.

He'd interfered, simple as that. He couldn't keep his nose out of it. Oh no, he had to act the beneficent patron, and now a good man was dead because he'd misjudged the danger. He really had believed it was all over, that there could be no harm in treating the Haydens to a shopping trip, especially after everything they'd been through. It was a moment of weakness, a whim that was out of step with everything he'd preached over a lifetime of trying to protect his men.

It was time for him to walk away.

Alfie Cheadle and Tim Halloran sat at the opposite end of the table, each alone with his own thoughts, which were all to do with feeling sorry for their boss, and not knowing how to snap him out of the cocoon of misery that held him in its grip.

"Look, sir, what's done is done," Cheadle offered with more hope than expectation. "There was simply no way of second-guessing this one. It looked like everything had been mopped up and we still don't know how this Todd Hamilton managed to track the team to Harrods."

"Thank you for trying, Alfie, but we both know I made a wrong call. I've been out of the field long enough to realise that things have passed me by. There are new technologies and new ways for our enemies to keep track of us. I should have known that, and I should have acted accordingly."

"If you don't mind me saying so, sir, that's a load of codswallop. One of the first things you taught us is that hindsight is always twenty-twenty, and when things go wrong, you fix it and move on. Sure, learn from the mistakes, but don't let them tie you up in knots by being afraid to take a decision. Those were your exact words. Maybe you should listen to them."

Before the General had a chance to reply, a mobile phone danced in front of Halloran. He moved his fingers deftly across the small keyboard before glancing up at a large wall-mounted monitor. "Seems we have another two gentlemen to identify."

All eyes turned to a cloudy image, backlit by the glare of marina lights which cast shadows over two faces emerging from a yacht. Halloran sighed in exasperation. "We'll never be able to enhance the quality enough to run this through our recognition software. There's not enough to go on here."

Sandford bolted from his seat and rushed towards the monitor. "There's no need for all of that, Tim. I'd recognise those characters anywhere. Christ, they're members of the Shannon Club!"

Chapter 44

IT TOOK TWO WEEKS to track their quarry to a log cabin nestled deep in the Adirondacks, a six-million acre spread of protected natural countryside in upstate New York. Former DHS agent Robert T Younger had acquired the modest property through a convoluted land deal that kept his name off deeds and licences, leaving him free to come and go without fear of discovery.

It had proved to be a useful weekend retreat and summer vacation spot for a number of years. Now it was a hideout, a prison without bars, as he attempted to stay one step ahead of his former colleagues. He'd stocked up on provisions, drastically altered his appearance, and settled in for the long haul, knowing he needed to stay off the radar for at least four months. Perhaps when the snows melted he would risk breaking out for Mexico, or maybe head north into Canada. At the moment there was no rush.

A federal arrest warrant on Younger was issued forty-eight hours after his abduction of Alan Doyle, activated by no less an authority than the President, following a phone message from the British PM, who had transferred a complete transcript of the Hayden dossier to the White House. Things had moved fast after that, including a nationwide manhunt for more than a dozen American bankers and investors, several highly-placed diplomats, and two State Department officials. The only name missing from the list was Senator Theodore Armstrong, though by then he would have had problems accessing his overseas bank accounts, which had been frozen in six separate countries.

Armstrong was left at large, under twenty-four-seven surveillance, which included phone and electronic tagging, in the hope he would help the authorities to spread the net even farther. At some point, when it was judged his usefulness was at an end, he would be reeled in to face the music.

Despite the Teflon-coated Senator's apparent immunity, he remained uncontactable by Younger. Calls had gone unanswered, emails remained unread, and even FedEx-couriered letters had been ignored. Younger was on his own, and that suited him just fine. Somewhere down the line, he would use his knowledge of the Senator's deals to plea-bargain his way out of a federal lock-up. There was no way he was doing time for that fat fuck!

Younger had spent his days catching up on some fishing, or reading from an extensive library of spy novels in the cabin's small study as he gazed out the window across the peaks, and dreamed of the first days of Spring. Patience – that's all he needed. *There's no way anyone will find me here.*

But Tim Halloran and his team of techies at *LonWash* in London *did* find him.

Working under one of Halloran's lateral-thinking strategies, the team looked for anomalies among what they dubbed the three Cs - *complacency-causes-cockups.* Ignoring all the usual lines of enquiry, Halloran went hunting among records that had often proved fertile ground in tracing a suspect who didn't want to be found.

Sure, they could change their name, get false papers, open fictitious bank accounts and credit cards, use burner phones, create fanciful email exchanges, swop their cars for payment-by-cash run-arounds, and even replace their fingerprints with latex guards. For someone like Younger, who knew his way around all the usual law enforcement trigger points, the exercise to make himself disappear was not a complicated one. Provided he stuck to some general rules.

Biggest of these was to let go of baseline data. Don't employ any variation of previously-used passwords; don't visit past internet sites; don't check what's happening to your old persona on social media platforms, or utility accounts. Above all, do not reference your actual date of birth – a lazy mistake made by people who were convinced they've thought of everything, though often it was little more than a defence mechanism to ensure they couldn't be caught out on a minor detail. A date of birth is engrained in the psyche, something that rolls off the tongue without thinking – an engrained fact that's hard to suppress or overlay with new numbers.

Halloran loved birth dates. In his experience, too many criminals held on to them when creating new identities, often resulting in their pursuers turning up when least expected. Get a date of birth; eliminate either male or female fields, depending on the quarry; narrow down geographical locations; scan for absence of dependents; look for recently-created paperwork; and concentrate the search to a manageable level.

By the time Halloran had run his algorithms using Younger's known date of birth, he was left with just twenty-eight names, all of them tied to addresses in North America. After applying an additional series of filters, he became convinced that a man known as John Harding was currently living under a business sub-let in a cabin in the Adirondack Mountains.

Devon and Doyle parked in a wooded area about a mile south-east of the cabin. They ignored a small country lane which led to a handful of adjoining properties, deciding that stealth was the only way they could hope to take Younger by surprise. They couldn't rule out the possibility that he'd mounted cameras or tripwires near the compound, or even that they might run into him on a casual morning walk. This would have to be done by the book; a typical military-style insertion that left nothing to chance.

The first part of their trek was relatively straightforward, thanks to the treeline shelter which took them within five-hundred yards of the cabin, sitting in a clearance with a three-sixty view across marshy fields. Hidden behind dirty lace curtains, Younger could spot an approach from any one of the dozen windows which surrounded the building.

An infra-red imager picked up Younger's heat signature in

a room to the right end of the cabin. If he stayed in that spot for at least fifteen minutes, it would make life easier for the *LonWash* duo who agreed to split up and approach from two routes on the north-east and north-west of the site.

They angled back into the trees and sprinted towards their left, negotiating several tree trunks and a fast-flowing stream that took them to the agreed starting points. Devon stopped to check the imager while Doyle continued for another fifty yards until he found a large boulder to rest behind while he waited for the all-clear.

The small red spot continued to flash at the same location as before, showing that Younger hadn't shifted position. Devon signalled a go, dropped on his belly, and began a slow crawl, careful not to disturb the tops of the reeds. If Younger was half the agent he pretended to be, he would detect the slightest disturbance, particularly on a morning without sufficient wind to rustle a feather.

It took them twenty minutes to reach the walkway surrounding the cabin. Devon mounted the boards at the front of the building while Doyle negotiated the creaky timbers at the rear. The slightest noise would carry in the still air like a rifle shot.

Step by step Devon edged towards the front door. Just as he was about to reach out for the handle, an ear-splitting screech cut through the silence and sent a dozen marsh hens fluttering from their nests in surrounding fields. Devon realised he'd missed a simple motion-detector siren built into the cabin's overhanging roof, a mistake that had lost them their advantage.

There was no time to worry about the consequences. He kicked open the door and sprinted to the room on the right with his Sig waving from side to side. To his surprise, Doyle was already ahead of him and charging through the opening in tuck-roll that cleared Devon's view of the room.

Younger leapt from a large chair in front of a log fire. Dressed only in a t-shirt and shorts, he lunged for a nearby table. Devon and Doyle both loosed off three-round bursts into the ceiling above his head.

Younger froze. "Don't shoot, I surrender!"

He threw his arms in the air and turned to face his assailants, his eyes ablaze when he recognised Doyle "You!"

"Nice to see you again too," Doyle intoned with chilling menace. "I think there's some unfinished business between us." He set his weapon down on the edge of the chair and dug into his sodden combat trousers, removing a length of heavy-duty hosepipe. "Recognise this?"

Younger's wide-eyed stare confirmed that he knew the hosepipe was the one he'd used on Doyle at the hostage house. "You wouldn't dare. I'm surrendering...I'll co-operate fully...I have information that will lead you to others far more important than me."

Doyle ignored the pleas and stepped forward, swinging the pipe in short arcs, with the full force of his considerable bulk behind every blow. It was a measured assault that moved from Younger's ankles upwards over his legs and across his torso. Despite the DHS agent's attempts to ward off the attack by curling into a foetal position, every lash of the pipe found its mark.

The screams give way to tearful cries. "Please stop, I've had enough. Look in the top drawer of the desk. There's a computer pen drive with details and dates of everything we did. I kept it as an assurance policy, but it's yours. I'm on your side now."

Doyle paused to wait for Devon to retrieve the item. He held it aloft and looked down at Younger. "Is there a password?"

"No, the files will open at a double click. It's a gold mine. I'll help to fill in any blanks and make sure everyone is brought to justice."

Devon looked across at Doyle. "It's your show, Alan."

Doyle nodded and shrugged at Younger. "That's not enough, friend, not nearly enough. The President has already agreed there'll be no deals and that you get to rot out your days in Leavenworth. Killing's too good for you, but here's a little taster of what lies ahead."

The assault restarted. It took another three minutes for

Younger to lapse into unconsciousness, his body weakened by several small-bone fractures to his arms and legs.

Devon and Doyle watched from the treeline as two DHS helicopters touched down in front of the cabin forty minutes later. They'd trussed up Younger, put in an anonymous tip-off, and waited around to make sure he was going nowhere until the cavalry arrived.

The former agent was carried out on a stretcher, apparently still unconscious, and was wedged into the rear floor area below the heavily-armed escort. Four agents remained on site for a follow-up search as the copter taking Younger to his new surroundings lifted off and disappeared across the treetops.

"Howya feeling, buddy?"

"I'm good," Doyle responded. "It was kind of nice to get that off my chest."

Devon smiled. "Remind me never to get on your dark side."

Chapter 45

THE OCEAN-FRONT house was the pick of Freeport's exclusive properties. Screened on three sides by palm trees, and with a clifftop view of the white-sand beach that circled Grand Bahama, it was the most stunning piece of real estate in the archipelago that was the Bahamas, nestled less than two hundred miles from the Florida coastline.

It was a place only for the seriously mega-rich, a category into which George Roper and Giles Grimand fitted snugly. Despite possessing a portfolio that covered homes, hotels and super-yachts around the world, this Freeport mansion was their favourite residence, a veritable haven to recharge batteries and plan their next, big assault on a global economy that had become little more than a chessboard game to satiate an endless power-thrill.

However, unlike previous visits to this hideaway heaven, Roper and Grimand were not making their usual short-stay stopover. Storms were gathering in their cloistered world, forcing them to stand still until they passed over. Events in both London and America had taken them by surprise, almost to the point that they were beginning to question if they were as insulated from the fall-out as they'd always believed.

But if the pair had learned anything in their cut-and-slash careers, it was knowing when to put on the brakes and take stock. A period of calm reflection away from the limelight was what was needed now. Yes, they'd sit back at a distance and watch what unfolded, knowing there would still be plenty of meat on the table by the time the vultures were done feeding.

"You know, Giles, it's probably all for the best. I could do with a bit of a break. A few weeks of sun, wine and those lovely little Bahamian models is just what we both need. I don't know about you, but I intend to partake copiously in everything that's on offer."

Grimand was standing by a window overlooking the front of the property. Just as he was about to reply, a silver Rolls Royce snaked up the driveway and braked to a halt at the front door. He watched bemused as a tall, silver-haired man emerged from the vehicle and walked confidently towards the front door.

"We have a visitor, George, and you're not going to believe who it is."

Roper rushed to the window and stared incredulously at the arrival. "That's General Sir John Sandford. How the devil did he track us down?"

"Why not answer the door and find out?"

Both men spun around to face Alfie Cheadle, who'd walked in from the balcony to cover them with a suppressed Glock 22.

Sandford eased back in the large wicker chair and sipped from a glass of brandy, his eyes holding steady on the thunderous faces of his hosts. Both men were seated opposite, transfixed by the menace of Cheadle's weapon.

"I'll not beat about the bush," the General told them. "Your antics have caused a lot of pain and misery, too much for me to attempt to enunciate, although I dare say you'd probably relish a recount of what you've managed to achieve. Let's just agree that we all know what I'm talking about. It'll save some time while we figure out what we're going to do about it."

Roper started to lean forward, but held back when Cheadle extended his gun arm. "I don't know what you think you have, Sandford, though if I were in your shoes I would listen carefully to what you're about to be told."

"I'm all ears."

"Very well. The bottom line is that you can't touch us. All you've got are smoke and mirrors. We, on the other hand, have many powerful and influential friends who will see to it that you and your organisation are ruined. You're dealing with something that's frankly incomprehensible to a limited intelligence such as yours. In short, General, you're way out of your league, and I suggest you take a step backwards before things get really ugly."

Sandford nodded in acknowledgement. "You're darned right that this is a spider's web far beyond my comprehension. The more I look at it, the more I know it would take me years to unravel its subtleties, much less even understand how you were able to weave such a tangled web. I don't mind telling you it got me down just thinking about it. I realised several days ago that I would not be able to get to the bottom of everything you pair have had a hand in. But then I realised something else."

"I'm sure you're itching to tell us what that was."

"Yes, of course. Last night, before leaving for here from London, I had an epiphany. I decided I don't want to understand it, or to contemplate spending fruitless weeks and months trying to get to grips with it. No, sirs, I don't need to do anything of these things. All I need to do is put a stop to it."

The chilly finality of the General's words caused Roper's heart to miss a beat. "You're bluffing! You just can't waltz in here and take the law into your own hands. We're not some pissant investors to be rode roughshod over, much less worry about the idle threats of a washed-up soldier."

Sandford sighed. "I see you doubt my resolve. Perhaps this will help you to understand things." He lifted his hand and waved in Cheadle's direction.

Giles Grimand died without realising Cheadle had fired the single round into his forehead. His eyelids drooped closed, the sound of a small expiration of air escaped from his lips, and his shoulder sagged over to prop against Roper. The back of the settee turned crimson as Roper leapt from the seat and stared down at his dead colleague.

"For pity's sake, Sandford, just tell me what you want. We don't deserve this. There must be something I can bargain with."

"Now that you come to mention it, there is something I would like you to do for me. I have a firm resolve that all the money you stole ought to be returned to its rightful place, to compensate the British taxpayer and British industry with the millions that have gone missing. I have an account number here for the transfer of funds, something you could manage to do within a few minutes, if you've a mind to."

Roper didn't need any additional encouragement. "Yes, yes, let's make compensation. If I transfer the money, will you promise to let me go?"

"I promise to kill you if you don't make the transfer. In the end, the money doesn't matter as much as the principle, so it's your choice."

"I'll do it," Roper almost screamed as he raced to a nearby desk and fired up a computer.

Fifteen minutes after Roper began attacking the keyboard, a grand total of £2.1billion had crossed the ether into a special offshore account. As usual, the General would deduct ten per cent commission against *LonWash* expenses before transferring the cash into a Whitehall reserve fund.

Roper watched his deposits deplete to zero, but he had still an ace up his sleeve. "There's more where that come from, General. Give me a few weeks and I can access other accounts, as well as safety deposit boxes filled with gold and jewels that will make this look like chicken feed. You need me alive to see this through."

"I'm afraid," Sandford said without a hint of remorse, "you've run out of time. I could try to get you to understand why it has to be this way, but they would just be meaningless words. Your moral compass is so off-kilter that I doubt you understand any longer the basic concept of right and wrong, or good and evil. Suffice to say, the balance of things is about to be restored."

Roper's last words were strangled in his throat. The nine-mil parabellum smashed through his Adam's Apple and blew a hole in the back of his neck. For good measure, Cheadle fired a second round directly into the financier's heart.

Sandford looked down disgustingly at the corpses. "What's the world coming to, Alfie? Imagine the Shannon Club allowing these two sick apologies for human beings to be members?"

Chapter 46

SENATOR THEODORE ARMSTRONG had become a pariah. No-one was taking his calls. Invitations to dinner parties, and political meetings, and public ceremonial events had all dried up. He was not just pushed to the fringes; he was shunted all the way into the wilderness, a sure sign that the Capitol Hill grapevine was in overdrive about his fall from grace.

His long-time aide and protégé had taken an extended leave of absence due to some mysterious illness, and what remained of his skeleton office staff were left to deal with juggling a diary full of trivial appointments and meeting requests that were far removed from the high-level activities that usually filled his working day.

He was back in Washington, holed up in his Georgian mansion at Bethesda, a half-mile west of the Potomac. To all intents and purposes, he might as well have been on the moon, such was his isolation from erstwhile friends and colleagues.

He'd already learned about his frozen bank accounts and credit cards. Apart from a few thousand dollars stuck in a wall safe behind a framed print of Abraham Lincoln, Armstrong was flat broke. Despite all his years of nest-feathering, there was no fall-back position. He was ruined. Worst still, through the fugue of whiskey and cigar smoke that hung around the large drawing room, he could see no way out of his present predicament.

Except of course for the .44 Magnum Colt Anaconda revolver that sat atop the room's centrepiece marble-topped desk.

Twice in the last hour he'd hefted the walnut handle, forced the stubby barrel into his mouth, and tried to exert pressure on the silver trigger. But he couldn't do it. This was no way to go; he'd figure something out. Hadn't he always?

He gulped down the last dregs of his tumbler and reached out for the bottle of Jack Daniels just as the chimes of the front door pealed across the room. He glanced at a CCTV monitor, noticing a uniformed delivery man standing in his porch clutching a bouquet of flowers. He hit the intercom button.

"What do you want?"

"Delivery for Senator Armstrong."

"I can't come down. Leave it on the porch."

Armstrong watched the man set his package on the ground and walk back to a delivery van parked at the kerbside. He waited until the van disappeared from view and then walked to a window to look up and down the busy road. Nothing seemed out of place.

He waited another five minutes before walking downstairs, the Colt wrapped in his chubby fist, and quickly opened the front door. He bent to retrieve the package, hurrying inside before anyone had a chance to approach.

Back in the drawing room he placed the bouquet on the desk and pulled a card from between the arrangement of roses and orchids. One line was scrawled across the plain surface.

Don't despair: Salvation is at hand.

Armstrong's face brightened immediately. He was not alone! There were still friends out there willing to help. Suddenly there was a way out – it was an opportunity he'd grab with both hands.

His desktop telephone rang. It was the first call he'd received in three days. He grabbed it eagerly and shouted into the mouthpiece. "Who is this?"

"Did you receive my package, Senator Armstrong?"

"Yes, yes, who is this? Can you help me?"

"Did you read the card?"

"Yes, what salvation are you promising?"

There was a five-second pause before a reply came. "If you've opened the envelope and read the card, you have been exposed to a rather nasty strain of Ricin, which has already started seeping through your pores and entering your bloodstream. In just a matter of minutes you will experience extremely unpleasant symptoms, starting with a high fever, followed by pains in your chest and arms."

Armstrong jumped from his seat, frantically wiping his hands on his trousers. "I don't understand, why are you doing this.... you have to stop this...I need an antidote...who are you?"

"I'm afraid there's no antidote, Senator. The poison will attack all your vital organs. It will turn your liver and lungs into mush; it will erode your veins and cause massive internal haemorrhaging, although that will be the least of your worries. Your body will go into full paralysis, which unfortunately won't save you from at least two hours of excruciating pain before you finally shut down."

"Oh, my God, please have mercy. Don't do this!"

"Too late for all that, Senator. Call it payback for past sins and misdemeanours. You could, of course, save yourself from these agonies by choosing your own way out. It's your call."

The phone went dead. Armstrong stared at it vacantly for several seconds before becoming aware that sweat was dripping from his forehead onto the desktop. He felt spasms in his chest and was struggling to breathe. The lower half of his body seemed to be on fire.

He tore buttons from the front of his shirt to relieve the constriction around his neck. He was hyperventilating. His respiratory rate had climbed alarmingly during the past few minutes, his airwaves crushed by some inner pressure that was choking his life away. He knew he was nearing the end.

Tears started to flow as he realised the hopelessness of his situation. This wasn't fair. *I don't deserve this.*

Armstrong summoned up a last vestige of resolve and reached forward to pick up the Colt Anaconda, ramming the barrel into his mouth without a moment's hesitation. This time, he didn't stop to think. There was nothing left to do; nowhere else to go. He pulled hard on the trigger.

The boom from the heavy-duty weapon reached the ears of two people sitting in a car fifty yards from the entrance to the

Senator's house.

"I can't believe he actually fell for that."

Marta Tessler looked across at Don Hill and smiled. "The mind is a wonderful thing. I remember a friend who was once placed on her belly under a heat lamp to ease a severe back-pain. She was told by the physio to turn over when the heat became too intense, but she stuck it out for more than twenty minutes. When she could finally bear it no longer, she turned over to discover that someone had forgotten to turn on the lamp. Her mind had convinced her she was heating up even though there was nothing there."

Hill shook his head. "Yeah, but imagining you're going through the horrors of a Ricin attack and putting a gun to your head to stop the pain, is a different animal altogether. How could he have really believed his whole body was shutting down?"

"Mind over matter, Tony. It's a bit like a frail woman lifting a car to free her trapped son. There's no logic involved. Nothing can explain where she got the strength from, yet somehow she managed to do what several men around her couldn't do."

"Okay, we both know there was no Ricin. It was a mind trick by General Sandford, something that even he didn't think would work. How come the fool didn't simply jump in his car and drive to the nearest hospital for a check-up?"

"He was told there was Ricin, he believed there was Ricin, and he accepted there was nothing he could do about it. Coating the card with a mild neurotoxin produced the incentive needed to kick him over the edge, although by the time an autopsy is carried out, all traces will have disappeared from his bloodstream."

Hill was unconvinced. "But what if he hadn't been fooled?"

"No big deal. It was meant to be the start of mind games. We'd have followed up with other little stratagems, all designed to point the Senator towards the only exit door left open for him."

"It would have been easier to just kill him ourselves."

"No, the General had promised there would be no reprisals

against Armstrong. The Americans wanted to keep him to themselves to wring out every last drop of information they could get. Sandford was worried the whole thing could play out for years, with Armstrong sitting in some cushy country-club prison, immune from the consequences of his actions."

"I thought the President had promised full prosecution?"

"Just words, Tony. The old *Senate Shuffle* would have protected Armstrong somewhere down the line. At the end of the day, they watch each other's back."

"*Senate Shuffle?*"

"It's a loose term for the political shadow-dancing that goes on behind the scenes. Sometimes, despite best intentions, it's not the done thing to air dirty linen in public. If the full extent of Armstrong's treason ever reaches the front pages of *The Washington Post*, this whole place would go into meltdown."

She glanced up at the front window of the Armstrong residence. "This way, everybody gets what they wanted. A nice clean suicide covers the General's back, while Washington grinds on as if nothing had happened."

Chapter 47

CHELSEA HORGAN walked proudly down the aisle, her hand curled inside her father's arm as he beamed a cheesy grin to guests on both sides of the packed church. It was a small, timber-frame structure dwarfed by the vastness of the open Missouri countryside that grew around it as far as the eye could see in any direction, and which had spawned its congregation back to War of Independence days when it had played its part in staging meetings of the state's revolutionary army leaders.

General Stan Horgan's family hailed from these parts. One of his forebears had sat in these pews plotting the downfall of the British, and starting a family military history that had been handed down through the generations. If Horgan thought it strange that this happiest of days should be shared with so many new-found Brit friends, his face give nothing away. In many ways, it was fitting that his daughter should help bring history to a full circle.

Chelsea had made a remarkable recovery. With typical Horgan stoicism, she had started jogging within a week of being discharged from hospital, confounding doctors with her punishing schedule of physiotherapy and intense aerobics. Within six weeks, she was into full-blown cross-country treks and mountain-climbing, always with Alan Doyle at her side pleading with her to slow down. Nothing, however, could dissuade her from the goal of attaining peak fitness again.

The old General had marvelled at his daughter's transformation. The sparkle had returned to her eyes, keeping pace with her fierce desire for independence. It was great to have her fully restored, even if a blazing row lurked around the corner.

"You can't be serious, Chelsea? You're not going back. You've done your bit. Your mom and I have gotten used to you being around."

After returning from a full weapons session at an FBI gun range she'd announced her intention to return to London to pick up her *LonWash* career. She had put off the news as long as possible, knowing it would hurt her parents, but equally sure she could never be fulfilled if she stepped away from the only life she'd ever really enjoyed.

"Dad, please understand, my life's with Alan now, and he belongs in London. We'll be happy there and I promise to visit more often. When we get back and settle in, why don't you and mom come for an extended vacation?"

Horgan tried unsuccessfully to mask his disappointment. "I'm just being a selfish old fool. You must do what's best for you and Alan. I want you to be safe and happy, even if that means you're four thousand miles away."

Doyle saw the anguish in the old man's face. He wanted to say something to help, but words couldn't get around the fact that a daughter, who had almost been lost to them a few months ago, would soon be torn again from their embrace. He hoped to never have to face a similar situation as a father.

He'd shared his concerns with the only true friend he had. Was it fair to marry Chelsea and rip her from the bosom of her family?

Mike Devon didn't have an answer, but he knew someone who would. In typical fashion, General Sir John Sandford didn't see a problem. "I think it's time we opened an office in Chicago, where I believe the soon-to-be Mr and Mrs Doyle would be the ideal candidates to run the operation. I think maybe they could spend six months there and six months here."

Two weeks before the wedding, an official appointment letter was sent to Doyle, along with the deeds to a luxury studio apartment overlooking Lake Michigan.

General Horgan had wept openly when the news was read out to him.

Devon stood shoulder-to-shoulder with Doyle as Chelsea glided down the aisle. "There's still time to back out, big man!"

Doyle responded through curled lips. "You're not getting out of your best man speech that easy."

Devon had got through his speech, prudently omitting the more raucous details of Doyle's chequered life, and taking care not to embarrass the shy giant of a man who'd with whom he'd shared so many exploits. He could have told them about the courageous, unflappable soldier whose actions had saved the lives of so many, not to mention pulling Devon himself out of harm's way on more than one occasion.

He could have told them about Doyle's horrific injury and the downward spiral of despair that followed. It was a period that would have ruined most other men, but had proved only to be one more challenge for the big ex-soldier to meet head-on and defeat with the same kind of determination that was fostered during his awkward teenage years when he'd been shunned by his Oxford-educated peers.

While others had taken to their books, Doyle stuck to his dream of joining the Army, walking into a recruitment office on the morning of his sixteenth birthday. He'd embraced life in a uniform totally, the only downside of which was losing contact with his parents, both of whom died within months of each other while he was away on yet another mission.

Devon smiled as he looked across the top table and realised Doyle had finally found a new family. Sitting beside Chelsea, and flanked by Stan and Barbara, he knew the Horgans would bring richly-deserved stability and happiness into the big fella's life.

All that mushiness would have been too much for Doyle to take. Instead, Devon shared a bit of barrack-room banter, a few snippets of Doyle's many awkward encounters with the fairer sex, and a previously-untold story of how he'd had to undertake a butt-naked trek through the snow-covered Brecon Beacons because an instructor had discovered he'd packed an extra pair of thermals!

It was time to wrap things up. "Ladies and gentlemen, I give you the best soldier, the best friend, and the most uncomplicated man you could ever wish to find." Glancing at Chelsea, he stole a quote from Jane Austen, one of his wife's favourite authors, and told Doyle: *"I could not part with you to anyone less worthy."*

The newly-weds left the Kansas City hotel shortly before midnight to catch a honeymoon flight to Hawaii. By the time Devon extricated himself from the other guests and returned to his third-floor suite, Emma and young Michael were fast asleep in the double bed.

He'd left Generals Sandford and Horgan to their stories and anecdotes, marvelling at the stamina of the old war horses as they regaled guests with tales that often bordered on the fanciful, if not downright manufactured. A genuine, warm friendship was blooming easily between them.

Throughout the evening, Devon had carefully monitored his alcohol intake. Something had been nagging at him all day. It was almost at the surface, though he needed a few hours of study before snapping it free.

He walked quietly to his briefcase and extracted a copy of the Hayden manuscript. There was something in there that rang alarm bells when he'd reread it for the umpteenth time two days ago. He needed to know what was hiding below the surface.

It had been a frantic six months since Matthew Hayden's revelations first surfaced. The aftermath investigations had been conducted mainly by MI6 and the Metropolitan Police, though Devon's team had kept a close watch on developments by logging arrests, mapping key players, and watching to see if anything was missed.

He had to admit it was a thorough operation. The PM had stuck to his promise of full disclosure, even going so far as to make several key announcements about the conspiracy at PMQs - the quaintly ritualistic weekly Prime Minister's Question Time in the Commons. Any embarrassments suffered by the Government were quickly overtaken by popular acclaim for the way in which it had been open and transparent about all wrongdoings. As the investigation started a slow wind-down, the media was already turning its attention to other matters.

But Devon couldn't shake the notion that he'd missed something.

He turned on a small desklamp and began reading a section of the dossier. The more he read, the more convinced he became that the former Home Secretary, Charles Manning, could not have single-handedly thrown a veil over certain events. He was not a details man; he would have needed someone else to help cover his tracks.

The dead financiers, George Roper and Giles Grimand, were the ultimate puppet-masters, but Manning had needed someone below his level to carry out their orders. The various junior ministers and Whitehall officials, who'd been implicated in a number of schemes, were not the kind of players he was looking for either. This was below their level of responsibility and expertise.

The more he thought about it, the more animated he became. He began frantically to draw rings around sections of the manuscript, scribbling names and dates stretching back more than five years. By the time he finished, there were lines of arrows pointing to three names. One of these was the man he was looking for.

He stared at the sheet for more than five minutes before it hit him. Of course, it couldn't be anyone else! He stabbed the point of his pen into one name. *You've been there all the time! Hiding in plain sight.*

Chapter 48

THE LOW-RENT AREA of Holborn, North London was the last place Devon expected to find his man. If nothing else, he was doing a good job of hiding what must have been considerable pay-offs among the rundown terraced housing and litter-filled streets of a borough that was hardly renowned for sheltering high-flyers.

He'd checked the address several times. It was the only property registered in the man's name, a curious anomaly Devon hadn't time to reflect upon. He was here now, and the place had to be checked out.

Standing in the early-morning shadows of an alley directly opposite the front door of his target, Devon noted the absence of lights or movement behind closed dirty curtains. Given the nature of the man's job, it was probably par for the course to pull late-night shifts, or maybe not even get home at all for days on end.

Devon checked the street to make sure no-one was watching before he crossed and walked down a sloped pathway to a paint-flaked door. There were no security cameras or alarms, another anomaly that caused him to shake his head in disbelief. It took less than twenty seconds to by-pass the standard lock and step into a hallway cluttered with boxes and full of the stench of stale cigarette smoke and alcohol fumes.

A pencil-thin torch beam took him to a cramped living room that just about managed to accommodate the normal bare-essential furniture of a settee, armchair, ancient television set, and a pine wall cabinet with very few ornaments or photographs on its stark shelves.

Devon wedged the torch between his teeth and shifted the armchair to a point where it faced the room door. He sat down, pulled out his Sig Sauer P226, and threaded a Rimfire 22LR suppressor into place. He placed the weapon on his lap and pressed a push-button illumination dial to check the time on his wristwatch. It was shortly after 2am.

He could afford to be patient. This was where he wanted to confront his man and, if need be, he would return each evening until he finally made contact. What he had to do had to be done away from public glare. This was more than vengeance; this was about settling the books and restoring the balance.

An hour passed before Devon heard the sound of footsteps and the rattling of keys. He straightened in his seat, grabbed the Sig, and adjusted his vision to the glare of hallway lights. Shoes clomped on the wooden floor as the house-owner strode to the room entrance, his arm reaching inside to hit the wall-mounted light switch.

The man froze instantly when he saw Devon. He already knew the answer, but asked anyway. "What are you doing here?"

"As they say in your world, this is the end of the line."

Peter Ramsden, head of MI6, the clichéd title for Britain's Secret Intelligence Service, flicked a sad-eyed acknowledgement as he walked forward.

"Stop right there!" Devon ordered. "Let's do this by the book. Take off your jacket and shoulder holster and dump them on the settee. You know enough about me to know you won't get a chance to do something stupid."

Ramsden peeled off his coat and unbuttoned the holster straps, careful to show no sudden movements. He placed the items on the arm of the settee, inched across to the pine cabinet, and raised an eyebrow. "Mind if I get a drink. I think I'm going to need it."

"Be my guest. Judging by the smell of this place, you've been spending a lot of time lately looking down at the contents of a whiskey glass."

"Yeah, well, I've had a lot on my mind."

Devon felt the first stirrings of anger. "Spare me the self-pity. I've got just one question; why?"

Ramsden chugged down a half-tumbler of whiskey, refilled his glass, and walked back to the settee, slumping down at the end away from where his gun was draped. "I needed the money, simple as that."

Devon looked around disgustingly. "Doesn't look like you put it to good use."

"It wasn't for me, it was for Margaret, my wife. She developed cancer five years ago and I needed to send her for this revolutionary new treatment in Switzerland. It was a private clinic that took all our life savings, and then some. I needed more, and somehow Charles Manning found out about my predicament. He arranged funding through some corporation or other, but of course there was a price to pay. I was in the bastard's pocket and he was not shy about keeping the squeeze on me."

"So, you sacrificed other lives for that of your wife? How'd she feel about that."

Ramsden's eyes clouded over. "She never knew about it. She thought the money came from re-mortgaging our previous home. She begged me not to put ourselves into debt; said she'd rest happily knowing I wouldn't be burdened by bills we couldn't afford. She was that kind of a woman, but I couldn't just watch her wither away."

"And yet the treatment wasn't successful." Devon knew that Margaret Ramsden died almost five years ago, though he hadn't been aware of the circumstances until now.

"She lasted barely three months. It was all through her body."

Devon needed to change tack. "What exactly did you do for Manning, and why did you hang Matthew Hayden out to dry?"

"I swear, Mike, I never took a penny for myself, and at the start I thought Manning just wanted an inside track on security issues to make himself look good as the new Home Secretary. I passed on low-level stuff, but gradually he kept pushing for more. He got me to steer a few investigations away from some of his cronies, although at the time I never imagined he was involved in treason to the extent he was. Things came to a head when Hayden started his investigations into a lot of random events that were eventually traced back to Manning."

"So, he got you to shut Hayden down?"

"They wanted to kill Matthew. I pleaded with them to call off the hit. I told them I would expose them if anything happened. I tried to keep Matthew safe by drumming him out of the service and cutting him off from his information supply. I figured he'd be better off by staying alive and turning his hand to another career. I never knew he was still chasing down his research until....until....."

Devon jumped from his seat and almost pulled the trigger. "Spit it out! Until they blew him to smithereens and went after his wife and son. Why didn't you come clean and help us to protect that family? It's no thanks to you they are still alive, although several very good men died to protect them."

"I know, I know, it all happened so fast. There wasn't really anything I could do. It was too late by then."

"Not quite – there was still time for you to try to cover your tracks."

Ramsden looked puzzled. "I don't know what you mean."

"It was you who cleaned out the servers at MI6. All that hogwash you gave me about strange things happening after Hayden had left was just a load of hogwash. When you heard he'd been killed, you went into the basement at Vauxhall Cross and expunged everything he had worked on. Not a lot of remorse there, eh Peter?"

"I know you won't believe me, Mike, but I thought cleaning the servers would put an end to it. I saved everything to an external hard drive, which is in a safety-deposit box at my bank. I'm happy to hand everything over in case there's something that's been missed in the current investigations. I would have liked some time to make things right with Matthew Hayden's name and reputation, perhaps rename the server room at Vauxhall Cross in his honour, and offer his son a job with the agency."

"Jesus, you make me sick!" Devon almost choked on the words. "You're a fucking hypocrite. The PM's already taking care of honouring Matthew Hayden, and you don't need to worry about his son Christopher. He starts a new career on Monday under Tim Halloran at *LonWash*. Something tells me that young man will be every bit as diligent about protecting this country as his father was. You're out of the picture, Ramsden."

Ramsden swallowed the last of the whiskey, setting the tumbler at his feet, and standing to face Devon. "Get it over with."

Devon levelled the Sig at Ramsden's head. "I came here to kill you, and nothing you've said has made me change my mind. However, if there's one thing I learned from Matthew Hayden's work is that he did what he did, not for personal glory or recognition, but because he felt it was his duty. He was a non-violent man who would have abhorred the body count that has grown around the work he started. I'm not prepared to let his memory be sullied further by adding one more death."

"You mean you're...you're letting me go?"

"You don't get off that lightly. I want your resignation handed in by lunchtime tomorrow, along with that external hard drive. You'll take full responsibility for everything that's happened, after which you can wallow here in shame remembering how you betrayed a thoroughly decent individual, as well as the country you swore to defend. I wonder how your wife will look down on you now? Frankly, Peter, I think she'd agree with me that you don't deserve a quick way out. You can live with your ghosts, drink yourself into oblivion, or do whatever the fuck you want. But remember this: I might change my mind tomorrow, or the next day, or God knows when. Keep looking over your shoulder and one day I might be there."

Ramsden fell back onto the settee and began sobbing, his face covered by trembling hands. "I don't know if I could face a future like that. I don't think I could......." His voice tailed off at the sound of his front door slamming.

Mike Devon had already left.

EPILOGUE

EXERCISE YARD B at HMP Belmarsh was one of two generous-sized, open-air rectangles cramped between buildings that housed some of Britain's most notorious prisoners. With over eight-hundred inmates, the yards were constantly in use, releasing controlled numbers on a shift system that stretched from breakfast to lock-down at 5pm.

It was what was known as *sky-time* – the population's caustic description for the one-hour-per-day privilege of shuffling around the perimeter. More than a third of the prisoners passed up the chance of fresh air, either because they couldn't be assed, or because they didn't need reminding of what they were missing on the other side of the walls.

The mid-morning session in B Yard was reserved for the inhabitants of HSU, the High Security Unit that housed Belmarsh's most violent guests. Among their number were Dave Millward and Mark Jennings, each serving five life terms, with a minimum tariff of thirty years – an odd addendum of British legal jurisprudence, which recognised that life didn't always mean life.

Millward and Jennings were under no illusions about not serving the full tariff – and then some. Cop killers were low down on the totem pole when it came to persuading the appropriate authorities about learning their lesson and no longer posing a threat to the public.

The prospect of sitting out his days in this hellhole was not one either man was prepared to contemplate. One way or another, the pair intended to be free long before the grey hairs came and senility set in. Going over the wall, figuratively speaking, would be preferable. The alternative was an early drive through the gates in a pine box, an altogether much-better outlook than gradually withering away.

Not that Millward and Jennings were prepared to throw in the towel just yet.

There were no guards in the compound. The prisoners were simply let out through a side door and left to entertain themselves, a euphemism for spending sixty minutes on one of a dozen bench seats while they choked on cigarettes and took advantage of the only worthwhile association they had with other human beings. The screws didn't come into that category; they were the enemy and there were no brownie points to be earned by fraternisation.

Millward sat down on his customary bench and cast a doleful look at a bright summer sky. It was the beginning of June, a time when he should have been looking forward to an upcoming birthday, swinging on a hammock on a Spanish beach, and trying to decide if he should prepare a barbecue, or just book a local tapas bar for the celebrations. With luck, that would all come to pass in due time.

He waited for Jennings to sit down before passing on his latest news. "It's all fixed. Our appeal hearing is set for next week at the Old Bailey. Looks like we're going to get another outing."

"Fuck that!" Jennings snarled. "These appeals are useless. It's not as if they're suddenly going to find there's been a miscarriage of justice. Best-case scenario is that they drop one life sentence, as if that'll make a difference, but more likely they'll find a reason to add something to what we've already got. Come to think of it, that won't make a difference either. We're here for the duration. I told you we should have taken our chances at that SAS ambush."

Millward flared. "Will you stop banging on about that! They'd have cut us to ribbons before we got ten feet outside the back of the lorry. What good would that have done?"

"Anything's better than this, Dave. I can't do the time, I just can't. One of these days you'll hear they've found me swinging from a blanket, or lying in a pool of blood from cut wrists. I don't know how much more I can take."

Millward slapped a comforting palm on his partner's knee. "Keep the chin up, Mark, all is not yet lost. What would you say to a sure-fire plan to get us out of here?"

Mark Jennings's didn't realise his jaw had flopped open. He was transfixed in a wide-eyed stare for ten seconds, his emotions dancing between hope and despair. "Don't fuck with me, Dave. You can't break out of this rat-trap; it's never been done. Stop trying to make me feel better by making me feel worse. All you're offering is a glimmer of hope that will be snatched away before I could even get used to the possibility. That's cruel."

Millward forced a smile. "Will you stop feeling sorry for yourself and listen? Of course, the appeal will get us nowhere, but it *will* get us out from behind these walls long enough to put my real plan into action. I've arranged it so that we never reach the Old Bailey. A lot can happen between here and there."

Jennings leapt from the bench and stared down at his friend. "What have you got cooking? Please tell me it will work!"

Millward tugged at Jennings's trousers. "Sit down and stop drawing attention." He looked around to make sure no other inmates were eavesdropping, though judging by the hang-dog expressions within different huddled groups they all had their own problems without worrying about what anyone else was getting up to. Prisons were like that – full of cliques, and testosterone, and fanciful notions of power and independence. The mind could transport caged men to wherever they wanted to go, usually to parallel worlds that served as escape valves for pent-up emotions. They lived in a bubble-wrapped existence, often no longer in touch with the realities of their situation, getting by on the basis of one day at a time. Was Millward getting caught up in a delusional trap?

"Don't worry, I'm not going stir-crazy," he told Jennings forcefully. "Why do think I've been pushing for an appeal? I needed regular access to my brief so that he could carry out my instructions for an escape. That man is more bent than the whole of this place put together. All I needed to do was wave enough cash in his face to get his attention."

"How'd you manage that?"

"Those stupid pricks never got wind of my offshore bank

accounts. I was able to arrange for the solicitor to transfer tidy sums into his own coffers. He's been using the money to recruit eight mercenary pals of mine to spring us from the prison convoy, and he gets a nice tidy bonus when we're free and clear. We know the date and time, the route that will be taken, and the vehicles to be used. They won't know what's hit them."

A spark returned to Jennings's sad eyes. "Can this be true? We *really* are going to escape? How will we get out of the country? How will we stay one step ahead? How will we...."

"Slow down, Mark. The first thing you should know is that we're not leaving the country, at least not until we take care of some unfinished business. We have a secure hidey-hole to lie low for a bit, after which there are things I need to do before we start thinking of departing dear old Blighty."

"Are you talking about this unfinished business? What is it?"

Millward clasped his hands behind his head and peered up at the cloudless sky. "My solicitor tracked down everything there is to know about *LonWash Securities*, the bastards who helped put us here. No-one's ever got the better of me before, and I'll be damned if I just walk away without settling the score." He tapped the side of his head before continuing. "It's all up here; names, addresses, family members. They'll rue the day they fucked with Dave Millward."

Jennings giggled. "That would be a delicious irony. Who exactly are we going after?"

"I'm only interested in the top two men. The owner is a retired Army General by the name of Sir John Sandford, but the real big bull is his enforcer, a guy called Mike Devon. He's the brawn behind the brains, although from what I gather he's just the same as you and me, a gun for hire, nothing more than a paid assassin with a badge."

"I'd love to meet this Devon character."

"You'll get the chance, my friend, but just remember, he's mine. You can take care of the wife. I hear she's quite a looker."

THE END

A BONUS READ

Introducing Garda Detective Mick Boyle.....

Meet Mick Boyle, a decorated detective consigned to a backwater posting in the West of Ireland. Once one of An Garda Síochána's brightest and best, he is struggling to overcome a past blighted by alcoholism, indiscipline and a failed marriage. Just when he starts to believe he can sit back and let the world pass him by, Boyle is confronted with a serial killer investigation, a drugs war with a high body count, and the theft of priceless paintings that leads the world's press to his doorstep.

There's no hiding place. Is this Boyle's chance for redemption? Or is he a spent force?

Turn over for a bonus read...........

SPENT FORCE
By Joe McCoubrey

PROLOGUE

THE MAN HITCHING a ride made three crucial mistakes.

The first was sticking his thumb out at the wrong car, not that he was spoilt for choice on a rainswept March morning along a shoreline stretch still bereft of traffic, two hours away from the breakfast time of normal people.

He needed a fix. The kind that can only be provided by watching the glassy-eyed stare of a fellow human being fighting for a last breath of air. The coppery smell of blood elevated the sensation to a level of sheer ecstasy that seemed to satiate his inner demons, at least for a short while. It was now five weeks since his last kill. And five weeks was way too long.

That was probably why he made his second mistake. He climbed into the welcome warmth and dryness of a battered blue Audi and took stock of the man squeezed behind the wheel. This would be easy pickings. He smiled at the thought of what was to come. A quick dip into his pocket, the flash of a wicked-looking flick knife held against the throat, and - just like the others - the driver would do exactly as he was told.

Five minutes into their journey the hitchhiker maintained the usual idle chatter about the Irish weather just long enough to wrap his fist around the hilt of the knife and withdraw it in a blur of movement from the pocket of his greasy donkey-jacket. With the tip of the blade firmly in place above the driver's shirt collar, he issued calm instructions about what was to happen next.

"All I want is your wallet and your car. Do what you're told and you can walk away unharmed. Try to be a hero and I'll stick you like a pig."

He boasted about how often he had done this before. Men, women, young, old, it didn't matter to him.

That was his third mistake.

Instead of reaching for a wallet inside the coat of his suit jacket, the driver delivered a surprising offer. "There's ten thousand Euros in an envelope taped to the underside of your seat. Take that, but please don't hurt me."

It was jackpot day! The man's eyes lit up with greed and expectation. It was a natural reflex for him to move his left arm under the seat in search of the treasure he believed was within his grasp. The movement took the knife blade fractionally away from the driver's throat. It was only a fraction, but it was more than enough.

It was what the driver was waiting for and why he had feigned submissiveness. Moving his left hand from the steering wheel, he wrapped it around the knife wrist and slammed hard on the brakes. Unlike his passenger, he was ready for the sudden jolt forward. Keeping a firm hand on the other man's wrist, the driver waited for the forward momentum to reach stalling point before twisting his passenger's arm and pulling him backwards.

Something popped in the man's shoulder as he crashed against the seat's backrest, the knife spilling out of his hand and careering into the rear compartment. The driver moved his right hand to join his left and yanked the man towards him in an awesome display of brute force.

As the hiker's face hurtled towards him in wide-eyed shock and bewilderment, the driver moved to meet it with his forehead. The force of the blow flattened the man's nose in a crunch of bone and gristle, and rendered him instantly unconscious.

The driver pushed the limp body away from him. Then he reached across and applied firm pressure with his thumbs against the man's carotid arteries, either side of an unwashed neck. It was just enough pressure to ensure the comatose state would remain long enough for him to do what he had to.

He rummaged through the man's pockets, finding an array of credit cards, identity cards, and even an old-age pension book – the macabre mementoes of a sick mind. One frayed driving licence card caught the driver's attention and his eyes misted over. He stared at the grainy photograph before putting the card in his pocket. He pushed everything else back where he found them.

There was still no other traffic on the road. The driver restarted the stalled engine and accelerated towards the growing light of what would be another typically overcast Irish day.

Six miles later he turned into a picnic area, switched off the engine and climbed from the vehicle. He walked around to the passenger side, unhooked the unconscious man from the seatbelt, and pulled him out onto the gravel. With his hands gripped under his erstwhile passenger's armpits, he dragged the deadweight across a narrow strip of grass onto a sandy laneway leading towards the thunderous roar of waves breaking against rocks about a hundred yards away.

The exertion didn't seem to faze the driver. He was scarcely out of breath by the time he threw the man on the ground and stood on a clifftop overlooking the crashing white horses far below.

He calmly lit a cigarette and waited for the hiker to regain consciousness. After a few minutes there was still no movement so he aimed a kick at the man's exposed ribcage. There was a soft moan as the eyes flickered and tried to focus. Suddenly, the prostrate figure bolted up into a sitting stance.

"What's happening? Who are you?"

The driver knelt on one knee and wrapped a bear-like hand around the man's neck. With his free hand he pulled the driving licence card from his pocket and held it in front of his victim's face. "Remember her? Remember what you did to her? She was probably nothing more than a plaything for your sick apology of a mind, but I want you to take a good look because she's the reason you're going to die here today."

The hiker's eyes blazed in fear and he began to squirm and twist, his legs thrashing frantically against the damp ground. Nothing he did could free him from the chokehold. He was aware of being dragged to his feet and feeling the weight of two hefty blows to his solar plexus. The hand clamped on his throat was released and he was spun round to face a deep inlet cut into the rocky shoreline. Far below, he could see rolling waves foaming against giant boulders.

His assailant's hands dug into the collar of his jacket and the waistband of his trousers as he was frogmarched to the edge of the cliff. He felt as helpless as a rag doll. "Noooo, please don't. Take me to the police. I'll admit to everything. I know I deserve to be punished for what I did."

The car driver moved his mouth close to the man's ear. "This *is* your punishment. Look on the bright side. You get to meet your maker at the site of one of God's great natural creations. Well, I can't stand here all day chatting to you. I've things to do and you must be on your way."

Without another word the driver flung the man out into space.

He listened to the screams echoing off the cliff face and watched the body bounce off several outcrops before it plunged from sight.

Chapter 1

DETECTIVE INSPECTOR MICK BOYLE of the Garda Síochána took his third call of the morning in a cramped office at the back of Castlebar police station. *Surely not another burglary*, he muttered as he slammed his coffee mug down on the cluttered desk.

"DI Boyle here. How can I help you?"

"Nice to see we've got our polite, public face on this morning," a less than cheery voice snapped back.

Boyle sat bolt upright. The unmistakeable twang of Chief Superintendent William – *'my-friends-call-me-Bill'* – McCloskey always caused the same reaction. He rated the man as nothing more than a supercilious, pen-pushing waster who didn't have much time for rank-and-filers, and even less for Boyle whose detection methods he considered belonged in the dark ages.

Boyle was quick to get over the shock of a phone call from the great man holed up in his plush Dublin office. Might as well have a bit of fun with the braided pipsqueak. "Good day sir, what can I do for you this fine December morn? Are you out and about in this glorious sunshine?"

Boyle knew fine well it was chucking it down in the capital, but the man on the other line was not one to correct the banalities of a rural copper. The comment was ignored. "I'm sending some trained murder detectives your way. We have reason to believe that a serial killer is on the loose and heading in your direction. I want you to give these men all the assistance they require."

The stress on the word *trained* wasn't lost on Boyle, but he was damned if he'd let the man off with the insult of breaking procedure.

"Serial killer, you tell me, and why am I only informed about this now?"

"Don't be impertinent. We've just learned he could be heading into the Galway or Mayo areas."

"I'll remind you, sir," Boyle said as reverentially as he could muster, "that you did say serial killer?"

"So?"

"So, the term serial implies that he's killed before. My question still stands. Why am I only being told about it now?"

There was silence at the other end of the line before it exploded with a tirade that would have smothered Boyle with spittle were it not for the fact that sixty miles of telephone wiring separated the two men. "I could have your badge for such insubordination. For your information, the previous killings were outside your jurisdiction and we had no need therefore to tell you anything. Come to think of it, I'm only telling you now out of courtesy because you will have nothing whatever to do with this investigation."

Boyle smiled and switched on his best reasoning tone. "You mentioned these other killings took place in other jurisdictions."

"That's what I said. Have you been paying attention?"

"I'm hanging on every word, sir. It's just that your use of plural jurisdictions leads me to believe this man is roaming around carrying out homicides in various parts of the country."

"That would be a deduction, Boyle that I would expect even you to grasp."

"Quite, sir, but I'm sure you understand that under Garda Síochána standard procedures for the potential commissions of crime or flight risks in multiple jurisdictions, all offices must be immediately notified of said threats, must implement be-on-the-look-out-for actions, and must post notices for the attention of all personnel, both uniformed and plainclothed. And that brings me back to my first question."

"Boyle, you're skating on thin ice here. There's really no need for us to be falling out over this." The tone had dropped a notch, a definite mellowing, Boyle thought. Time to put the boot in.

"Sir, you can't expect me to be happy with clear breaches of procedures. The Commissioner himself implemented the new guidelines and there's not a man on the force who doesn't back them."

The mention of the Commissioner had the desired effect. "You're quite right of course, Boyle, and I'll get to the bottom of this. Someone has failed to pass on the information in timely fashion and I'll see they pay for it. I'm only glad that I thought to contact you the minute I heard of the likelihood of this spreading into your patch."

Back-covering bastard, Boyle thought. Well, you're not getting off that easy! "You did say you're sending two detectives from Dublin to handle any investigation from my station?"

"Yes, but only because we've had to put together a special response team to deal with the matter. There's really no telling where this perpetrator will turn up next. I expect your full co-operation and I'll see to it these men respect your position. Now I have other pressing matters to deal with it."

"Just one more question before you go sir."

"Yes, what is it now?" Exasperation dripped from every word.

"You said *he*, do we know it's a man and not a woman? Come to think of it, do we know it's only one person and not more than one?"

"The detectives will bring the file with them. Everything you need to know is in it." The line went dead.

Boyle drove through the large gated entrance and dropped into second gear for the long pull up a gravelled driveway to the imposing house on top of the hill. He had heard the property changed hands last year for just over five million Euros but had yet to meet the new owner, rumoured to be a bigwig in the English music scene.

The call about the theft of valuable oil paintings from the house had come in two hours ago, immediately after Boyle's verbal sparring with the Chief Superintendent. Apart from uploading a log of the incident, Boyle had to sit twiddling his thumbs until a forensics team from Galway got off their asses and paid a visit to what he had no doubt they would regard as the wilds of Mayo.

When they did show up, Boyle had ordered the station sergeant to have the men transfer their gear to his car in the rear compound. He then leaned back in his seat, finished a cup of lukewarm coffee and allowed the minutes to drag on. Satisfied he had made his point, he walked slowly through the station and out into the car park where his silver Toyota Rav4 was kept unlocked.

Two Scenes of Crime Officers were already suited and booted in the back seat, holding large suitcases on their laps. They were covered in white, plastic overalls which included one-piece coverings for their shoes. They were a taciturn pair, new to Boyle, but it suited him just fine if they weren't the talkative type. He wasn't exactly known for the social graces himself.

The passenger seat was occupied by a twenty-something Detective Sergeant, a fresh recruit straight out of university with an armful of degrees in criminology, criminal justice and forensic psychology. Boyle knew how this new fast-track breed of coppers had their careers already mapped out. This young man would be an Inspector in little more than a year and a Superintendent before he was thirty. Provided he kissed all the right asses, he'd make it all the way to the top by the time he was forty.

To be fair to DS Paul Brogan, he had been respectful and keen to learn since being dispatched to Castlebar to link with Boyle in an operation to track down the source of new designer drugs heading from the West to Dublin. They both knew it was a crap assignment and that the real supply chain started in Galway where a number of Latvians had settled in the past five years. But some higher-up had decided to stretch the net into more rural parts. The fact that he or she knew it would piss Boyle off was an added bonus.

Spread across the passenger footwell was Boyle's crime suit, to be donned only when he reached the crime scene. Damned if he'd drive down the main street of Castlebar looking like a fancy-dress cut-out!

The journey to the big house took less than fifteen minutes. By the time Boyle parked at the front entrance only a few words had been uttered between the four men.

"About time too," a plaintive voice squeaked from the main door of the big house as the group alighted from the car.

Boyle switched to his best beaming smile as he approached a dapper little man wedged between two burly minders on the top step of a large porch. The man was barely five-two, with a smooth porcelain face below a mop of curly hair, dyed to an extravagant shade of light tan. He wore a pink golf sweater draped over powder-blue slacks and sported enough jewellery to fill the window of Madison's in Castlebar's High Street. Boyle guessed his age at mid-sixties, though he looked more like a lost schoolboy beside the two brutes standing splayed with arms folded across their considerable chests.

"Sorry we're a bit late, sir, but we had to bring in some experts from Galway."

"Late! This is beyond late," the man responded in a high-pitched moan as he repeated the words "Peter and Paul...Peter and Paul."

"Excuse me, sir?"

The little man seemed to snap out of his distraction. "Don't you know this is probably the biggest burglary ever to have happened in Ireland?"

"Home invasion, sir," Boyle said with a grin.

"What, what are you talking about?"

Boyle maintained his cheesy face. "Blame it on the Americans, sir. It used to be burglaries or even just good old-fashioned break-ins, but now it's known as home invasions."

"The hell you say. I've just lost some of the rarest paintings in the world and you stand there talking gibberish."

The man was on the verge of tears, and for a moment Boyle almost felt sorry for him. "Let's start again, sir. I'm Detective Inspector Boyle. Are you the owner of this house?"

The man relaxed, but Boyle could see he was struggling to maintain composure. "Yes, I'm the owner. My name's David Bicker, of Bicker Recording. Surely you know about me?"

Boyle was tempted to say he had never heard of him. Instead he nodded knowingly and invited Bicker to show them around. Twenty minutes later he was alone with Bicker in a large drawing room while the forensics team went about their painstaking routine of dusting, scraping, moulding and photographing. He had directed Brogan to take witness statements from the two bodyguards in an adjoining room.

Boyle extracted a notebook. "How much were the paintings worth?"

"Peter and Paul, they were Peter and Paul."

Boyle shot him a quizzical look. "You mentioned those names when we first arrived. Are they your two bodyguards?"

Bicker waved his hand dismissively. "Goodness me, no, they're my paintings. One is a Peter Rubens and the other is a Paul Cézanne. They're my life!"

Boyle struggled to stifle a smile before composing himself to ask: "How much are they worth?"

"They're invaluable!" Bicker exploded. "You can't put a price on these masterpieces."

"I'm sorry sir, but we need an estimate for the records. Surely you have them insured for a precise sum?"

Bicker thought for a moment. "About one hundred million, give or take."

Boyle was stunned. His first thought was to look around the room and out the window to rolling lawns at the rear of the house. "If you don't mind me saying so, you don't appear to have the proper levels of security that would be necessary for the kinds of valuable objects that are being kept here."

For the first time Bicker looked uneasy. "That's just it, inspector. The paintings are usually held at my London home in Chelsea, but since I was coming here for a few months I couldn't bear to be away from them. I decided to take them with me on the spur of the moment."

Boyle digested the impact of Bicker's words. "Doesn't that mean your insurance cover will be invalid?"

Bicker buried his head in his hands. "I'm afraid that's all too true. If you don't recover the paintings I'm ruined."

Boyle leaned back in his seat and studied the pathetic figure slouched in the armchair. Now he really did feel sorry for him. The news could mean only one thing. It ruled out the likelihood of an insurance scam.

"Tell me about your bodyguards," Boyle said as he turned a page in his notebook.

"They're not bodyguards; they were hired as a security detail to guard the paintings during my stay in Castlebar. There are three of them, but one had the night off to go to a pub in the town. He hasn't been back since."

"What!" Boyle leapt from the seat. "Why haven't you told me this before now? Don't you realise this third man could have had something to do with the theft of your paintings?"

Bicker smiled. "No chance Inspector. Philip has worked for me for many years. I would trust him with my life. He probably met some girl and spent the night at her place. He's a bit of a ladies' man is Philip."

"Just the same, sir, I need his full name and details. Do you have a photograph of him?"

Bicker rose and crossed to a writing bureau in front of a large bay window. He rummaged for a set of keys, bent to open the top drawer, and carried a passport back to Boyle. "Here you are Inspector. Philip always leaves his papers with me for safekeeping."

Boyle studied the burgundy British passport. The face which stared out at him was that of a man in his late twenties, certainly not more than thirty, Boyle decided. The date-of-birth entry confirmed he was in fact twenty-eight. Dark brown hair appeared to have been subjected to a number-one clipper setting, which matched perfectly with a designer stubble that give the bearer the look of a Hollywood A-listed brat. All in all, Boyle thought, a man who would indeed have little trouble with the ladies.

Boyle kept studying the face as he rose from his seat, crossed to the large window, and withdrew a mobile phone from his pocket. He was grateful to hear the voice of Sergeant Colm Moriarty, one of the few officers he liked and trusted at the station. He explained the situation quickly.

"Sarge, I need you to get out an all-points on a Philip Langton. He's gone missing from the big house and I need to track him down. Chances are he's already fled the area, but get some uniforms to check the local bars, and send someone up here to collect a passport photo."

"What's the score Mick?"

"Dunno yet, Sarge, but this Langton seems to have disappeared around the same time as two very valuable paintings. We need to account for his movements."

Boyle cut the connection and turned to face Bicker. "I need you to tell me about the other two members of your security detail and about the arrangement you have with their agency in London."

Bicker seemed to need a moment to compose himself. When he finally spoke, the voice was low and sorrowful. "Not much to tell Inspector. I have used the agency on a number of occasions before, including protection for some of our major stars on gigs and overseas trips. They are a highly-respected agency."

"So what about Tweedledum and Tweedledee?" Boyle asked nodding towards the nearby room.

Bicker smiled. "They do look like a couple of storybook characters. I don't really know them that well. This is the first time they've worked for me and they seem to know what they're doing."

"The jury's still out on that one," Boyle responded with derision.

"I'm sorry, what do you mean?"

"Well, if they knew what they were doing they wouldn't have allowed someone to waltz in here last night and make off with two priceless paintings from right under their noses."

Spent Force, and other titles by Joe McCoubrey, are available as eBooks or Paperbacks.

ALSO BY Joe McCOUBREY.................

www.ingramcontent.com/pod-product-compliance
Lightning Source LLC
Chambersburg PA
CBHW062110170626
46813CB00002B/382